DADDY'S BOY

BOOK TWO OF THE ARIZONA SERIES

ROMEO PREMINGER

CONTENTS

BOOKS IN THE SERIES

THE ARIZONA SERIES

Sins of Yesterday
Daddy's Boy
Ties That Bind
Promises We Keep
When Fallen Angels Fly

1

I'M ASHAMED TO say I wasn't looking forward to going home to Louisiana for the summer. I'd finished my junior year at Middleton Academy in Massachusetts, and I'd made so many friends and settled into such a fine routine, I'd rather have kept going with it. At school, I had my people, who were Jonathan Gutierrez, Dale Knox-Levy, and Russell Thorne. We were together every day from breakfast to late night carousing. At the top of the year, I thought I'd never fit in at that fancy school, but I'd done fit in and I was proud to be a big blue gorilla, which was what we called ourselves after the school mascot.

Let me fill you in on an important fact about me. I'm gay and proud. Through a whole lot of trials and tribulations, I came out in my first two months as the first openly gay student in Middleton's history. Then Jonathan came out, then Dale, and then Russell. Well, we like to say Jonathan and Russell only got one toe out of the closet. But what a miracle we found each other. It was 1985, and Middleton Academy for Boys was just about the straightest place you could find on the map.

The four of us looked out for each other. Jonathan and Russell looked out for each other a little extra, having decided to be boyfriends, which was cute as heck. We even started the works on a school-sanctioned Pink Triangle club. I ain't saying we painted the school pink. There were plenty of ignorant students and ignorant teachers who gave us ugly looks, but we were making strides and having loads of fun. Some Saturdays we hopped on the train to Boston where you could have some real fun in the South End. That's the gay neighborhood in town.

It wasn't just my friends I'd be missing that summer. I'd joined the equestrian club, and call me a nerd, but I liked being in school and knew I'd be missing my teachers. Especially Miss Antonelli who taught English literature and who I told about my big dream of being a writer like Mr. Thomas Wolfe. He was my favorite writer at the time, though I was such a bookworm, ask me another day and I might tell you different. Anyway, it was one sad morning on moving out day, and I'm not too proud to admit I wept saying goodbye to Jonathan, Dale, and Russell. Three months felt like forever. We swore we'd write letters and talk on the phone from time to time.

Jonathan was going home to Los Angeles where he'd be saving up money washing dishes at his uncle's restaurant. Russell's family was taking a month-long trip to Europe. Dale, our aspiring actor, was enrolled in a pre-college theater program at Yale. Me, I'd be spending the summer at my daddy's house in Darrow. I had a lot to do and not much to do at the same time, which I'll get to later.

Some days I tripped out remembering what my life had been like just one year ago. I'd never dreamed I'd be in a first-class seat on a plane from Boston to come home from school for the summer. That year hadn't been all roses. I'll try to stick to the short version and fill you in along the way.

I was born Arizona Fanning and spent the first fifteen years of my life living with a family I thought was blood. You can't do worse than be a Fanning in Louisiana low country. My great granddaddy Luke was an evil, twisted man who kidnapped little girls to do dirty things to them. When he got tipped off the sheriff was coming to lock him up, he murdered the six girls he kidnapped, and then he took his shotgun and shot his wife, his daughter, his sons, and then himself. Just my Grandad George survived. Growing up, I didn't even know that was why people hated us. I just thought we were poor John's Island trash, which was where all the broke-ass bayou folk in Le Moyne Parish lived.

My Mama Lou died in a car accident when I was thirteen. My Grandma Tilly and Grandad George died in a fire the summer last. I was raised by no-good drunk Gus Fanning, my stepdaddy, though I thought he was my real father up until last year. Last year, I also found out my birth mama was Philippa Bondurant, and then my life changed forever when a man named Gaston Polydore Bondurant showed up to claim me from Social Services on behalf of his wife, my grandmother Virginia. I'd been removed from home after brawling with Gus Fanning, and my siblings had been sent off to foster families. My life was complicated, and that's no lie.

Then, I come to find out Gaston Polydore Bondurant is my daddy, not my step-grandaddy. Here's where things get real Southern. He fell in love with my mama after he married Virginia, and my mama, carrying his baby, ran off at sixteen years old and took up with Gus Fanning, telling him I was his. Philippa died, birthing me. You might think I'd hate Gaston Bondurant after hearing all that, and we did have a score to settle for a time. But I came to understand my daddy is a good man. He loves me as his own. We got closer after his younger brother Nicolas killed himself last Thanksgiving. Nicolas and I were in love. That was before we knew Gaston Bondurant was my father. You can bet that's a story of its own, and I'm only getting started on the kind of drama I was born into.

I'll get to that, but this here part of the story begins with me landing at New Orleans International Airport and Daddy's chauffeur, Buck, driving me back to Whittington Manor.

The first time I saw that big estate, I just about broke my jaw gaping like a country fool. Gaston Bondurant is the CEO of B&B Sugar, which is on the shelf of every grocery store, five and dime, and gas station across the South. Whittington Manor comprises one hundred acres of land. It has a big, white columned main house, a half dozen outbuildings, stables, wooded riding trails, a chapel and a family cemetery, and its own lake. But sadness hangs over that estate. As grand as it is, it's an empty, lonely place. I felt that hollow ache in my gut as soon as Buck drove my daddy's Bentley through the gates and down the tree-lined road to the main house.

My daddy wasn't there to welcome me home. He told me he'd be back next Thursday evening when he finished some business he had in Houston. That was typical. Daddy was always working. He'd said he'd make more time for me after Nicolas died, but as much as we swore we'd be there for each other more, we both fell back on our old ways. It's not that we didn't love each other, and it's not that I didn't wish things were different. But deep down, I knew the man he was. Him not being around didn't mean he didn't care. He'd never learned how to be a father. He'd only been one a little short of a year. He accepted me for who I am, and if he could do that, I figured I should accept him for who he is, too.

As for my grandmother, Virginia, she lived in the house year round, but she was hardly the type of grandmother to welcome me home with a hug, a glass of lemonade, and a plate of cookies. We hated each other. That's a story for another time as well.

Mr. Wainwright, the estate's snooty manager, helped me hike my luggage upstairs to my room and get unpacked. The two of us had a checkered history, so that wasn't a warm welcome either. He told me my daddy had sent ahead a request for the cook, Mrs. Gundy, to make my favorite dinner which was lobster bisque, fried chicken, and a Bananas Foster sundae for dessert. Then Mr. Wainwright said I should follow him down to the car lot behind the house. That had me mighty curious.

When I stepped outside, I set my eyes on a royal blue, Chevrolet Corvette convertible parked in the middle of the lot with a big red bow around the hood.

"A gift from Mr. Bondurant," Mr. Wainwright said.

I was so excited, I ran over to the car and checked it out from different angles, taking in every detail of that thing of beauty. My favorite color was blue. Heck, I was ready for the speedway, and lucky I'd gotten my learner's permit during winter break. I opened the driver's side door and sat inside. It had a gold-brown steering wheel, a radio and a cassette player, marbled brown consoles, plush seats, and it smelled brand new. I'd be driving around town in style. Heck, I'd be driving around like a millionaire.

Mr. Wainwright came over to the driver's side, eyeing me carefully. For a minute, I forgot he didn't like me. I gave him a grin.

"Don't this beat all? Can I take her for a spin? Just around the grounds. I never drove stick."

"And you won't. Not today. Unless you want to destroy the transmission. Buck will be giving you lessons, beginning tomorrow morning."

"I reckon that makes sense." I laughed to myself. "I wouldn't mind sleeping here till he comes by."

Mr. Wainwright frowned.

"I ought to give my daddy a call to thank him. How 'bout taking me to his office so I can ring him up?"

Daddy had a mobile phone for reaching him. I was getting ideas about calling Jonathan as well to give him the good news.

Mr. Wainwright nodded stiffly. I climbed out of the car and followed him into the house.

2

I TOOK MY driving lessons with Buck that week. That sports car was a little beast, itching to be opened up on the highway. Her engine knocked and growled while Buck directed me along two-lane country roads. He said I was doing real well, getting the hang of a manual transmission. By Saturday, he told me I was ready to drive it on my own, even on the interstate. I'd take my road test at the end of June, and I'd have my own driver's license when I turned seventeen in August. Then I could drive anywhere I wanted, maybe even all the way to California to visit Jonathan. And wouldn't that be something? We could drive through Hollywood and Beverly Hills and over to the beach by the Pacific Ocean.

I had things to sort out that summer before I made plans for road trips, though. I wasn't supposed to be driving without an adult in the car, but my daddy told me he was driving on his own at sixteen, and he didn't see a reason why I shouldn't. So, first thing Sunday morning, I drove out of Whittington Manor, took the Sunshine Bridge across the Mississippi River and took Route 70 over to county highway 90.

I wanted to find my brother Duke. I hoped I'd have some luck in Le Moyne Parish where we'd grown up. We hadn't seen each other in nearly a year, and he'd been hard to track down. Last I'd heard, he was on the road with Gus Fanning as a traveling carny. I'd tried talking sense into Duke, telling him to stay in school and not trust Gus, who'd sold off our little brother Douglas. The only thing that man loved was money.

Duke and I had always gotten along. There was only a year between us, and he respected me in a way our sister Dolly never did. He hadn't been sore about Gaston Bondurant taking me in, though he didn't know yet the man was my father. Duke was sewn tight to his own daddy. It didn't make no sense to me, though I supposed it made sense to Duke. Gus Fanning was the only daddy he had, no matter that he was a drunk who never cared about his kids.

Driving into Le Moyne Parish, all kinds of feelings bubbled up inside me. I was what you'd call nostalgic seeing familiar things like the Marlboro cowboy billboard, Clemmon's roadside diner where Grandma Tilly took us kids for special occasions, and Le Moyne Senior High with its football field and bleachers.

Then, a sort of identity crisis set in. That country parish had been all I knew up until last year. But I'd seen more of the world since then, and part of me was embarrassed of the place where I'd grown up. All them rickety old houses with grisly folks sitting on their porches. Dirty-faced, shirtless boys running around the yards. Confederate flags on pickups. I was seeing everything with new eyes, and I'd only driven a few miles into town. Things would only get worse when I drove over the bridge to John's Island where I'd grown up.

Arriving on the main strip with the Piggly Wiggly on one side and Our Lady of Grace cathedral on the other, I decided to pull into Merle's Gas and Go and Bait and Tackle Shop. If I found Duke, I didn't want to be empty-handed. I'd pick him up some Bazooka Joe bubble gum and a *Sports Illustrated*. My brother lived for playing baseball. He'd had his sights set on being a major league ballplayer someday.

I parked my Corvette in front of the store and stepped out. One thing you can count on finding in front of any country store across Louisiana is a pair of old men sitting on the front bench with nothing better to do than stare at passersby all day long. That day was no different. I'd dressed casual in a white polo shirt, a pair of running shorts, and my tennis shoes. Still, those two dusty oldsters fixed on me like I'd dropped down from outer space. I'm sure it was on account of my fancy convertible, which you didn't see in Le Moyne Parish every day of the week.

I tipped my hand and gave them a friendly "how do you do?" That got the two of them hiking up smiles, recognizing my local accent. I went into the shop.

I found the bubble gum and magazine, and headed to the cashier counter. Then I stopped short and froze.

Behind the register, in a New Orleans Saints baseball cap and a Merle's T-shirt was Preston Montclair. I saw him before he saw me, which gave me a precious second or two to work out how to compose myself. I'd never figured out if I'd done Preston wrong or he did me wrong or maybe we both done wrong by each other. We'd been secret sweethearts from sixth grade through tenth, but when Social Services took me away from Gus Fanning's house last summer, we fell out of touch. Part of me was terrified to face him again, and I almost turned on my heels, put the gum and magazine on the nearest shelf, and slipped out of the store like a bandit.

Then Preston's gaze landed on me, and I had no choice but to face him.

He squinted at first. I'd started cutting my hair different, long up top and short on the sides, which might've thrown him off. I'd never worn Lacoste polo shirts before, and I guess if he looked close at my sneakers, he could see they were expensive, the kind worn by boys from good families in Franklin Acres, who Press and I used to make fun of. As for Preston, he'd sprouted a little, and he still had cowlicks of wavy brown hair sticking out of his cap and the same heart-breaking good looks.

I smiled. He didn't smile back.

There was nothing for me to do but march up to his counter and set down my bubble gum and magazine.

"How do you you, Preston?"

He gave me a nod and started ringing me up.

I took a glance around. Not a soul in the store. I tried another grin. "It's been a long time, hasn't it?"

He said nothing.

"Preston Montclair, you gonna tell me you got nothing to say?"

His face flushed. "How do you do, Arizona? That'll be one dollar and eighty-nine cents."

I scrounged out my wallet. But my pride wouldn't let me just pay and go about my business.

"It's good to see you, Press. I guess I should've gotten the picture when you never returned any of my phone calls or letters."

He rolled his eyes and glared at me. "I ain't stupid."

"Who's saying you are?"

Preston looked at me, lopsided. "Phone calls and letters? What kind of crap is that?"

I'd called him at least three times when I got placed with a foster family outside Baton Rouge. His mama always answered the phone, and after she told me to stop calling, I just hung up when I heard her voice. I'd written him a half dozen letters last summer, including an invitation to my sixteenth birthday party. I told him all that.

"Well, I never got none of them." He crossed his arms over his chest.

"Maybe your mama didn't want you to."

"You sayin' my mama's a liar?"

He looked keyed up. I didn't want to fight. I wanted to make him understand it hadn't been my fault we lost touch, but that was going to be a long story, which I wasn't sure he'd believe.

"Could be the letters never made it to the post office." I told him I'd asked other people to mail them. It was awkward. I didn't want to say I had a house butler to handle my mail. I was hoping to ease into explaining what my life was like since I'd left Le Moyne Parish.

"Well, you got my ear now. What you got to say to me, Arizona?"

I fumbled a bit. "Press, I suppose I got a lot of things to say. But I don't think this is the time or the place."

He found something amusing about that. I had no idea what it was, and I told him so.

"What you doing in town?" he said. "You gonna say it was on account of me? You looked like a jailbird caught in the searchlights when you saw me in this here store."

"What was I supposed to do? I told you when we last saw each other, I *had to* move." I pointed my finger. "I never heard one word from you."

"Where'd you move? Darrow, you say? Why don't you come by the house, and I'll show you a stack of mail marked 'return to sender.' I called that number you gave me, and every time a man told me there was no Arizona Fanning living there."

Now I understood, and my heart sank. That bastard Mr. Wainwright made sure nothing from Preston got through to me.

Preston put my bubble gum and magazine in a paper bag and pushed it across the counter. "That's one dollar and eighty-nine cents."

"Press, won't you give me a chance to explain?"

He sucked his teeth. "I don't have time for things that ain't worth hearing."

"How you gonna know if they worth hearing unless you willing to listen?"

"Fool me once, Arizona Fanning, shame on you. Fool me twice, and you can bet you're gonna have a problem on your hands. Now you wanna step out back and see how well you do, we can do that. But I can't promise you gonna make it out of town walking on two feet."

I won't lie. I hadn't thought about Preston Montclair for a long time, and a whole lot had changed in my life since we'd last snuck off to the woods behind our houses to mess around and talk about our future together. But Preston was the first person I ever told I was gay. We didn't call it gay, actually. We just said we loved each other, and we'd always be true. I was a different person back then, but seeing Preston again, I realized I still had deep feelings for him. So while the old me probably would've told him where he could stick my one dollar and eighty-nine cents, I drew a breath and kept my cool.

"I'm not sure what I got to apologize for, but I'm willing to be a man and say it, once and for all. I'm sorry, Press. For breaking your heart and whatever else I caused you. I never meant to hurt you, but you're making it plain I did. So for that, I'm sorry."

We looked at each other squarely for a breath. His eyes trembled and got a little misty. Then he turned his head and hardened again.

"Pay for your things and go on. What're you doing back in town now you got family in Darrow?"

"I was hoping to track down Duke." I pulled two dollars out of my wallet and handed them to Preston.

"You wasted the trip. Duke and Gus been on the road for at least a month—Kansas, Oklahoma, Missouri. You'd have to go over to the post office. They got one of them Ringling Brothers posters up on the wall with the itinerary printed on it."

That was disappointing, though I was grateful he'd saved me from running around town on a wild goose chase. Just then, the bell above the door jangled, and a lady with her little daughter came in to look around the store.

"Thanks for letting me know. What time you get off work?"

Preston fingered the change in his hands, looking like he was considering whether or not he wanted to answer me. Eventually, he reached over the counter to give me my dime and penny.

"I'm here till close. Seven o'clock."

I remembered how early everything closed down in a little town like Le Moyne. Except…

"How 'bout you let me pick you up after work? I'll take you to Clemmon's for a milkshake and something to eat."

His eyes widened. Then he scowled. "You got a car?"

I nodded and watched him while he shifted his weight.

Finally, he sighed. "This is probably the worst decision I'll ever make. But all right, Arizona." He raised his eyes to me. "You be here seven thirty. I gotta sweep and straighten out the store 'fore I close up."

My face stretched wide with a big smile. "You won't regret it, Preston Montclair. Seven thirty. I'll be back."

I HAD NINE hours to kill, which is a lot of time in a town like Le Moyne. I strolled over to the Piggly Wiggly to buy some flowers, and then I drove crosstown to Gideon Cemetery to place them on the graves of my Grandma Tilly and Grandpa George. I knew now they weren't my grandparents by blood, but my Grandma Tilly had been much more of a grandmother to me than Virginia Bondurant, and I loved her.

It was one of those late May days when the sun was pounding down fierce, and the sultry summer heat was grabbing hold of the inland Louisiana countryside like a great big terrarium. I sat down at the graves, paying my respects and baking in the sun until I couldn't take it no more.

I drove over to the post office to check out that Ringling Brothers poster Preston told me about. But, of course, it was closed on a Sunday. I tried peering through the glass doors of the building, but it was too dark to make out anything.

Next, I took a drive over the bridge to John's Island and found the dead-end street where I'd grown up. Grandma Tilly's house was still an empty plot, razed by that terrible fire one year ago. Next door, I could see a new family had moved into Gus Fanning's house. They'd put on a new asphalt roof, tidied up the yard, and installed a flagpole. Looked like good people had moved into that little ranch house.

I was hit by a whole lot of memories, good and bad. My Mama Lou filled that house with love, showing me how to help her out in the kitchen, giving me hugs, and sending us kids to play out in the yard with water pistols, wiffle bats, and bouncy balls. But when Gus Fanning was home, the place took on an entirely different climate, with everyone walking on eggshells, him running his mouth, breaking things, and not a few times raising a hand to Mama Lou and later me and Duke. The corners of my eyes burned, and I couldn't stay looking at the house too long. I turned my car around and drove off.

The only thing I could think to do was drive over to a spot along the road by Bayou Teche where I used to go with my brother Duke and take a swim. No one else was around so I stripped down to my boxers and trudged into the water. I laid on my back and treaded water, looking up at a kaleidoscope of colors through the sheltering beech and magnolia trees. It was peaceful, but I missed my brother Duke. We'd cannon-ball off the bank and wrestle in the water. I'd always been able to dunk him, though he was growing to be strong enough to overtake me.

I dried off on the hood of my car, and when the sun was setting, I got back inside and drove back to Merle's Gas and Go.

I made it over there a little after seven. The parking lot was empty, and I stood outside the car until Preston finished closing up and came out to lock the front doors.

He did a double take when he saw my convertible, and then he slunk over to the passenger's side door, pulled it open, and piled in. No hug. No handshake. Not even a how do you do. Inside the car, I tried prying out a grin from him, but he was cold as ice.

I turned on the ignition, gave the gas pedal some taps to make the engine roar, and I barreled out of the lot, tires screeching and smoking against the blacktop as I took the wide turn into the opposite lane without touching the brakes. Preston went white as a corpse, and he grasped the door handle for dear life.

"You lookin' to get a highway patrolman on your tail?"

I chuckled. Then I cranked into fourth gear. The speed limit in town was thirty mph, and I was pushing fifty. But we had the road to ourselves. There's no such thing as traffic in Le Moyne Parish, unless they've got a Friday night football game going on at the high school.

"Knock it off, you damn fool," Preston said.

"You turn into an old lady on me? You used to say you wanted to be a Daytona race car driver when you grew up."

"I'd like to live to see that day. Now slow down."

"Aw shut your pie hole, Minnie Pearl."

Preston stared at me indignantly. Made him look even more like Miss Minnie Pearl from the Grand Ol' Opry, if you ask me. I laughed. Then to lower his hackles, I slowed down. A little. Press braced himself in his seat with his eyes shifting around.

We got to Clemmons in a jiffy.

I parked and stepped out of the car. Preston came over to me, took off his baseball cap, and swatted me twice in the head.

"What the heck was that for?" I grumbled.

He swatted me again on my back side. "For near wrapping your car around a tree with me inside it."

"Now don't be sore at me, Preston Montclair. I had to find a way to get you talking."

He thwapped me on the side, and I jumped.

"You gonna ruin your hat." I smirked. "Though maybe that's just as well. The Saints always been a suck-ass team."

I sidestepped his next attempt to hit me, giggling. He had steam coming out of his nostrils, and his hair was flat from wearing his cap.

"Better fix your hair," I told him.

"Eat shit."

"I'm only trying to help you. You go into Clemmons looking like that, people are liable to think you're from Arkansas, and they might not serve us."

Preston rolled his eyes.

I eased up in front of him. "Lemme see what I can do."

He shoved my hand away. "I'll do it myself."

I watched him pick at his hair to get it fluffed out some. I was grinning the whole time.

"You gonna tell me what's so damn funny?"

"There's a difference when I'm smiling because something's funny as opposed to smiling on account of something being cute."

"You're cute all right."

I smiled. "You've got a point there. Y'know, the word 'cute' comes from '*a*cute', which also means shrewd or clever. Not a lot of folks know that, wouldn't you say?"

"I'll be sure not to use that word around you from now on. C'mon. Let's get this over with." He started toward the diner.

I couldn't say I liked his attitude, but I was feeling warm and eager being around him. He sure looked good in his Wranglers and that crew neck Merle's T-shirt. There were reasons I'd risked my neck to be with him for close to four years, and I was discovering them all over again.

Inside the diner, the hostess seated us at a corner booth with a pair of laminated menus and gave me a wink. I'd been to Clemmons two dozen times or more and never been treated so friendly. Then again, I'd never pulled up to that diner in a spanking new Corvette, wearing a shirt with that little alligator on the upper left side. When the waitress came by, I asked her for a Coca-Cola, and Preston said he'd have the same.

"You can order anything you want," I told him.

He buried his gaze in the menu. "Are the stories true? You a millionaire now?"

"My daddy, I mean my granddaddy is. Isn't the worst thing in the world, is it?"

"I can tell it's changed you. Driving like you above the law. Like you above everybody."

Before I could snap back at him, the waitress returned with our drinks and pulled out her order pad. I told her I'd take a fried oyster po'boy, a side of hush puppies, and a chocolate milkshake. My stomach was growling. I hadn't had Louisiana road stop food since last summer. Preston just asked for some sweet potato fries.

"That it?"

"I ain't hungry."

I touched his shoe with mine under the table, and he kicked it away. I drew a breath to even myself out.

"Preston, explain something to me. What did I do to you?"

"Nothing."

I pointed my straw at him. "Oh, it's something. And it's not fair you keeping it to yourself. Now you tell me what it is."

"You left, Arizona. After giving me a promise." He glared at me. "Couldn't even be bothered to say goodbye."

I'd promised to wait for him the last time we'd seen each other. But I hadn't known what was in store for me moving across state after my daddy had worked things out with family court.

"Whose choice was that? You answer me. You know what I went through last year."

"Well, you made out all right in the end, didn't you? With your preppy clothes. Your preppy haircut. Got a nice set of wheels. Couldn't have come by any sooner? It's been a year."

The corners of my eyes burned, and I sprouted tears. Angry tears. I wiped my eyes with a napkin and glared right back at that boy.

"You got no idea what I been through, and don't pretend you do." I threw up my hand. "And some things you know real well, Preston. I shouldn't have to remind you, but I will. Gus Fanning assaulting me. Losing my grandparents. Getting taken away in handcuffs after hitting Gus, and spending weeks in a psychiatric hospital, and another week with a family that didn't want me. But I 'left you.' You gonna say that to me again? Or we could step outside like you were interested in doing earlier today."

"Arizona—"

"I should've listened when you told me to beat it. Best advice I heard all year." I perched in my seat, looking around for our waitress. "I'll settle up, and you can take your fries to go."

"All right. Maybe I shouldn't have said it that way."

"What was the moody, wounded act for? Nonsense. You never cared about me one bit, and don't be putting on like you did."

"Now hold on, Arizona. You know that ain't true. Ain't nobody can get me angry like you can, and you know the reason. I told you I was sorry when all them things happened to you. You settle down for crying out loud."

I was in such a state, I was only hearing every other word he said. "Press, I pined for you all last summer. You gone and made me feel like a fool for doing it."

The tears came out again. I'm just that way. When I get wound up, whether it's from anger or sadness, I can't help bawling like a child. It made me feel ashamed out in public at that diner. Probably scared the living daylights out of poor Press. And here's the sad truth: it wasn't all for him. Sure, I'd loved him and missed him something awful for the first few months, but I had other heartaches coming back to me from that past year. One of them, Nicolas Bondurant, was something Press knew nothing about, and I wasn't eager to fill him in.

"C'mon Arizona. I never could stand to see you cry."

I awakened from his voice and pulled myself together.

Preston gazed at me kindly. "You tell me what happened. And I'll listen." He nodded at me encouragingly. "I'd take it all away if I could."

Now it was like he had swung too far in the other direction, hard to gentle. Got me feeling guilty, though I couldn't say if I ought to feel that way. Anyway, another thing about me is I've always been the kind of person who clears his plate of the yucky-tasting food first to get it over with.

"I ain't been true." I had a lump in my throat, which I tried to swallow down. "I had to have a difficult conversation with myself. Do I wait on someone who ain't giving me the time of day, or do I lick my wounds and call it quits." I raised my hand because I could see he was fixing to break in. "I know now you got turned around trying to reach me. But the point is, I didn't know at the time, and you best sit there and listen because this ain't easy for me to say. I met someone, Press. Even fell in love. It wouldn't be a man of me to lie to you about that."

My head was so heavy, I could barely hold it up straight.

"Who? Someone you met at school?"

I shook my head. "It don't matter. It's over. He died."

We said nothing for a while.

"You kill him?"

My eyes flared. Then I saw the quiet humor on Preston's face. "Know what? You a rat bastard, and that's the truth."

Preston chuckled. "Well, the way you drive, I thought you might've run him over pulling into the driveway."

I scowled at him, and then I got to snickering myself. "Don't keep me in suspense. How'd he die?"

Nicolas Bondurant done took his life. On account of me. As much as I made a big deal about being honorable and honest, I couldn't bring myself to tell Preston that part.

"Drowned." It was medically accurate. Nicolas downed a bottle of his psychiatric pills and waded into the lake by his cabin at Whittington Manor.

"I'd be lying if I said I wasn't pleased to hear you ain't with nobody no more. But I'm sorry, Arizona. Sorry for your loss."

That was right decent of him to say. I was remembering more and more what a good person Preston was. Well, when he wasn't being a pain in the ass.

"What was he like?"

I peeked at Preston. I was timid about that line of conversation. Nicolas being thirty-one years old and technically my uncle and all.

"I'm not sportin' for a fight," Preston said. "I'm just curious is all." His face darkened, and he leaned closer and lowered his voice. "Since you left town, there ain't another queer in Le Moyne Parish 'sides me. I couldn't find another fella to be with if I tried."

A mischievous ember lit up inside me. "Did you try?"

Preston gaped. He slyly gazed around our booth. The only other people were on the other side of the diner.

"No, I didn't try. I ain't lookin' to get lynched." I watched him hemming and hawing on the inside, warming up to say something private. "That's what made you leavin' so hard. I lost you, and I lost any chance of happiness. Some nights, I thought real long if there was any point in waking up the next day."

I leaned my foot against his. This time he didn't push me away. "Press, you look me in the eye and tell me you ain't never gonna get those foolish ideas in your head."

He shifted his gaze. I kept my eyes square on him and touched his calf with mine under the table. He glanced at me and gave me a little nod.

"There's a whole lot of people like us out there in the world." I told him about Jonathan Gutierrez, Dale Knox-Levy and Russell Thorne, and all the kids we met at the gay youth center in Boston. I also told him what I'd learned about the Stonewall riots, the Gay Liberation Movement, and Mr. Harvey Milk who was the first openly gay man to run for mayor. Preston brightened a little, but then he looked glum again.

"Press, there ain't no reason to be ashamed. God made us who we are. Anybody who says different, that's their own problem. You just let 'em jog ahead."

That was an expression I'd picked up from Nicolas, but I didn't mention that. Preston looked like he was breaking down. I wanted to reach across the table, grab his hand, and show him how much I cared for him and that he wasn't alone. But we were in Clemmon's diner in Le Moyne Parish. I'd be asking for trouble in that backward town.

The waitress brought over our dinner. I gave Press half of my po'boy. Like my Grandma Tilly used to say, them po'boys at Clemmon's could feed a family of five. I chowed down and went to heaven. They had good seafood in New England, but nothing like a po'boy with French bread, fried seafood, mayonnaise, pickles and hot sauce. I was happy as a pig in mud and even happier to see Preston wolfing down his half. I spread my leg so that our knees were touching. Thank god for that table. I was stiff between the legs.

Preston belched, and then he looked at me with a humorous gleam. "I guess this ain't half bad." He reached his hand under the table to squeeze my knee. "We never had a proper date in all these years."

"You play your cards right, I'll take you to a fine restaurant in New Orleans. Tablecloths and all. Right there in the Vieux Carré."

I wriggled my eyebrows. "Laissez les bon temps roulez."

Preston's eyes widened. "You been to New Orleans?"

I remembered then we'd always said we'd go to New Orleans together. "Now don't be sore. I wanted to go with you."

"What's it like?"

I grinned. "It's big. And colorful. And loud. They got street performers on every corner. Every half block, really. But what they don't show you in the movies is they've got men like us walking the streets together in the middle of the day and not caring a whit."

That got Press blushing and smiling. "Folks been talking. They say you been all around the world."

"I don't like being the subject of idle gossip. Who been talking?"

Press shrugged. "Just...folks. Don't happen every day that a boy from John's Island finds out he's related to Gaston Bondurant. By marriage you said, right?"

I nodded, but I decided he ought to know the truth. "He told me he married my grandmother. But Press, he's my daddy. Came out around Thanksgiving." I smirked. "Turns out it's not just the Fannings know how to make a soap opera out of their lives. My daddy, he had an affair with my mama, my grandmother's child. Then my mama ran away and took up with Gus Fanning. Told him she was pregnant with me, and I was his."

I don't think I'd ever seen Preston Montclair so flabbergasted. His hush puppy fell right out of his hand.

"That means—"

I finished for him. "Duke, Dolly, Little Douglas and me, we ain't blood."

"Why, you ain't a Fanning at all."

"No, sir. I'm Bondurant through and through. I even changed

my name. But you keep that under your hat for now. I haven't told Duke and Dolly yet."

Preston gave me a couple nods.

"Enough about me. How about you tell me what all you been up to?"

"Not much. I'm working full time at Merle's."

"For the summer?"

Preston didn't answer.

"Press, don't tell me you dropped out of school."

He fussed on the other side of the table. "I was no good at school. You know that."

"I sure don't. You were doing real well in them vocational classes. Got medals and everything."

"You don't need a high school diploma to help out at an auto shop."

"Look here. A high school diploma's free. Why give up on that? It's something to fall back on. You'd be done next year."

"Arizona, I turned seventeen at the start of the month, and I signed myself out. I ain't going back. I'm making money. My uncle gave me his old pickup. It needs a new engine, but Merle's going to give me a good deal and show me how to install it myself. I'm saving up to get my own place. A trailer or something like that."

"Right here in Le Moyne?"

He gave me a crooked smile. "Oh, that's just for the summer. At three dollars and thirty cents an hour, you think I could buy one of them mansions over yonder in Darrow?"

He was getting me riled up again, which I didn't want to be. We had some things to work out, but I figured I'd leave well enough alone.

We ate every morsel on our plates, and then I took the bill over to the cashier. We hopped back in my car to drive Preston home.

WE TOOK A detour on the way to Preston's house, back to that
nook off the road by the Bayou Teche. We closed up the roof of
my car, rolled back our seats, and we went at each other like two
octopuses in heat. There's a lot better places to mess around than a
two-seat convertible with a damn console and stick shift getting in
the way, but we was lusting for each other fierce.

I missed Preston. Not just being with each other like that,
though that all came back as good and easy as I remembered. I
missed that boy for all the things about him, even his thick-headed
stubbornness. I used to think Preston Montclair was all the happiness I needed in the world. I felt that again that night.

I showed Press a thing or two I'd learned that year, and with
the aid of a scoop of my hair gel, I gave myself to him. Snuggled
inside me, Preston beamed so bright, I laughed out loud.

"I'm starting to think you enjoying this."

He gazed at me gently and held my face. "Arizona Fanning, I
never stopped loving you."

I curled my neck from blushing so much. "It's Bondurant now.
And I think you love *this*."

"No sir." He held me tight while he pushed in deeper, slow and
gentle. "I'll always love you. Don't tell me different. I love you like
this and every which way."

I gave him a smirk. "We could try some other ways. But we
best wait till you get your uncle's pickup fixed. Have a little more
elbow room."

He laughed. God, I loved watching Preston laugh. I loved all
the expressions on his handsome face, and I got some motions
going to get him grim and moaning, lips parted, clenching his eyes
shut and thrusting needfully.

Things went quick after that, and we jumped in the river to
wash up. It was dark, and there didn't seem to be nobody around
besides the bullfrogs and the minnows slipping by our shins. So I
gripped his shoulders and wrapped my legs around his waist to feel
him up close again. We kissed some more. I don't think I'd ever
seen Press so happy, and that made me happy too.

"I better not be dreaming. Arizona, I didn't think you'd ever come back to me."

I combed the side of his hair. "You understand now, don't you?"

He nodded and nuzzled his nose against mine. "You feel different now, being a Bondurant?"

That was a tough question to answer. "Sometimes. But I was raised a John's Island swamp rat. I think that'll always be part of me."

"Handsomest swamp rat this side of the Mississippi."

"They like me fine on the other side as well. Don't forget, I been to Baton Rouge, and I'm living in Darrow now."

Preston hooted. "Don't get me jealous. I'll fight any man who's got ideas about making you his."

I felt his bicep. He'd always been lean and well-proportioned, and now he was bulking up and hardening like a man.

He pulled back from me a little. "Arizona, I can't expect you to answer me right away. But I'd sure like to pick up where we left. Y'know, how things used to be. You think about that?"

"Press, I can tell you this. You're stuck with me this summer. I got wheels and nothing to do but get into trouble."

That made him smile. Though only for so long. I could tell he was thinking about the distance between us, not to mention me going back to school when Labor Day came around. I hurt thinking about those things, too. So, I kissed him and got him awake downstairs so we didn't have to worry about that situation, at least for the night.

3

I HAD A whole lot of things to think about after that night with Preston. That boy hadn't even been on my mind since last summer, but the fact he was the first person I ran into back in Le Moyne and the way we got along so well after patching things up, I wondered if we were meant to be together. Preston knew me better than anyone in the world, even my new friends at school. He was kind and loyal and made me feel like I could be myself. After we'd really made love, I was thinking, like he said, maybe we ought to pick up where we'd left off. It sure was easy being with Press.

Still, I had doubts and fears. We were a ninety minute drive away, and that was just to get together on the slip. Preston's family couldn't know about us, and with his work schedule, he couldn't make the trip to Darrow unless I picked him up. We'd be spending more time in the car than visiting each other.

And that was just the dog's whiskers on the problem we were facing. I'd be going back to Middleton for my senior year and only coming home around the holidays. After that, I was planning to stay up north for college. Miss Antonelli told me I should apply to a top tier school like Columbia or Brown, which had the best creative writing programs in the country.

I was in anguish lying in bed the next morning. I hated the

thought of leaving Preston again, but I didn't want to regret not going after my hopes and dreams. I was looking forward to my daddy coming home later that week. I sure could use his wisdom and experience to help me figure things out.

I might've stayed in bed till noon since I had nothing better to do, but I heard footsteps pass by my room, headed to the wing where my daddy and my grandmother slept. I jumped out of bed and threw on a bathrobe to take a look. Maybe Daddy made it home early.

Whoever passed down the hall was long gone by the time I got out there.

Something about those heavy footsteps got memories percolating inside my head. *Boots?* It couldn't be. I ran over to my balcony, which looked out back and to the side of the house clear over to the car lot. Sure enough, I spotted a fire engine red Ford Ranger, which belonged to none other than Mr. Dan Jolly.

Dan Jolly and I had a history, and one I'm none too proud of. My daddy hired him to exercise his horses, and last summer he asked Dan to teach me equestrian lessons. Well, a few weeks into my lessons, I went on like an idiot confessing I was in love with him. That was short of my sixteenth birthday, so you have to keep in mind my brain wasn't fully formed. Other parts of me, well, that's a different story. Dan Jolly was as handsome as a Hollywood actor and boy, did he ever fill out his riding britches nicely. He was the finest specimen of manhood I'd ever seen. As if that wasn't enough, he had a smile that could charm a cow into buying milk. I'll call it an infatuation on my part, and when I blubbered to Dan about it, he told me he wasn't that way, but it'd be fine with him if I gave him some relief in the stable shower every now and then after our lessons.

And like a craven fool, I took him up on that offer, dreaming it would turn into something more.

That wasn't even the main reason I was hopping mad to see his gleaming sports utility vehicle that morning. I wasn't the only person in Whittington Manor Dan been giving the how-do-you-do with his willy. I searched my room and pulled down one of my daddy's old boxwood croquet mallets, which were mounted on the wall for decorative purposes. Then I marched down the hall in my bathrobe until I came to my grandmother's room.

The door was closed. I shoved it open and sized things up. There was Dan, stripped down to his blue boxer shorts with his hands inside Virginia Bondurant's lace nightie. They were both frozen to stone from me breaking in on them. I stared at Dan and clopped the hardwood mallet hammer in my palm.

"Arizona? Good golly. You home from school already?"

Dan had always been slick as oil with his big, handsome grin. It made me want to send him off for dental work.

I pointed the mallet at him. "Get out."

Dan held up his hands. "Now, son, don't be getting the wrong idea. I was just giving your grandmother a muscle massage. Getting her limber. You know she suffers aches and pains after riding."

"You get the hell out 'fore I break both your kneecaps, and you'll be needing a wheelchair to roll over to the Workforce Commission."

He smiled nervously.

"You wanna test me?" I stalked toward him with the mallet raised to my shoulder.

"Boy, you simmer down. Ain't nothing going on here that can't be explained."

Virginia cowered behind him like the snake she is.

"You gonna leave?"

Dan was too slow to answer. I swung for the closest thing I could shatter, which happened to be the china lamp on Virginia's dresser.

She shrieked. Dan waved his hands, sprouting sweat on his temples.

"That's your three second warning."

"All right. I'll just get dressed."

I whipped that mallet into the bedpost, no more than a hand

spread from where Dan stood. The canopy collapsed on one side, and Dan jumped like a leapfrog.

"You leave here in your drawers like the filthy swine you are."

Virginia screamed for help. "Somebody call the police. The boy gone and lost his mind."

I'd put a thing or two together. She must've sent Mr. Wainwright away that morning so she could have her tryst with Dan. Maybe the housemaid Mrs. Laroche would come to her aid, but we both knew she'd be no better for it in the long run.

"Call the police? You go ahead, grandmother. We'll get this little social visit on record. Might even make the *Weekly Citizen* police blotter."

She hollered at me through tears. "You no good country trash. I'll talk to Poly. Have him send you back to the swamp where you belong."

I ignored her because meanwhile Dan was bending down to grab his riding britches from the floor. I hammered my mallet, just missing his stinking hand.

"What did I tell you? Get out."

He shook his head. Looked like he might start crying himself. I threw a play jab at him, and he skittered toward the door. I grabbed the keys to his pickup off the dresser and followed behind him like a prison warden moving a man along to the gallows. Gave him a prod in the back every now and then for a little extra motivation.

Mrs. Laroche had come out of her sewing room from the commotion. But when she saw Dan Jolly stumbling down the hall in nothing but his blue boxers, and me, pointing that big, hardwood hammer at his back, she shrank against the wall with her hand trapping her mouth. I gave her a wink as I passed by.

Out back by the car lot, I tossed Dan his keys, which he fumbled to catch and had to scrounge up from the gravel. He righted himself and pointed a finger at me.

"This ain't right, Arizona, and you know it. I always been a friend to you."

That left just one last thing to do. I strode over to his pickup, busted both his headlights and gave that shiny, waxed hood a great big dent. The hammer came off the stick with that whack, but I still had the long, splintered handle, which looked something like a spear.

"You come over here again, it'll be a rifle you see pointed at your head. And don't expect to be getting any references from my daddy."

Dan scurried to the driver's side door, climbed in, revved up, and careened out of the car port down the drive to the gates.

NOBODY IN THE world could get me angrier than Virginia Bondurant, and keep in mind, I'd had my share of fools and bullies in my life. Gus Fanning who'd punched me in the face and collapsed on top of me in a drunken stupor, moaning my mama's name and groping me between the legs. Christopher Watts-Jennings who got everyone at Middleton Academy calling me a faggot until we came to fists, and his father sent him away to a military academy. And I can't say I had any warm feelings for Mr. Wainwright, who must've tossed every letter I wrote to Preston and my siblings in the trash.

Still, Virginia Bondurant would always be my enemy numero uno. I could live with her hating me for being a reminder of my daddy's infidelity. But I was not going to abide her disrespecting the man who'd turned my life around and made me special.

I marched up to her room as soon as Dan's Ford Ranger disappeared down the drive.

Mrs. Laroche was already in there with a broom and a dustpan to clean up the destruction I'd wrought. Virginia was nowhere to be seen, but then I heard the shower in her adjoining bathroom. Just like her to leave a mess for someone else to fix.

I apologized to Mrs. Laroche and sent her away. I didn't have regrets about what I'd done, but it wasn't the poor woman's responsibility to clean up the lamp and bed I broke. Shards of that lamp had scattered helter-skelter. I swept for near a half hour to clear away every last one. Then I surveyed Virginia's bed and frowned. The bed post was splintered like it had been struck by lightning, and I had no idea what to do about that.

The bathroom door opened, and Virginia strolled out in a robe and a towel wrapped around her head. She glanced at me and startled.

"What in the name of God are you doing here?"

I straightened up from my hunched position beside the bed. "I want to talk to you."

She grabbed one of her glass bottles from her tall, mirrored vanity. I thought she might throw it at me, but she just uncapped it and rubbed the lotion into her elbows. I'd never seen her out of her makeup. Virginia Bondurant was a former Miss Louisiana and a runner-up in the Miss America beauty contest. She minded her figure and never looked her age. But that day, I could see the fifty-something woman she was, and it might not make sense, but I was ashamed for both of us seeing her that way.

"I've got no interest in talking to you. You've done enough damage this morning. Go on and bug off."

I watched her uncap a brown bottle of pills from the pharmacy and swallow a pair of them down with a glass of water from her desk. My daddy had told me she had a nervous condition, but I'd never seen it. I think she just liked being hopped up on pills and liquor.

"This affair with Dan Jolly is over," I told her. "I'm not letting you break my daddy's heart."

She sat down at her vanity and uncorked another bottle to rub some unguent into her face. "The things you don't understand could fill the Library of Congress. Now, leave me to my peace." She took up one of her brushes to make up her face. "Surely you can entertain yourself elsewhere, wrestling in the mud with your country kin."

"What're you gonna tell your husband?"

She said nothing. I took a careful step closer.

"Arizona, you may have had the upper hand this morning. But that was round one. I've handled crooks and triflers all my life. I always come up on top." She snorted mirthfully. "Sixteen years old and you think you run the roost."

I'd be lying if I said she didn't strike some fear in me. That woman could cut a man down with just a look. I think she'd been born with venom instead of blood.

She went on making up her face with a ghost of a smile. "Now, the first thing we're going to do is get you enrolled in a nice summer program. Seems you like outdoor sports. We'll find a ranch that takes students for the summer somewhere nice like Montana or Saskatchewan."

She couldn't do that, could she?

"My daddy knows I wanna stay here. I ain't budging."

She laughed. "You can try."

"I'll tell him about Dan."

She pivoted toward me in her seat. "Arizona, you ever heard the expression about shooting the messenger? You said yourself you don't want to break your Daddy's heart." She turned back to her mirror and focused on plucking her eyebrows.

"I'll do it 'cause he's got a right to know you been running around making a fool of him."

She sighed. "So young and naïve. You resemble your mama in that way, thinking she had Poly all to herself. Thinking she could take him away from me. But you go on and tell your daddy what you saw this morning. While you're at it, ask him about Philippa and why she really left him. Ask him what he's up to on all his long business trips." She clucked. "As if I'm the only one breaking marriage vows."

That fear inside me wound up tighter. I couldn't discard the possibility she was right. That whole house was full of ugly secrets I didn't want to know.

"What're you thinking, Arizona? You going to have that talk with your daddy? Could be quite the drama. Poly knows I could ruin him if certain things came out. Why do you think he tells everyone you're his grandson?"

I was suddenly freezing cold. I'd thought everything was out in the open about me, but Gaston Bondurant being known to have gotten his sixteen-year-old step-daughter pregnant would be disastrous for his reputation and his company. I felt ashamed and helpless.

"Here's what you're going to do," Virginia said. "When your daddy gets home, you're going to tell him a bat flew in from the attic. Happens all the time in this old house. You tried to kill it with his croquet mallet and ended up tearing apart the room. You'll get a tongue lashing, but he won't be too sore. I've been eyeing an upgrade on this old bed set anyway. You do that, and we'll see about me reconsidering telling him about that dude ranch."

I didn't know what to say. I was ready to be done with her. I stepped out and went to my room.

4

LATER THAT WEEK, I heard goings-on outside the house. I stepped out and saw Mr. Wainwright directing a team of men setting up an outdoor barbecue. I guess my daddy wanted a big party for his return from Houston. They were setting up chairs and tables for ten dozen people or more.

So much for having a private conversation with him. Truth be told, I was split down the middle about doing that after what Virginia said to me. I couldn't tell him about Dan Jolly. I didn't even want to ask him what I should do about Preston anymore, either. I wasn't sure I knew my daddy as well as I thought I did. I'd known he cheated on Virginia to be with my mama, but I hadn't thought on that too hard before. They say once a cheater always a cheater. Could be he'd cheated on my mama, too. I was feeling low, wondering if he even cared that much about me.

I stayed in my room all day just writing a letter to Jonathan and paging through a book by John Irving, which Miss Antonelli had loaned me. When Mr. Wainwright came along to tell me to get dressed for my daddy's arrival, I had to fight through my gloom to shower and shave, fix my hair, and put on the aquamarine madras dress shirt and seersucker suit Mr. Wainwright had set out for me. At least I looked good on the outside.

I heard Daddy's booming voice as I came down the stairs and walked over to the men's parlor, which was done up with mounted buck heads and muskets on the walls. For the first time in history, Virginia beat me to a gathering. She was sitting snug as a bug at an overstuffed chair in the corner, wearing a Grecian white dress, working on a martini. Daddy looked slick in his blue vested suit and bow tie. He set down his highball, came over and gave me a hug that lifted me off the floor.

"I won't be able to do that for long," he said. "You're growing by the day and getting twice as handsome."

I turned my head, grinned and blushed.

"Well what you got to say to me, Arizona?"

"How do you do, Daddy? Welcome home."

He gave me a play uppercut to the chin, and then he pulled me into a big hug again. "I'm so happy to see you, son." He walloped my back with his hand. I think he was a little drunk. "How you like your birthday present? It came a little early, but I knew you'd need something for getting around town this summer."

My birthday wasn't until August 12th, but I sure didn't mind. "I love it, Daddy. Thank you."

"I heard you already took her on the road. How's that five-speed manual transmission?"

"I'm getting the hang of it." I laughed. "It's something else. You shouldn't have spent so much money on my birthday, but I'm glad you did."

"You earned it. I saw your grade report. You keep up those straight As, and you'll have your pick of top colleges." He waved a servant along to fetch me a glass of lemonade and moved us over to a pair of Chesterfield chairs closer to Virginia. I was hoping he wouldn't, but it was the only polite thing to do.

"I'm so proud of you, son. Now tell me all about your year at Middleton, and don't leave out the fun parts. I know them Yankee boys can stir up some trouble."

I didn't want to say anything in front of Virginia. She was watching me with a false smile and sure to make a wise comment.

But I couldn't say nothing. I told Daddy about my friends, the equestrian club, and all the good books I read in Miss Antonelli's class.

"He must be in seventh heaven living in close quarters with all those boys," Virginia chirped. "I bet he's made a name for himself in the bathroom stalls."

I stared flames at her. Daddy chuckled uneasily, playing things off. "Where do you come up with these things, Ginny?"

"I like keeping up with popular culture. Did you know Rock Hudson's a queer? I read it in *People* magazine. This gay plague is sorting everyone out. I had to hire a female hairdresser for fear of catching it myself."

"It's not a plague," I told her. "It's a virus." I fixed a long stare at her. "The kind you catch through sexual relations."

My daddy patted my knee. "How'd we get on such a morbid topic? Tonight's a celebration to ring in Arizona's return from school."

Virginia took a draw of her martini. "We should've had the servants dress in pink. And ordered feather boas for the guests."

I grinned at her. "Now, that would've been fun. But luckily we've got a female impersonator in residence right here. All you need is a bigger set of bosoms, and you could put on a revue." I frowned thoughtfully. "Maybe the Camellia dining room would go best with your lipstick."

"All right, you two. You're giving me a headache, and I haven't even had my third Johnnie Walker. Ginny, the guests are due to arrive any minute. How about you go on to the south lawn and make sure everyone feels welcome. I intend to walk in arm-and-arm with the guest of honor."

He gave me a wink. Virginia downed the rest of her martini, and one of the lady servants came over to escort her from the room. I hoped she didn't have quick reflexes if Virginia happened to stumble drunkenly in her heels.

Daddy had another servant line him up a refill on his whiskey. Then he looked at me confidentially.

"If I could change anything in the world, it would be you and your grandmother's relationship. That's something money can't buy. It breaks my heart the two people who mean the most to me can't help sparring all the time. Well, I suppose the two of you will come along to an understanding at your own speed."

I'd never get along with that woman. I wanted to point out it would be nice if he defended me now and then when she said cruel things, but I didn't want to spoil my daddy's good mood.

He stretched a hand over to wring my shoulder. "I've got some people I want you to meet tonight. Arthur Ruben is my vice president for communications. Steel Linklater and Leroy Price lead the sales team. Now, the decision's up to you, Arizona, but I was thinking you could do an internship at B&B's marketing department this summer. I know you've got the head for it, and it would look good on your college applications."

My insides sank. I had no interest in business. I wanted to be a writer, and besides, I didn't want to spend the summer working in my daddy's corporate office.

The disappointment must've been showing on my face. Daddy smiled wryly, and I could see thoughts churning in his head while he tipped back his highball.

"I'd sure like to get you involved in the company. But you don't have to give me a yes or no right away."

"Daddy, it's just...I've got things to take care of this summer."

He looked at me expectantly, and I went on.

"I'd like to visit Duke, Dolly, and Little Douglas. It's been near a year since I saw my brothers. Little Douglas is all the way in Texas. Dolly, well, she's due to birth a baby any day now up at some Baptist home for girls in Mississippi."

I told him about looking for Duke earlier in the week and wanting to see if I could track down the itinerary for the traveling circus where he was working. Then I drew a deep breath and mentioned I had a good friend from school back in Le Moyne.

Daddy shrugged. "Nothing saying you couldn't take a long weekend, even a week to travel. And as for your friend, we could

have him over for Sunday dinners. You've got the horses and the
lake for fishing and swimming. Lots of things two fellows can do
while getting caught up." He threw back the rest of his drink. "You
think on it. I know you've got ties to them Fannings. And Gus
Fanning's kids are carrying the burden Gus put on them with his
bad decisions. But don't you forget, you've got a family by blood.
And like the Bible says, blood's thicker than water."

I was even more out of sorts after that. I'd sworn I would take
care of my siblings, but now I had two families, and he was saying
I ought to put my effort into one over the other?

Daddy stood up. "I think it's time. You hear the band? You
ready to make your entrance?"

I stood and followed him along out to a party with people who
were strangers to me.

THAT WAS ONE big, dizzying night. Daddy had invited dozens
of his executives from B&B, and they all had wives and children of
different ages. He had hired none other than Mr. Wynton Marsalis
to lead the jazz band for a private concert. They played inside a
covered pavilion with a dance floor and lights, and they sure did
raise the house. The chef stations had barbecue pork, chicken,
gumbo, rice, fried fish and oysters, everything gourmet quality.
They were setting off fireworks at dusk, and I knew everybody
would be dancing until late in the night.

My daddy brought me around to his associates, and like he'd
said, they were important people with titles like VP this and execu-
tive that. Daddy always said I was his grandson, and the few times
he had to elaborate, he said I'd grown up with his aunt Gertrude
due to my mama's passing. I'd heard him spin that tale before, but
not since he'd told me the truth last Thanksgiving.

I went along with the story and tried being friendly for his
sake. The men he worked with seemed real happy to meet me and
keen to know how I was doing at school, though I could see why

they treated me so graciously. That's what you did when you were introduced to the grandson of a rich and powerful man.

They did start looking a little restless when I talked about my interest in being a writer. I noticed Daddy tighten up a bit, too. From that point on, I spared the businessmen that story, and I managed to carry on some conversations about manly things like horseback riding and college football.

One of them fellows, Steel Linklater, was eager to introduce me to his daughter, Fiona, who was also going into her senior year. She went to a Catholic school in Metairie called Our Lady of the Immaculate Conception, and she was one of them society girls with curled strawberry blond hair and a ruffled dress. I was happy to have someone my age to spend some time with, but Fiona gave off strange signals. It felt like we'd been set up for a date, and I had to skate over lots of things about where I was from and who I was. It didn't help I couldn't stop watching my daddy work that party.

I'd always admired his charm and sociability, wanting to be the kind of man who filled up a room like him. Everyone loved my daddy. But watching him that night was different.

I noticed things I hadn't before, like how he got the ladies smiling, especially the young, pretty ones. He did it in a way that didn't disrespect their husbands or daddies, but I could tell those girls were mesmerized by him, idling around to hear him talk, their eyes wide and grinning, shifting this way and that to give him views from different angles. I caught Daddy gazing across the tent at a young redhead in a green, peplum dress that hugged her body, and she was sneaking glances back at him.

"You got a girl up in Massachusetts?"

I jolted. I'd forgotten Fiona was sitting next to me at a table where we'd stopped to have coffee and cake.

"No. Well, Fiona, you're a real sweet girl. But you should know there is somebody. We just got back together when I came home. We'd been going steady for four years."

She sighed. "Always my luck. All the good ones are taken. Didn't someone write a song about that?"

"Ian Hunter." I knew my British rockers thanks to Nicolas.
She nodded glumly.

"We can be friends," I told her. "What do you say about
having a dance?"

"You think your girlfriend wouldn't mind?"

"It's just a dance. I won't get fresh if you don't."

I took her by the hand and led her over to the dance floor. We
danced a sloppy kind of swing all the way through the band's third
encore.

Things started breaking up after that, and I exchanged phone
numbers with Fiona before she had to leave out. It would be nice
to have a friend who lived nearby, and her house was just down
Route 10 in Metairie. Then Mr. Wainwright came by while we
were saying farewell.

He looked harassed, which tended to make me smile. I snuck
off with him outside the tent away from the guests.

"Have you seen Mr. Bondurant?"

"No."

He drew my attention to a receiving line at the path to the car
lot where valets were at the ready to retrieve the guests' cars.
Virginia was standing over there chatting with some well-dressed
ladies.

"He's needed to see the guests off. I don't have time to search
for him. I've got to settle up with the band, and all the staff are
clearing the buffet and packing up the rental gear."

"I'll look for him. Where you last seen him?"

Mr. Wainwright shrugged. "One of the servers thought he
might've seen him headed to the house."

I gave him a nod and started off in that direction. Maybe doing
him that little favor might ever so slightly improve his treatment of
me. Anyway, I was intrigued. Daddy had perfect etiquette. It wasn't
like him to leave his own party.

I didn't find him back in the men's parlor, and then I thought
to check his private study. It could've been he needed to have a

conversation about the company with his executives, and they lost track of time.

As I came down the back hall, the place was awfully dark and quiet. But I noticed a sliver of light cast out from the study, and I gained up on that room. I still didn't hear any voices, but the door was partially open and lights were on. Cigarette smoke hung in the air. His study was the only place Daddy smoked one of his unfiltered Camels, and the few times I'd caught him smoking there, he had serious matters on his mind.

Then I heard his voice, and call me a weasel, but I drew up close to have a listen before making my presence known.

"I been telling you that since September...I know...yes ma'am...Honey, what do you want me to do? I can't just race over to Chattanooga at the drop of a hat..."

I didn't hear any other voice. He must've been talking on the phone. He sounded keyed up and a little drunk. I could hear the clink of ice cubes in a glass. I skulked past the door to take a peek into the room. Daddy was leaning on his desk with his back turned to the door, a telephone receiver in one hand and the other alternating between his cigarette and his tumbler of Johnnie Walker on the rocks. It wasn't right for me to eavesdrop, but that conversation had me as nosy as a bloodhound. It had to be something real important for Daddy to run off from his guests, and it was going on midnight.

"Cher, don't I always make it up to you? What do you say to taking a trip to Bermuda next month? Book a suite at the Hamilton Princess with all that pink sand you like? You know I'm crazy about you. I'd fly up tonight if I could...Now don't be talking that way. You know it's a complicated situation, but I'll be up to see you as soon as I can...You've just got to be reasonable..."

I stepped away and headed back outside. I'd heard the gist, and I didn't need to know anything more about that conversation.

5

I COULD TRY to explain my relationship with Gaston Bondurant in a hundred ways, but not one of them would come out right. Looking back, I should've been angry he couldn't own up to being my daddy in front of his friends. I should've been sore he barely made time for me, and meanwhile he was keeping a mistress in Chattanooga and maybe he had other girlfriends like Virginia had implied.

Truth was, those things confused me, but it wouldn't have occurred to me I had a right to complain. I idolized that man for all his wealth and accomplishments. I felt I owed him my loyalty for taking me in. He spared no expense to give me a good life, and most of all, he loved me no matter I'd grown up in the poorest country parish in the state and come out as gay. He was the only decent father I'd ever known, so I suppose I made allowances for him.

But we shared something even deeper that went beyond being blood, though it could've been related to that. It had always been his responsibility to take care of everyone. Nicolas had told me about their mama not being right in the head, and their father dying so young and Daddy having to run the company as a young man in his twenties, all the while looking out for his twelve-year-old brother and his sick mama.

I knew what that was like, having lost my Mama Lou at thirteen, leaving me and my siblings with Gus Fanning who terrorized us, while I had to keep Duke, Dolly, and Little Douglas fed and keeping up with school. It was hard and so lonely at times, I felt hollow and nothing could make the ache in my gut go away.

I guess I first felt the pain we shared when Nicolas died, and I don't just mean the regular kind of grief people go through. He felt like he'd failed his brother, and he needed me to hold him and say everything was going to be all right. I think he was chasing after something he needed, hoping he'd get it by keeping people happy. But that was never enough, and maybe he was blaming himself for things in life he couldn't control.

My grandma Tilly used to say the same thing about me. I blamed myself for my Mama Lou getting in a car accident, and I blamed myself for my Mama Philippa dying in childbirth, and then I blamed myself when Grandma Tilly and Grandpa George died in a fire. Being the older brother, I always felt it was my job to make sure my brothers and sister were taken care of, and sometimes I felt selfish for wanting things just for me. So, hearing Daddy was trying to hold on to that woman in Chattanooga got me thinking about him differently. Like, maybe that woman gave him something he needed. He didn't mean to hurt anybody by it, and didn't the man deserve some happiness? He tried to make my grandmother happy, but that woman would never forgive him for being with my mama. Daddy and I didn't have anybody to look out for us besides each other.

Anyway, when we had breakfast together Sunday next, I told him I decided to do that summer internship at B&B.

I knew that would make him happy, and I also knew he was a businessman who liked making a deal. So, I proposed I'd need next week to visit Dolly in Mississippi, and I wanted my Fridays to Mondays to spend time with Preston or see my brothers. We worked things out over Mrs. Gundy's blueberry cornmeal pancakes, and Daddy was mighty pleased. He told me he'd have Buck drive me to his corporate headquarters in New Orleans the following Tuesday so I wouldn't have to rack up mileage on my car. He was taking a trip to Canada that week, but he said when he got back, we'd plan a big party for my seventeenth birthday, which was coming up in less than two months.

On Monday, I packed up for my drive to Fernwood, Mississippi, which was where Dolly was living in that Baptist home for wayward girls.

It was a two-hour drive, and I don't know what I was expecting, but the little, two story Victorian white-sided house where I pulled up seemed too ordinary for a home for girls who had gotten into a bad way. They had a cross over the front porch, but it looked like every other house on the block otherwise. I parked my car across the street and stepped over to ring the bell at the front door.

A wide-hipped woman with short, gray hair and a plus-sized Jesus T-shirt answered the door. I introduced myself. The lady looked past me to my Corvette and doubled back over my sports jacket and leather penny loafers.

"I came to see my sister Dolly Fanning." I tried out a smile. "This is my first time in Mississippi. You heard of Darrow? That's where I come from. It's a small town just upriver from New Orleans."

"Come in." She stood aside so I could enter the foyer. The house stunk like it had been run over by an old, dirty vacuum cleaner too many times, but I told her everything looked nice.

"I'm Mrs. Witt. It woulda helped if you called ahead. Can I get you an iced tea?"

I wasn't fond of iced tea, and I already wasn't fond of Mrs. Witt. I suppose it wasn't her fault, but Dolly hadn't wanted to get shipped off to that house like she was so tarred with sin, she needed to be hidden from the eyes of good people. I tried my daddy's approach of killing your enemies with kindness.

"Why, that would be mighty kind of you," I told her. "I apologize for not calling ahead. I only had the address, and the telephone operator couldn't find a number for the house."

I followed Mrs. Witt as she waddled toward the kitchen. "It's private," she said. "For the protection of our girls. Visitors supposed to contact the church office on Maple Drive. Dolly shoulda told you that."

"My apologies again." I took a gander around while I passed through the house. It was awfully quiet for a house full of teenage girls. No sounds coming from upstairs. Maybe everybody had gone out for the day. I sure hoped Dolly was around.

In the kitchen, Mrs. Witt poured me a glass of Country Time iced tea. My eyes skimmed over the linoleum tiles, olive green cabinets and sunflower wallpaper. Over by the sink, a girl with a big bump in her stomach was peeling potatoes. She couldn't have been older than fifteen. She looked kind of glum in her dowdy smock, and Mrs. Witt sent her away before we could say hello. She was the kind of woman who probably worried about the perils of boys mixing with girls, which was funny seeing as her wards had already gotten in a bad way, not to mention, she had nothing to worry about with me.

I took a few sips of the sickly sweet iced tea and told Mrs. Witt it was delicious. Then I asked her very nicely if I might see my sister, having traveled so far to do so.

"I don't recall an Arizona in the Bible. Are you a Christian?"

"Yes, ma'am. Roman Catholic. That's part of the big Jesus rainbow, wouldn't you say?" I wriggled my eyebrows. That woman was as uptight as a nun at Mardi Gras. She frowned like I was being fresh with her, which I was getting close to doing.

"Dolly's not well," she said. "It happen sometimes when the baby come, but she got it a little worse. She resting in her room."

"I'd like to cheer her up. And see the baby." I brought out of my jacket pocket a rattle I'd picked up at the pharmacy in town.

"The baby's not here."

"Is she all right?"

Mrs. Witt said nothing. She looked like she was enjoying

keeping something from me. "Best let your sister tell you the news. The girls only get forty-five minutes to visit. I'll bring you up to her room."

My heart started doing skips. I followed Mrs. Witt upstairs where it looked like they had four or five bedrooms. Everything was very tidy, and the doors were closed. She brought me along to the last door at the end of the hall, and she knocked and told Dolly she was coming in. Then she brought out a big ring of keys from her skirt pocket and fiddled out the one for the room with her fat fingers. I nearly gasped. Was she running a home or a penitentiary?

It was dark as night inside. The blinds were drawn over the room's two windows. The room smelled like stale sweat and unlaundered clothes. Mrs. Witt clicked on a light. She gave me a firm look.

"Forty-five minutes. I be timing. Door stays open."

Now she was giving me the heebie-jeebies. She stepped out into the hall, and I came over to the side of my sister's bed.

Dolly had her bedsheet pulled over her head. I had to give her a rustle.

"It's Arizona. Your brother."

When she showed herself, I was disturbed, though I tried to not let on about that. She had unwashed hair matted to her face. She was pale as milk, and she didn't smell too good. She propped herself up a little. She hadn't lost the baby weight, and she'd put on a lot since I'd last seen her almost seven months ago. The worst was the hollow look in her eyes. I noticed a bottle of pills from the pharmacy on her nightstand. Could be those were making her groggy. My sister and I had our ups and downs, but it was hard to believe seeing me didn't stir up any emotion. No reaction at all at first, as a matter of fact.

"Don't tell me you don't recognize your own brother."

She pulled her sheet back up to her neck. "I didn't want you to see me looking like this."

"Dolly, you're a sight for sore eyes no matter how you look." I felt brittle thinking about what she'd gone through. My baby sister. Still a baby at thirteen years old. "Was the birthing hard?"

She shook her head. "Dinah. That's what I named her."

"That's a real pretty name."

She hiccupped tears. I fumbled to say something.

"When'd she come?"

"May 26th."

That was just over a week ago.

I smiled at her, and she sniffed away some tears. "She was tiny. Five pounds, ten ounces."

"She doing all right?"

Dolly's face shrank up again, and she curled over on her side.

I sat down next to her on the bed, trying to look her in the face. "Dolly. What happened?"

"They took her away," she sobbed.

"How you mean?"

"The Landrys. The pastor and his wife."

That was the Jonesville couple Social Services had placed her with. I remembered my visit the past Thanksgiving. Pastor Landry had a little house behind his cinder block church. I also remembered Dolly saying they wanted her to give up the baby, and she was hell-bent on keeping it. She never did say who the father was, but I had an idea, and I didn't like it.

"Well, you'll get to see Dinah when you go home, won't you?"

She shook her head. "They don't want me no more. All along, he just wanted his baby and to get rid of me."

My stomach turned. I almost couldn't bring out the words. "Pastor Landry's the father?"

She broke down in tears again.

I wanted to kill the man. Then the lump forming in my throat got bigger and achier, and I couldn't stop myself from choking out a sob.

"Dolly," I sputtered. "What kind of man would do this to you?"

Like she'd been possessed by a demon, her tone changed on a dime.

"What you crying for?"

I stared at her.

"Ain't your problem, is it?"

I tried to clasp her arm. She ripped it away from me.

"Dolly, I came here because I wanted to see you," I said with a squeak in my voice. "I ain't here to judge. I'm here to help."

"You wouldn't be here to judge, having all them sins of your own. I don't want your pity, neither."

I drew a breath. As much as it tore at me that she hated me for being gay, I wasn't going to fight with her in her condition.

"Who came to see you, Dolly? Not Gus Fanning. Not Duke. I'm here because I love you, and you tell me who else you got?" I swiped my face and tried to calm myself. "Just let me know what I can do. I promise, I'll do anything I can."

She propped herself up to look at me. "You gonna get my baby back?"

I fumbled for words again, and then I held her shoulder. "Dolly, what Pastor Landry did to you, that's rape. It's against the law."

"He don't say so. He say I got in trouble with a boy."

"But you didn't, did you? That's what you're telling me, isn't it?"

She looked away from me, but I could see her chin quivering. "He came to my room at night. Told me he couldn't help himself. That I was like Jezebel in the Bible, making him sin. Then, when the baby started growing in me, he said it was my shame for being a temptress. But that's what the Lord wanted for me, and I oughta have a baby to love. Isn't that right?"

I didn't know what to tell her. Part of me was reeling from the fact a man who was supposed to take care of her like a father did that to her. Another part was reeling from the idea that she could be a mama at such a young age.

"I know it ain't right for a grown man to put a baby in you. First thing I'm gonna do is settle that fair and square."

"I don't want nothin' to do with that man. I just want my Dinah."

I tried to comfort her while she cried. "I told you before, you need a mama, not to be one yourself. When you get older, you can be a mother to that child. But right now, we need to bring Pastor Landry to justice and find a good home for both you and your baby."

She turned her yellowed, watery eyes to me. "Where am I supposed to go? You gonna take me in?"

I was ashamed I had no answers for her. Then she gripped me tight and started bawling again. "Please, Arizona. I ain't got nowhere to go. They gonna send me off with some family, and I never gonna see Dinah again. No family's gonna take in a girl with a child."

I hugged her and gave her a kiss on the cheek. "I'm gonna make this right. You just stay strong, you hear? Ain't nobody treats my sister this way."

I made her give me a nod, and I went to look for Mrs. Witt.

I FOUND HER in the kitchen tinkering with pots on the stove. I told her as politely as I could what had happened to my sister, and there was no way another child belonged with that monster Pastor Landry.

I'd known several ways the world can cut you down to size before that day, but I learned a new one with Mrs. Witt. I explained what Dolly had told me, and that cruel woman acted like I was the one in the wrong.

"Pastor Landry's a man of god. He was called by our Lord." She fixed on me squarely. "Now, you best not repeat anything Dolly told you. The girl's delusional, and I won't let either of you ruin that good man's reputation."

"I think I understand, but I just want to make sure. You calling my sister a liar?"

Her eyes flared. She was a big woman. Probably had beat a lot of girls in her time. But I wasn't scared of her.

"She's thirteen years old. And I know about your family, young man. With no mama to teach her right from wrong and a father who's an adulterer and a drunk, it's no surprise she turned out to be a whore. And now she's blaming a good Christian man who tried to set her right?" She shook her head. "The girl belong in an institution. We'll find a good Christian treatment center where she can work for her room and board."

"What kind of place you run here?" She gaped at me. "I'm asking you a question. Where's Jesus in this house?"

She clucked. "You questioning me, boy? I'm sorry to inform you, I ain't intimidated by a sixteen-year-old from Darrow, Louisiana. You might've landed better than your sister with all them people flashing around their wealth and breaking the commandments of our Lord, but you ain't free of sin. I see it in your eyes."

I had to remind myself of the impropriety of striking a woman. I didn't even trust myself to open my mouth for a count of ten. I took a step away from her, drew a breath, and tried to put two and two together. Then I came back to her.

"I'm taking Dolly home. We'll pack up her belongings, and we'll be on our way."

"You'll do nothing of the sort. You a minor, and in the state of Mississippi, it would be against the law for me to release that child to you."

"How old I got to be?"

"Eighteen. Now I say it's past time for you to be on your way."

I couldn't move. I was so flustered and defeated.

"I say it's time for you to leave, boy. And you think twice about bothering that good man Pastor Landry. First thing I gonna do is ring him up so he can have the police on the lookout for you."

I raised my gaze to her. "I learned some real good wisdom from a man I used to know. There's people beautiful on the outside, but they're rotten ugly on the inside. Then, you have your people who are ugly outside, but they're beautiful the other way around. You, Mrs. Witt, you ugly outside and in, and that's the truth. I'm not as religious as you, but you can bet I'm gonna pray for any girl who ends up in your care." I pointed my finger at her. "I see what's on the inside, too."

I staggered out of her house, hopped in my car and drove off. When I was a quarter mile down the road, I pulled over to the shoulder, beat my fist against the steering wheel so hard, my hand throbbed, and I crumpled in tears.

6

I DIDN'T KNOW what to do with myself after that morning. I was in some kind of haze like I'd just crawled out of the wreckage of a ten car pile-up on the highway. There was nothing physical wrong with me, but my head wasn't working properly. At some point, I made a turn in the direction of Le Moyne Parish. I guess deep down, I had an inkling of what to do. I drove to the cemetery where I'd been a few weeks ago, and I walked over to Grandma Tilly's grave and sat with her again.

I told her everything that happened, and I looked up at the sky, hoping for a sign. Somebody had to tell me what to do. Should I kill Pastor Landry for what he done? Go back to Fernwood and break Dolly out of that rotten house? I was all she had. Her big brother. I had to do something, but I didn't want to make her situation worse than it already was. I was real angry at God. What good was he if he couldn't protect a thirteen-year-old girl from getting raped and treated like it was her fault?

I shed so many tears, I felt like there was nothing left inside me.

Toward dark, I realized they'd be locking up the cemetery pretty soon. My watch read 7:20. I could rush over and catch Preston before he got off work at Merle's, so that's what I did.

He scolded me about showing up out of the blue, but he looked real happy to see me. I sure needed to be around someone happy to see me. I waited for him to call his mama to say he wasn't coming home for dinner. Then I drove us to our spot by the Bayou Teche and told Press about my day. I was wrong. I still had tears left.

Press took me in his arms and tried talking some sense into me.

"You ain't murdering Pastor Landry, cher. You wanna get yourself on death row? And you ain't stealing Dolly out of that house. You take her over state lines, and that's a federal offense."

I peeked at him. "For someone who dropped out of school, you kept up with your civics lessons."

"Nope. I just have cousins who've had their share of trouble with the law."

I straightened up in my seat. "What am I supposed to do? That woman said I have to be eighteen to take her in."

"It's only a year."

I kept my thoughts to myself for a while. I was supposed to be going off to college in a year. I couldn't take Dolly with me, and I certainly couldn't take her along with her baby, if there was a chance she could get Dinah back.

Was it wrong for me to not want to sacrifice going to college for my sister? If I took responsibility for my sister and her child, I'd have to come home after I graduated from Middleton, and I'd already asked and been told no about Dolly living at Whittington Manor. I'd need to get a place for us to live. Find some low-paying a job, get Dolly enrolled in school, and help out with her daughter. I'm ashamed to say it, but picturing that future had me feeling worn out and sick.

Blood's thicker than water.

"Arizona, what's stirring in your head? You ain't back to hog-tying that pastor somewhere in the woods and cutting his throat to let him bleed out?"

"Huh? No." I scratched my head. I hated lying to Preston, but that's what I did. "I was just thinking about talking to my daddy about this. Not looking forward to it. Last time Dolly was at Whittington Manor, we got to sparring so bad we brought my whole birthday party to a halt."

Preston wrapped his hand around mine. "I'm gonna give you something to think about, and like I said the other night, you don't have to say one way or the other right away. In a year, I'll have money saved up to get my own place. Well, to get *our* own place if you'd have me. With both of us working, we could get a good house here in Le Moyne. You only need to come up with ten percent. That's two thousand dollars with a ten-year mortgage of just one hundred fifty a month. And that's a ranch big enough for all three of us plus Dolly's baby."

He might've caught the blank look on my face. "I been looking into these things, but we don't have to talk them it right now."

I gripped his hand. He was so damn sweet. "I told my daddy about you. He said you should come over for Sunday dinner."

Preston beamed. "Sunday dinner at Whittington Manor? Now that'll be something to tell my folks."

I described the place, which I'd done before, but I knew he liked hearing it. I liked seeing him with a big boy's grin on his face and stars in his eyes. He'd never rode horses before, but he'd always wanted to.

"You gonna have to help me figure out what to wear." He gave me a crooked glance. "If this is what you wear to drive to Mississippi, I reckon I need a tuxedo to come over for dinner."

I poked him in the ribs. "Clean shirt. Button down is best. Belt and slacks. No sneakers, boy. Leather shoes."

He laughed. "Well howdy-do. Now, how am I supposed to talk?" He put on an imitation. "Pleased to meet you, Mr. Bondurant. My, my, you've got a house to beat the band." The damn fool knit his brow. "He's a proper Frenchman, isn't he? Not like the broke-ass Acadians 'round here, huh? Think I should try out my French? Bonjour. A little comment t'allez vous?"

"Just try proper English, and you do fine."

His face turned a little glum.

"Press, what you worried about? All you gotta do is be yourself."

He sniffed his shirt. "Wish I could take a shower. That's why you need to call ahead. I gave you the phone number at Merle's."

I smirked. "Then I best drive you home so you can get cleaned up. We can try this another day."

He grabbed my arm before I could twist on the ignition. "Don't be stupid. I got you now. You ain't getting rid of me." He glanced out the window at the river. "How 'bout we rinse off. See how things go from there?"

I looked at him funny. "I ain't taken you to dinner yet. And you best believe we ain't walking into Clemmon's stinking like we been wrestling in a swamp."

He giggled and placed his hand on my thigh, creeping his way up to the good parts. "What do you say to a couple burgers at Sonic? We don't even have to leave the car. They bring your dinner right to your window. Meantime, we can work up an appetite. That wrestling idea of yours sounds like fun."

I watched his hand find me between the legs. "Mmm. I guess you do have a point." I opened the car door, stepped one foot out and glanced back at him. "But I bet you can't beat me to the water."

I jumped out and started stripping down in a hurry. Preston never could resist some competition. He tried to catch up, but I was naked as a jaybird before him and went cannonballing into the river.

I DIDN'T GET a chance to talk to Daddy until Thursday that week. After he got back from Canada, he worked late every day, coming home after supper, and the timing never felt right. I hoped to catch him in a good mood so I'd have his full attention. I was scared to tell him about Dolly regardless of how he reacted.

I spent my days taking Duchess or Bonnie through the trails in the woods on the east side of the estate. Duchess was the brown mottled thoroughbred I'd learned to ride last summer. She was gentle and easygoing and would be perfect for Preston on his first ride. Bonnie was a taller girl, and she could kick up some speed when she wanted to. I'd gotten to be a better rider that year, and I had no problem getting her used to me. Funny, after a couple of days, I actually preferred saddling her up. When she opened up in a gallop, it was like flying in mid-air.

One of the trails had a clearing along the lake where I'd first seen Nicolas's cabin in the woods across the water. I reined in Bonnie to take a look and reminisce. Nicolas and I spent two glorious weeks together there last summer. Probably doesn't sound like much, but I loved that man. He was beautiful, and gentle, and kind, and smart. He loved reading just as much as me, and he introduced me to gay writers like Paul T. Rogers, William Burroughs, Gordon Merrick, and James Baldwin. He was my uncle and fifteen years older than me, which made what we did wrong. But that didn't make my heartache any less.

That gave me an idea. The next day, I brought a satchel with one of my school notebooks to the stables, and in the afternoon, I rode Bonnie over to the family cemetery. I spent all day under the giant willow tree by Nicolas's grave, and I wrote him a letter to say how much I missed him, along with all I'd done that year.

I lost track of time. I heard the clop of a horse coming down the trail, and when I glanced that way, I saw Daddy rein in Duchess and lead her over to a picket outside the cemetery. He done found me before I found him.

I stood and dusted myself off. My daddy had been a prize-winning equestrian in his youth. He looked the part in his sharp riding gear and the confidence with which he handled Duchess. When he walked over, he smiled and pulled me in for a hug.

"I had a feeling I'd find you over yonder. You've got Mrs. Gundy in a lather, son. Dinner was supposed to be at seven. She made her signature pork tenderloin and says it's getting all dried out."

"I'm sorry, Daddy. I got to writing and time just flew by."

He waved me off. "Mrs. Gundy will keep. First thing I should've done when you came home was take you here to pay your respects."

I watched him gaze at Nicolas's grave. December 18th, 1953 to November 28th, 1984. His headstone had veteran stars for his service in the Vietnam War. He'd been a medical officer, fourth class.

Daddy slung his arm around my shoulder. "You meant a lot to him in the short time you had together. I never told you that, but I think you know, better than anyone."

I was touched by him saying that but squeamish at the same time. Nicolas and I loved each other physically, and that was something I don't think I could ever talk to my daddy about.

"I was writing him a letter. To let him know I'm doing all right, and I still think about him."

Daddy nodded. "He'd like that."

"I bet you miss him, too."

He nodded again. His face turned grim.

"You can't blame yourself for him dying, Daddy. If anything, it was my fault."

"Arizona, it's nobody's fault. There's just one person to judge, and that's God himself. You remember that always, won't you?"

He kissed me on the forehead. "Now tell me what you've been doing with yourself. Mr. Wainwright said you been spending a lot of time on these riding trails."

"I have. I missed the girls. And that friend of mine, Preston, I invited him to come over Sunday. It'll be his first time riding a horse."

"I'm looking forward to meeting him."

I drew in a deep breath. I didn't want to keep anything from my daddy, but I was getting butterflies in my stomach.

"Daddy, Preston is more than a friend."

His face ticked, but he recovered with a grin. "Then I'm

looking forward to meeting him even more. Though he's got a lot to prove to say he's worthy of my son."

I gawped at him. "Daddy, you'll be kind, won't you?"

"I'm not making any promises."

"Preston's good people. He's honest. Hard-working. Got a good head on his shoulders."

Daddy patted my back. "Well if you like him, I'd say there's a good chance I will too. Let's say sixty-forty. Could be better odds if he's minding his education and planning on a good career."

I let that pass in silence. Time for a change in subject.

"Daddy, I don't mean no disrespect, but do you think we could skip introducing him to Virginia?"

He gave me a long, stern look, but I could tell he was in a playful mood that day. Sure enough, he couldn't hold out too long before snickering.

"I'd say why spare the boy the entertainment, but as it happens your grandmother's out of town. She heard about some dude ranch out in Montana. She's spending a whole month up there, if you can believe it."

That was the best news I'd heard all day.

"How 'bout we head back to the house before Mrs. Gundy throws that pork loin in the rubbish?"

I held him up. It seemed like I'd have no better chance to catch him about the situation with my sister. So, I told him. Couldn't look him in the eye the whole time, but I got out everything from A to Z. Then I asked him what I should do. He took a long time to form his thoughts, and I wasn't sure what to make of his shifty gaze.

"Arizona, I was trying to tell you the other day, you can't help people who can't help themselves."

"She been raped by that pastor."

"I understand that's what she says. But you don't know. Were you there?"

I couldn't help raising my voice to him. "No, sir. But she's my sister. Thirteen years old. How's she getting pregnant at that age?"

"Now, hold on. You know better than taking a tone with me, son. All I'm saying is you don't know. The sad truth is, this kind of thing happens to girls every hour of the day. I'm not acquainted with this Pastor Landry, but I'd say you've got one hell of a hill to climb trying to prove that child is his. It'll take a lot more than a thirteen-year-old girl's testimony, and in the meantime, you can bet she'll be dragged through the mud. I've seen these things happen, son. She'll be worse off than she is now, if the case even makes it to trial. I know it's not fair. It's just the way of the world."

"What am I supposed to do?"

"I can't see a stitch of good you *can* do. You said yourself she's not fit to raise a baby. Why not let it go, son? I know you and them kids been raised together, but here's the hard truth you need to put to mind—you're different, Arizona. You've always been meant for a better life. I know you see it. You're my son. Trying to change the fate of your sister and brothers is only going to bring you down. I won't have that. It's no good for you. I can see what it's doing to you already."

At first, I felt socked in the gut. I'd changed Dolly's diapers when she was little, played house with her and held her when Mama Lou died. But then things started getting muddled in my brain. Gus Fanning was her father, and he'd been nothing but cruel to me. Everything about that family had been cruel and miserable, and I didn't need to be part of it no more.

Still, I ached for Dolly. She was all alone in the world, and she didn't know we weren't blood. I trembled, and tears rolled down my face.

Daddy held me. "Listen. Listen here, son. You've got a big heart, and you've done all you could. I'll have some people check out this Pastor Landry. If there's anything untoward going on, you can be sure he'll answer for it. But don't let this situation get to you. You're a Bondurant. There's nothing in the world you can't have. Now, that's a privilege and a responsibility. You focus on that and be the best man you can be."

7

I WASN'T SURE how to feel after that conversation. Was I a lousy fink for abandoning my sister? Or was I best off leaving the past in the past? I had so much I wanted to do with my life. I wanted to go to college. I wanted to write novels and meet all types of interesting people. Heck, I wanted to see the pyramids of Egypt and go all around the world.

Forgetting about Dolly, Duke and Little Douglas would be easy. If I could live with myself for doing it.

I didn't sleep so well the rest of that week. To top things off, I was worried about Preston visiting. I'd told him all he had to do was be himself, and I thought I'd meant it. But now, picturing him meeting Daddy, well, you can call me a phony. Truth was, I was getting itchy.

I got over to his house about eleven Sunday morning, and it was a strange day from the start. My blue Corvette convertible caught a lot of eyes as I drove down his block. Ain't nobody nosier than folks on John's Island. It seemed like every one of Preston's neighbors was on their front porches just waiting for me to arrive.

At his house, I only opened the car door before Preston's entire family poured out to greet me. His daddy, Richard. His mama, Jean. His younger brothers, Earl and Harry. His aunt Regine, his uncle Willy and their four kids who lived just down the road. They surrounded me like I was a celebrity come home from Hollywood. Funny thing was, a year ago, after I bashed that liquor bottle over Gus Fanning's head, they didn't want Preston having anything to do with me.

"That's one beaut of a vehicle you got there," Mr. Montclair said.

I could see he was pining to take a closer look. I told him he could go ahead and hop inside. Pretty soon, all ten of them were taking turns climbing in behind the steering wheel. A group of neighbors drifted over to see if they could do the same thing. I didn't care. I waved them along to have their fun.

"Preston's taking forever getting dressed," Mrs. Montclair explained. She turned to the house and hollered for him. "We went to the mall over in Lafayette to pick out a new shirt and a pair of shoes."

"He looks like a fairy," Earl piped in.

His mama swatted him on the side of his head. "What I tell you 'bout talkin' like that?"

Earl was fifteen, the same age as my brother Duke, and he was a country boy through and through. Having to wear clean jeans with no holes was too fairy for him. He winced at his mama, but he shook it off real fast.

"Arizona, is it true? You Gaston Bondurant's grandson?"

That raised Mr. Montclair's temperature. "Listen here, dummy. Your older brother told you so. Why you gotta question the boy?" He fixed a friendly gaze on me. "It's mighty kind of Mr. Bondurant to invite Preston over for Sunday dinner." He nudged his son. "Go on and get your daddy's Polaroid. And tell your brother to get his butt out of the bathroom while you're in there."

Earl scampered away. Mr. Montclair kept beaming at me. "My older brother, Charles, he's a line supervisor over at Mr. Bondurant's refinery in Acadia. His two sons are working their way up the ladder as well."

I didn't know what to say to that. I think he might've been angling for me to put in a good word for his brother and nephews.

Preston's Uncle Willy came around. "Gaston Bondurant hire a lot of people. He's a good man. Keeps the economy a-runnin'."

Just then, Preston came out of the house. He had his hair slicked back, wore a starched, long sleeve button down and slacks, and looked about as flustered as a rooster in a lawn sprinkler. He ducked his head and strode toward my car with his gym bag from school, which must've been packed with his swimsuit and a change of clothes.

He shot a glare at his brother Harry. "What you do? Go house to house telling everyone my business?"

I popped open the trunk so he could stow away his bag. I felt bad for him. Everyone was laughing, and it's not that they were laughing at him, but I knew he hated the attention.

I stooped down in front of little Harry. "How'd you like I come back here on a Saturday and take you for a spin on the highway."

Harry's eyes grew the size of saucers, and he nodded his head vigorously. Preston shot a sour look at me and shut himself up in the car.

I went to drive us off, but we were delayed by one thing after another. Earl tramped out of the house with Mr. Montclair's Polaroid camera, and Mr. Montclair took shots of me and Preston in the car. Then he wanted a photo of his whole family standing around us, like we were driving off to our honeymoon. Uncle Willy cornered me with questions about the car engine, the transmission, and what kind of mileage I got. Mrs. Montclair ran cursing into the house and brought back a big green Tupperware container and handed it to me.

"Preston can't come to supper at Whittington Manor empty-handed." She grinned giddily. "I hope the Bondurants like pralines. I made 'em myself."

I thanked her and finally, they let me pull away from the curb and drive off.

After a count of twenty, I turned my eyes to Preston. His face was beet red, and he looked hopping mad. I tried not to, but I just couldn't help chuckling.

"It ain't funny."

I smirked. "If you say so."

Preston glared at me. "What kind of people do something like that?"

I minded my humor.

"It's plain ignorant is what it is."

We were silent for a while. Then I got to smiling and that led to chuckling again.

"What's so damn amusing?"

"You."

"Well ha ha. You go on laughing. I never been so humiliated in my entire life. But you just laugh."

"Earl said you looked like a fairy."

I was just teasing him for fun. Poor Preston didn't take it so well. Couldn't produce a word.

"Preston Montclair, I know you've got a sense of humor. They're good people, your family. Well, maybe except for Earl." I gave him a glance. "You sure clean up good. Handsomest fairy I ever seen."

He swatted me.

"Excuse you. I was paying you a compliment."

"I ain't in the mood for compliments."

"Hmm." I spotted a place on the shoulder of the road where I could pull over. I left the keys in the ignition, stepped out of the car, and came over to the passenger's side.

"What're you doing?"

"I drove all morning. I say it's your turn at the wheel."

Preston fussed at first, but I could see him warming to the idea, checking out all the gauges on the console, the stick shift, the gold-brown steering wheel. I opened his door, and he filed out and got back in on the driver's side. He took his inventory of things and broke out in a grin.

"Go on, country boy." I eased back my seat.

Preston very carefully pulled back onto the road, but by the time we were on Highway 90 out of Le Moyne, he got some wind whipping in our faces, and he howled like a hot rodder on a Saturday night.

I THINK PRESTON near fainted when he turned onto the drive of Whittington Manor. I'd just about done the same the first time Buck took that turn in Daddy's Bentley, saying it was my new home. It made me happy seeing that sense of wonder through Preston's eyes.

Mr. Wainwright met us at the front hall, and I told him we'd be changing into riding gear and packing up swimsuits and towels to take to the lake. To my surprise, the mean old meddler said he'd taken care of all that. Outfits were laid out in my room along with a beach bag. Mrs. Gundy had packed us a picnic lunch. Preston handed Mr. Wainwright his mama's pralines, and I led him upstairs and onward to my room.

When we had our privacy, Preston looked at me like he was about to burst.

"You putting me on?" He caught himself and lowered his voice. "You *live* here?"

"Mm-hmm." I sat down on the bed to take off my shoes. "You keep gaping, you're gonna catch flies."

He staggered out to my balcony, took a look, and staggered back to me. "Arizona, maybe I oughta go home. I don't think I belong in a place like this."

I shot up from my chair, grabbed both sides of his face, and shut him up with a deep, wet kiss. Then I pulled off my polo shirt and unbelted my pants to get into my riding clothes. Preston stood frozen where I'd left him.

"You gonna get changed? We already missed half the day driving 'cross state."

Slowly and blankly, Preston stripped down to his drawers.

I pulled my britches on, and then I couldn't resist giving him some more sugar while he was so handsomely indisposed. Soon enough, I was contradicting myself about getting a move on. I pushed Preston into my bathroom, shut the door and dropped my britches. I freed him of his briefs, and we went to town.

Afterward, I led him into my bathtub to take a shower. We nuzzled and kissed some more.

"Arizona, I don't think life gets any better than this," Preston said.

I snickered. I had half a mind to say we could forgo the horse riding and swimming and mess around in my room all day long. It felt so good being with Press. I had to summon every ounce of my willpower to move us along. We only had the rest of the day and that night. I was driving him home first thing in the morning.

So, we dried off, and I showed Press how to put on his britches, his undershirt and button down, and his riding boots and cap. I'd told Mr. Wainwright Preston was a little wider in the shoulders and chest than me, but otherwise the two of us were close in size. Preston's outfit fit him like a champion. I had to pull him away from admiring himself in my dressing mirror.

At the stables, I got Preston set up with Duchess. I helped him fix her saddle and reins and geared up Bonnie.

Press was a little stiff and timid on his horse at first, but he got the hang of things. I kept close to him at an easy pace and took the wide and level trail through the woods to the lake. It was a hot June day, but a little cooler once we got into the thick of the old oak trees and sycamores. Preston warmed up to Duchess, and I could see she liked him, too.

We reached a clearing by the lake, and I dismounted and helped Press step down and picket his horse. We'd both sweated through our shirts, so I suggested we cool off in the lake before having our picnic lunch. Mr. Wainwright had packed up a pair of swim trunks for me, but I had other notions in my head. I'd rarely encountered anyone on that side of the woods. A groundsman once in a blue moon, and who cared what any of them thought? I threw off all my clothes and waded into the lake. Preston followed suit and trudged after me.

That lake water was blissfully refreshing. I swam out deeper where I was covered to my shoulders but could touch the squishy floor. I dunked my head and hollered because it felt so good. Press swam up on me, looking mischievous, and we wrangled a little until we were just holding each other. I wrapped my legs around him to stay afloat, and soon enough we were pining for one another real bad and grinding and stroking to make each other burst for the second time that day.

I made Press carry me piggyback to the bank. We dried off with towels, and I unpacked Mrs. Gundy's picnic lunch. We devoured pork sandwiches, coleslaw, and her special beignets. We passed back and forth a thermos of fresh-squeezed lemonade to wash it all down.

I told Press some funny stories about life at Whittington Manor. I had plenty of material between my dealings with Mr. Wainwright and evil Virginia who swilled half her weight in gin most nights. I also told him about Mrs. Gundy, who was a character herself. She was a big woman, black as midnight on a new moon, and she was built like she could hold her own against a linebacker. The woman fascinated me. She had big, meaty hands that could probably strangle a horse the way she worked dough for hours, making biscuits and breads. She didn't have no recipe books. I don't know if she could even read. But there wasn't a better cook in all of southeastern Louisiana. I'd heard Daddy say it himself.

She took charge of her kitchen, and you best not get in her way. She was the only person in the estate who could put Virginia in her place. They'd get to arguing about the dinner menu, but no one could tell Mrs. Gundy different when she made up her mind. Virginia would hem and haw, but if she wanted Crab Louis and Mrs. Gundy wanted Shrimp and Grits Étouffée, you could bet you were getting shrimps for dinner. Virginia always ended up storming out of the kitchen, mumbling curses under her breath.

But the funniest story was when Mrs. Gundy's husband came by the house, usually after supper. He was an old bean pole of a man. He drove a United cab in New Orleans, but as he was getting on in years, Mrs. Gundy only let him drive during the day, and mostly just back and forth from the airport to the hotels in the center of town. They were Jack Sprat and Mrs. Sprat. Mrs. Gundy always heaped up a big plate and made him out to eat on the stoop outside the kitchen. He'd eat every morsel, and God only knew where it went. He always looked like he could blow away in a strong breeze and where Mrs. Gundy was loud and forceful, he was quiet and meek. Though one night, I heard him serenading his wife with some old folk song, and she got to singing along. That was just about the sweetest thing I'd ever seen.

Preston gazed at me. "You got a real home here now."

I shrugged. "Don't feel like it all the time. But I've got lots to be thankful for."

"You sure do."

Something was making him sad. I bumped my shoulder against his. "What do you think about going to New Orleans some weekend?"

We'd been talking about doing that since seventh grade. Preston grinned. "If I can keep up with you. Seems like in just a year, we're running at different speeds." He looked away and plucked idly at the grass. "You changed, Arizona. I ain't saying it's bad. I just think sometimes I might not have what it takes anymore to keep you happy."

I scowled at him. "Press, I wouldn't have asked you here if you didn't make me happy."

He glanced timidly at me. "Do I make you as happy as that fella you were with last year? What was he like? You said you fell in love."

I looked out to the lake. I wanted to be straight with Press. He deserved it. But it was an awfully hard story to explain. The two of us used to talk about everything real easy. It made me think he was right about me having changed.

From the spot where we were drying off in the sun, you couldn't see Nicolas's cabin. But during that quiet spell, with the low sun glinting on the lake and a breeze sighing through the woods, I felt his presence, or something like a benediction.

I pushed out some words. "He was a lot of things. He taught me to not be ashamed of who I am. That's real important. You should never be ashamed of yourself, either."

"Was he real handsome? You said he was older than you."

Did I? "Just by a few years."

Preston looked at me funny. "You said he worked at your daddy's company. He had to have graduated college."

I nodded.

"You think he was more the type of man you should be with?"

A breath rushed through my nose. "Press, you ain't got to be jealous. He's gone. I've come to terms with that."

Deep down, I knew he wasn't talking about just that kind of jealousy. But I didn't want to have a conversation about our relationship. Things were going fine. We had the whole summer together, and couldn't we wait to see how that turned out before talking about our future?

I reached over and turned his head toward me and kissed him on the lips. "You think too much. That's your problem, Preston Montclair."

"I ain't never been accused of that." He grinned at me.

I stood and held out my hand to pull him up. "C'mon. We gotta head back. Gotta get you cleaned up and dressed for dinner."

He took my hand, and we wrestled into our clothes and mounted the girls to trek back to the stables.

SUNDAY NIGHT SUPPER at Whittington Manor was always a fancy affair when Daddy was home. Preston and I got back to the house, and Mr. Wainwright informed me my daddy had invited a small assortment of people: his good friend, Lawrence Barbet, who was also the family lawyer, along with his wife Claudine. More interesting, the guest list included a famous jazz singer, Marguerite Francois, who entertained at nightclubs from New Orleans to St. Louis and all the way to New York City. Miss Francois was bringing along an entourage of three men. The nine of us would be dining in the San Francisco salon, which was an opulent room with red velvet wallpaper, a dining table for a dozen people, and a grand piano. I loaned Preston one of my sport jackets and assured him he'd look just fine.

We sat down for a five-course meal from Oysters Rockefeller to prime rib to Mrs. Gundy's famous Hummingbird Cake, which was just about the most delicious thing known to man. My daddy let Preston and me drink beer right there at the table, and soon enough, we were all in a festive mood. Mostly, the grown ups talked among themselves, but I glanced at Preston from time to time and could see he was enjoying himself.

After the dessert course, Daddy pleaded with Marguerite to do a number for us, and we all moved over by the piano where there were red upholstered settees and wingback parlor chairs. That Miss Marguerite was a stunning, dark-skinned woman and real fashion-able in her purple sequin dress with ruffled skirting. Her friends were three black fellows in colorful suits. I could've been wrong, but two out of three seemed like they might've been friends of Dorothy as they say. The youngest looking one sat at the piano and got to playing a song by Billie Holiday. Miss Marguerite took a place by the piano, and she sang along to that soulful melody, filling that big room with her beautiful voice.

She performed a couple of numbers, and we all stood up and clapped. I put my fingers in my mouth to give her a whistle. I'd never had two beers before, and I was feeling happy and drunk. When we sat back down, I even stretched my arm around Preston's shoulder on our settee. It was nothing so scandalous, and I felt like cozying up to him. We were seated nearest to Mr. Barbet who turned to us and started making conversation.

"How you making out at Middleton Academy, Arizona?"

"I'm taking to that school like a bee to honey, Mr. Barbet. I've got a straight A average. Try as they might, them Yanks can't keep a Southern boy down."

Preston hid his face and blushed. I guess I was a little cocky after my two beers, but everyone around us was all smiles.

"That's the right attitude," Mr. Barbet told me with a wink. "What're your plans for college? You see yourself as a Harvard man like your granddaddy?"

I wasn't too drunk to notice my daddy giving me a glance. But I was drunk enough to speak my mind anyway.

"Now I hear Harvard's the best university in the country. But I've got my sights set on Columbia in New York City. I intend to be a writer, and if Columbia was good enough for John Kennedy Toole, wouldn't you say it's good enough for me?"

John Kennedy Toole won a Pulitzer Prize for fiction, and he grew up in New Orleans. That got folks chuckling again. Except for Press.

"That's an admirable profession if you've got talent," Mr. Barbet said. "But it's not the easiest way to make a living. You don't think you've got business in your genes like Poly and every Bondurant who come before him?"

I considered my words, but not for too long. "Now, Mr. Barbet, you a lawyer. Is that something you always wanted to do?"

His face darkened, and he peeked at his wife. "I suppose when I was your age, I had my mind set on something different. I played basketball in high school. I made the team at Loyola University. But I was always second string and figured I ought to line up a back-up plan."

My daddy broke in. "I'd say that worked out well for you, Lawrence. You've got the top law firm in all of Louisiana, and there's people talking about you running for state attorney general."

"I don't know about all that, Poly. State politics always been a dirty business, and it don't help our governor, Edwin Edwards, is always getting himself in hot water. There's no dignity in being a Louisiana Democrat these days."

"That there is exactly why the party needs a man like you. And don't you worry about Governor Edwards. Them bribery charges won't stick. The man's slicker than a duck's tail."

"Poly, I think you're the one who's got the fire in his belly to run for office."

Daddy waved him off.

"Not so? Well, meantime, we were talking about your boy here. Got a good head on his shoulders. Might take some time, but I bet he'll come around to choosing a profitable career."

Everyone in the room was looking at me, including Miss Marguerite, who had a kind gaze as though to say, you do whatever you want to do. That was all I needed to run off my mouth again.

"Mr. Barbet, I reckon I could turn out to be a successful businessman like my granddaddy. But I don't think that's my destiny. I just know I was born to be a storyteller, just like the famous Marguerite Francois, who was generous enough to join us for supper." I looked at her. "'Cause that's what you do. A writer can write the lyrics and string along the notes, but it takes a magical voice to bring his story to life." She put a hand to her neck and gave me a smile. I turned back to Mr. Barbet. "What I'm saying is writing is in my soul, and I don't want to grow up regretting I was too scared to pursue my dream."

I caught my daddy glancing at me again. I was feeling like he ought to lay off. I already knew where he stood with my career, but shouldn't my opinion count for something?

Mr. Barbet fixed on Preston. "Let's hear about the other boy. Find out if he's another *artiste* or a more practical type. You keeping up your grades at school? Where you planning to go to college?"

Preston leaned forward and knit his hands together. "I was never good at school like Arizona. Could be I learn a trade. I work at my uncle's gas station, and he's going to teach me automotive repair."

"Don't count out college, son," Mr. Barbet told him. "Instead of spending your life as a grease monkey, you could get yourself a degree designing cars."

Our companions snickered. I felt bad for Press. There was nothing wrong with him pursuing a trade, but in our present company, I think it made him feel small.

My daddy called over a servant to put a jazz record on the room's antique record player, and then he took Mr. and Mrs. Barbet to see the renovated sun room in the back of the house before they left out for the night. That left Preston and me with Miss Marguerite and her three friends. I was feeling so high, I asked Miss Marguerite to dance. I'd learned the jitterbug at school, which was not to say I was any good at it, but my feet were performing wonders after those two beers. Her friends clapped along and hooted. I felt like Mr. Fred Astaire.

After, I plopped down next to Preston. A servant brought over two more glasses of beer for us, and Miss Marguerite and her entourage took seats on the adjoining settee and chairs. They were drinking bourbon and broke out cigarettes and offered them to us, but I'd never had an interest in tobacco. Preston took a Newport from one of the fellas, which surprised me.

One of the men looked eager to say something to me. He was a skinny fellow, at least twice my age, with slick jheri curls. We'd been introduced at the dinner table, and he'd said his name was Curly.

"Mr. Arizona, you what they call a Renaissance man. Writin', dancin', and runnin' your grandaddy's business." He pointed his cigarette at me. "Nothin' can stop you, can it?"

"Now that ain't true, Mr. Curly. I stop for a good time. I stop to let old folks cross the road, and every now and then, I stop when the light turns red."

That got people hooting and chuckling. Though Preston was quiet. I sat back and reached my arm around him. He seemed uneasy, but I didn't know why.

Curly took account of the two of us, adding up this and that.

"You like a good time, you boys should visit Café Lafitte in Exile. You pass a good time there twenty-four hours a day."

His friend Lucius, the piano player, chimed in. "And they got a literary history. Used to be frequented by none other than Truman Capote and Tennessee Williams temps passé."

I was pretty sure what they was getting at. That café had to be a gay nightclub in the Vieux Carré. Lucius was speaking my language, bringing up the two most famous gay writers in the South.

Johnnie, the other man in their trio, looked over at his friends. "Now, don't you go corrupting them boys. You knows Mr. Bondurant is a genuine French gentleman and a pillar of the community. He won't take kindly to hearing you been telling his grandson about the disreputable places you sneak off to late at night."

"Well, I got something to say about that." I pointed my finger at Lucius dramatically. "I don't like your insinuations one bit. So, let me settle something for you, and no disrespect to the lady in the room. I'm queerer than Mr. Liberace when it comes to the bedroom." I turned to Johnnie. "And as for being corrupted, I been corrupting men since I was fourteen years old. I don't give a fig who knows it, including my granddaddy."

Them three hollered and slapped their knees. Miss Marguerite raised her tumbler to me.

Curly laughed so hard his eyes teared up. "Mr. Arizona, you cut out to be a comedian."

I glanced at Preston. He looked like he wanted to crawl under a rock and die.

"How long you two boys been together?" Lucius asked.

I waited for Preston to answer so he didn't feel left out of the conversation. But he was too petrified to say a word.

"Well, Press here, he ain't told people yet. On account of his family that's not so broad-minded if you get my meaning. But we been together going on four years."

"You boys being careful?" Johnnie said. "There's men dropping dead left and right from that AIDS virus. I think it's a government conspiracy. You know that President Reagan would do anything to kill off all the blacks and queers."

I was curious to ask him more about that theory. But just then Miss Marguerite stood up and got everyone's attention.

"No politics. You know that's my rule. Now Lucius, you sit your ass back down at that piano. I've got a song to sing for Mr. Arizona and Mr. Preston, and ain't nobody gonna dance but the two of them."

While they were getting ready, I looked at Preston. He didn't say anything, but when I gave him a nod, his eyes told me he wasn't sore about everything coming out.

Lucius struck up the piano keys, playing a slow, romantic melody. I took Preston's hand and got him up on the floor, with his hands on my waist while I held his shoulders. Then Miss Marguerite started singing, real bluesy and tender, and Press trembled a little and held me tight with his head tucked into my neck.

It had to be you,
It had to be you,
I wandered around, and I finally found,
The somebody who,
Could make me be true,
And could make me be blue,
And even be glad,
Just to be sad - thinking of you.

Preston sniffled. I clasped him against my chest, rubbing his back and keeping him moving in slow circles.

"It's all right, baby. You gonna be just fine."

I swayed us along to that beautiful song.

8

THAT NIGHT WAS one of several new experiences I had that summer. The next weekend, I picked up Preston on a Saturday when he was off work, and we spent the day in New Orleans. We took a trolley car to the Garden District, and afterward we walked all over the French Quarter, stopping here and there at voodoo shops, quaint little boutiques, and dirty bookstores. We sat down on the steps of the big, white stone Louisiana Supreme Court to listen to a saxophone player and watch people passing by.

Later, I pulled Preston along to that Café Lafitte in Exile, which was a two-story hotel with a bar on the ground floor. Nobody asked us for IDs, and we slugged down beers right on the wrap-around porch, holding hands while men snuck glances at us passing by.

I started that internship at my daddy's company. He'd cleared out an office for me on the top floor of his corporate headquarters by City Park. Supposedly, I reported to the head of communications, Mr. Arthur Ruben, but his secretary told me he'd be in meetings all day and he'd left some notes to get me started on this and that.

It was nothing too much. I read through marketing reports and looked at advertising campaigns in newspapers and supermarket circulars. As far as I could tell, B&B Sugar sold itself. Everybody needed sugar, and when people went looking for it on the grocery shelf, the main thing they cared about was the price. My daddy's company manufactured some other products like candy bars and lollipops, so I jotted down some ideas about branching out to sugared drinks and popsicles.

Then one night, I got to looking at the phone number and address for the family who had taken in Little Douglas, and I made a phone call.

He was living in Wichita Falls, Texas. The woman who answered the phone sounded wary, but in the end, she said it was fine if I drove over the following weekend to visit my brother. So, that's what I did at six o'clock on a Saturday morning to make the nine-hour drive over to Wichita Falls.

Now, you cross the border to Texas, you're in an entirely different world. I don't think there's one hill in that state. It's flat as a pancake. Nothing but browned acres of land. I saw oil wells and cattle ranches while I was zipping down the highway, billboards for roadside barbecue restaurants, and dusty little towns. But it was a whole lot of empty space.

Wichita Falls was a small city, meaning it had three exits off the highway. Buck had given me a road map and highlighted a route for me. I was so nervous, I still found a way to get myself turned around once I got off the highway. I had to stop at a Gulf gas station to ask the pump boy how to sort things out.

He was a friendly kid around my age, and he got my map spread out on the hood and drew me a route with his ballpoint pen. I tipped him two dollars, which I think made his day. After that, I finally found my way to 12 Petunia Lane.

That street was part of a new development of aluminum sided homes on the outskirts of the city. It looked clean and kind of boring, every house with the same square yard covered with strips of emerald green sod and the same two story, twin steepled roof and attached garage. I was glad it was a step up from where we'd been raised. It was nothing fancy, but it was the kind of neighborhood where people with good jobs lived.

I parked my car in front of 12 Petunia Lane, and I walked up to the front door with a shopping bag full of things I'd picked up for my little brother.

A woman with a big helmet of feathered ash blonde hair answered the doorbell. Mrs. Cullins. She looked a little stiff at first, but I won her over with a great big smile.

"How do you do? I'm Arizona Bondurant." I reached out my free hand to shake hers. "I'm mighty pleased to meet you." I glanced around. "You've got a beautiful home."

"Thank you. Come on in and let me get you something to drink after your long drive." She led me into the air-conditioned house and over to the adjoining living room where there was a sofa and an easy chair, both wrapped up in plastic. Everything was as neat as could be, but I have to say that house was strange. It hardly looked lived in and got me antsy about touching anything. I was worried I'd dragged in dirt on my shoes.

Mrs. Cullins called out for her husband. "Steve. Arizona Bondurant is here." She turned to me. "You caught him during his Saturday baseball game. He never misses his Texas Rangers." She frowned to herself. "Now what can I get you to drink? I've got Crystal Light. The sugar-free kind. Orange juice? Coffee? Water?"

"A glass of water will do me fine. Thank you."

She wandered away to the kitchen and left me standing in the living room not knowing what to do with myself. I figured I ought to wait to follow her lead about the rules for sitting down on the couch.

I heard voices coming down the hall. They were bickering, Mr. and Mrs. Cullins. Then the man who had to be the husband came into the room. He was your average sort of man, thinning brown hair, brown-framed glasses, a weak chin, a little paunch. He wore a short-sleeve polo shirt, sweatpants, and slippers on his feet. I hiked up a big smile and waited for him to say something. He seemed more off-balance by our meeting than I was.

"How do you do? I'm Arizona. Pleased to meet you."

He stepped close enough to shake my hand.

"Nice to meet you, too."

He didn't sound like he meant it.

"How's Little Douglas doing?"

He scratched his ear. "I'll let Barb tell you about that."

I blinked.

"You come a long way?"

"Yes, sir. Darrow, Louisiana."

"That's right. Louisiana." He narrowed his eyes. "Though I thought your family was from Le Moyne."

"One side of the family. I'm living with the other now."

Mrs. Cullins swept in with my glass of water. She set it down on a coaster on the coffee table in front of the couch. "Have a seat, Arizona."

I gingerly sat on that crinkly couch and put my shopping bag on the floor.

"You interested in baseball? I've got the Rangers and White Sox game on in the den."

"Thank you, but no. I'm just looking forward to spending some time with my little brother."

Mr. Cullins looked from me to his wife.

"You go ahead and get back to your game. I don't mean to keep you from it."

He gave me a nod and ran along to the den.

Mrs. Cullins came over, looking chummy. "Darrow, Louisiana," she remarked. "That's one of them towns with all those antebellum mansions, isn't it? Along River Road?"

"Yes, ma'am, it is." I took a draw from the glass of water. "I don't mean to be impolite, but I'm just dying to see Little Douglas."

"Of course you are. I'll bring him down from his room."

I caught her glancing at my shopping bag. Then she strolled upstairs, leaving me alone in that sanitized living room.

I heard a slow progression of steps down the stairs, and then I turned to see my blond-haired little brother plodding along in orthopedic boots and a pair of metal braces for his legs. I shot up from the couch and swooped over to take him in my arms. He was heavy with all that medical equipment attached to him, but I gave him a great, big hug.

I looked to Mrs. Cullins. "What happened to him?"

"Oh, that's just corrective gear. The doctor's cure for his pigeon toes and weak ankles. We're getting his bones forming right."

I'd never known Little Douglas to have any sort of problems. He walked on his tippy-toes sometimes, but that was normal for little kids. My heart broke seeing him braced up like a cripple. He was only five years old.

I sat down on the couch with him on my lap. "You remember your big brother Arizona? How do you do, Douglas Fanning?"

He bowed his head and blushed. Something wasn't right with him, though.

I gave him a playful scowl. "Now what did I teach you about proper manners? What do you say when someone says how do you do?"

Little Douglas looked away. He'd always been on the quiet side, but he could speak when I'd seen him a year ago for crying out loud.

"How do you do?" I mouthed to him.

Mrs. Cullins had been hovering around us. "He gets in these moods sometimes. We're taking him to a speech pathologist."

I didn't have the faintest clue what she was talking about. Little Douglas just looked like he could use some cheering up. "Well, I been missing you something terrible," I told him. "I brought you some things. You wanna see?"

I reached down to my shopping bag. I pulled out a boy's size Middleton Academy T-shirt and a pair of Oshkosh B Gosh overalls. I knew he was growing, so even if they were a little roomy on him now, they'd fit him fine in a few months or so. The clothes didn't interest him, but when I showed him a squirt gun, he took it proudly in his hands. I'd also gotten him some He-Man action figures, gobstoppers, and B&B chocolate bars.

"We don't give him candy," Mrs. Cullins said. "He had a mouthful of cavities when we took him to the dentist last fall. It was the first time he'd been seen by a dentist by the look of him."

I cocked an eyebrow at her. I'd made sure Little Douglas kept up with all his annual appointments, just like I did with my sister and Duke. Then I cocked another look at her when she plucked the candy right out of my hands. I would've given her a piece of my mind, but Little Douglas let out a wheezy cough.

"It's his asthma. It gets set off by cologne and perfumed hair products."

Now I felt like I'd walked into one of them scenes from that TV show *The Twilight Zone*. Douglas had never had asthma. His pediatrician had always said he was healthy as a horse. And I didn't like Mrs. Cullins's tone one bit. It was like she was implying I was putting my brother's health in danger just because I'd dabbed on some of my Stetson for the visit and a little Dippity-Do for my hair.

"I'll get his inhaler." She left the room with the candies I bought, probably to throw them in the trash.

I studied Little Douglas. While we had some time alone, I asked him, "How you feeling? How you like living here?"

He made a face and shrugged. Then the little angel put his arms around my neck like I was his mama. "You take me home now?"

I had such a hollow feeling in my stomach I thought I might start sprouting tears. I looked him in the face. "I can take you for a visit sometime. I'll talk to your new mama about it. What do you think of that?"

He looked away from me and frowned. I was right concerned. Little Douglas was like a different child. He'd lost the brightness in his gaze, and he must've been miserable having to wear those heavy boots and leg braces all the time. I couldn't even get him interested in playing with his action figures.

Mrs. Cullins came back with one of them spray inhalers. She came over to Little Douglas and gave him a pump in the mouth. Then she stood no more than two steps away, not budging.

"Mrs. Cullins, you think I can have some time alone with my brother?"

"I don't." She crossed her arms. "You have no idea about his health problems. I prefer to be here."

I smirked. "I only been here for ten minutes and you told me about his bad ankles, speech problems, and asthma. What else am I missing?"

She fixed on me self-righteously. "He's anemic, he has a heart arrhythmia, and he's been diagnosed as developmentally delayed. Now that he's in our care, we're nursing him back to health."

"That's what you're doing? Because it looks more like you're making him a prisoner."

That definitely wasn't the right thing to say to her, but I couldn't help myself. She put a hand on her hip. "How old are you? Sixteen?"

"Yes, ma'am. I'll be seventeen in August. And I'll have you know I've been raising this boy since he was born. He ain't *developmentally delayed*, and he never once had a cough or a sniffle."

"There were reasons he was removed from your family. Douglas needs a safe, healthy, and loving environment. I seem to recall hearing you were taken away for juvenile delinquency."

That got me raging mad. Then a worse feeling came over me. I was helpless. Just like with Dolly, I had no legal right to do anything on my brother's behalf. The only thing I could do was try to make things better with his new mama, maybe talk some sense into her.

"Mrs. Cullins, I apologize for my words coming out hot. Little Douglas is my brother. He lost his mama when he was only two. Lost his grandma just last year." I peeked up at her. "I always looked out for him. He brings out protective instincts in me."

"All you need to know is he's got a good home now. A boy your age shouldn't have to worry about the welfare of his siblings. I'm sure you've got plenty of things to sort out on your own."

"That's right kind for you to be concerned, but I'm sorted out just fine. I'd like to take my brother for a weekend visit. I've got a good home now, too. With horses and woods and a lake for swimming. I know Little Douglas would just love it."

That terrible woman gave me a look like I'd suggested taking my brother over to some honky tonk bar and then bull riding.

"Young man, I only agreed to this visit because I'm a good Christian woman who believes in charity. But I can see now it wasn't a good idea. Douglas is a very sick boy. We're correcting things that haven't been right for a long time, and not just physical. After all the trauma he's been through, frankly I don't think he should be spending time with you."

My jaw dropped. I shook my head, and then I took a different tact. I pulled out my wallet.

"You're giving him a safe, healthy, loving home, huh? How much did you pay Gus Fanning for him? Couldn't have been more than a thousand. It must've been a good bargain to get you traveling cross state. But look here, I'll double it. I'll even triple it if I can get over to the bank."

She looked horrified by all the bills in my wallet. I'd cashed out my two week paycheck from B&B so I could take Little Douglas to dinner and over to a water park or something like that.

"I think you best leave."

I stared at her. "I think you best not speak to me like I'm some boy who delivers your papers. You know who my daddy is? Gaston Polydore Bondurant. He could buy up this crummy house a thousand times over and have you and your husband living on the street and standing in line at a soup kitchen."

"Get out before I call the police."

I regretted my damn fool mouth then. I was just so angry and scared. "He's my brother. My baby brother. Now I know I got a temper. Said some things I shouldn't have. But you can't just go on and separate us."

She called for her husband. I wasn't too worried about that based on what I'd seen of him, but Little Douglas had buried his head in the back of the sofa and started to cry. I didn't want to make him sad with all the fighting and seeing his brother get forced out of the house by the police. I took him in my arms, gave him a hug and made him look me in the eyes.

"I love you. You remember that, you hear?"

I gave him a kiss on the forehead, and I staggered out of that house, holding back the tears until I got into my car.

9

I WAS BACK to where I'd been with Dolly, not being able to do a damn thing for my little brother's welfare. I was so angry at the world, wondering what I'd done to have my heart broken over and over again. I got my car in fifth gear on the highway like I was daring God to put a truck in my path or have me swerve across the highway divider and end it all. At some point, I came to my senses and pulled onto the shoulder to sob over the steering wheel.

I got out of the car, kicked the tires, screamed and broke down again, kneeling in the dirt with the gravel scoring through my slacks. Life was so goddamn cruel. I didn't think things could be worse for me and my siblings after living with Gus Fanning, but don't ever ask how much worse it can get. Life's got an answer for that.

Around midnight, when I reached the highway juncture at Lafayette, I saw the sign to stay straight for Baton Rouge and New Orleans, which would take me back to Darrow. I thought on it a few seconds, and I veered right to catch Route 90 south. I drove all the way to Le Moyne and over to Preston's house. It was almost one thirty in the morning, but I couldn't be alone that night. I didn't trust myself.

Of course, all the lights were off in the house. I couldn't ring the doorbell and wake everybody, so I did what I'd done a couple times back when Press and I were going to school together. I skulked along the side of the house to his bedroom. It was a sultry night, and luckily he'd left his window open.

His bed wasn't far from the window, and I tried calling for him, keeping my voice barely louder than a whisper, which wasn't getting me nowhere. So I felt around the grass, found an acorn, and tossed that into his room, aiming to peen him sleeping under the sheets. It took two more acorns to get him rustling awake. I know it sounds reckless, but I'd run out of patience, and it helped some knowing that even if I woke up the whole house, his parents wouldn't be too mad at me. Based on the last time I'd seen them, they'd probably invite me in and fix me glass of lemonade and a plate of something or other.

Once Preston was up, I called out to him again from the window. He stumbled over in his pajama bottoms quicker than a rabbit with a fox on his tail.

"Jesus, Arizona. You tryin' to give me a heart attack?"

I couldn't muster a sense of humor. It was hard for me to even lift my head to look him in the eye. I asked him to come outside, and he climbed out of his window and followed me to my car. I closed the roof and drove us down the road to the parking lot of Christ the Savior church.

Poor Preston must've thought I'd come to tell him I'd murdered someone and was running off as a fugitive to the law. I explained everything about visiting my little brother. Press held my hand while tears streamed down my face.

"I'm sorry, Arizona. Little Douglas sure don't belong with strangers." He stretched out his arms. "C'mon over here."

I rustled around and fell back into his arms. "I didn't know where else to go."

"I'm getting used to you popping up out of nowheres. I'm glad you did." He kissed my head. "What kind of trouble you looking at when your daddy catches you coming home in the morning?"

"He don't care." I hated how pitiful I sounded. "He's out of town. Probably visiting his mistress."

"Well, that sounds like a story I might like to hear. But we oughta put you back together first. At least you're not getting grounded or having your car taken away."

I teared up again. "What am I gonna do, Press? It's my fault. All of it. If I hadn't hit Gus Fanning that night, Dolly wouldn't have gotten raped by that preacher and Little Douglas wouldn't be living with a woman who's got him living like a cripple."

"You just listen to yourself, Arizona. If you hadn't hit Gus Fanning that night, you might not be here right now. Tell me that's not the truth. And God only knows what kind of shape your sister and brothers would be in. You did what you had to do. Stop telling yourself different."

My heart wasn't quite believing it wasn't my fault, but it did feel good to hear him say it. I wiped my eyes. "Every time I think I'm doing right, I end up doing wrong. Maybe I should try doing wrong and play the odds."

"Stop talking nonsense. You're a good person, Arizona. You couldn't do wrong if you tried."

I turned my head to face him. "I did wrong by you. How 'bout that?"

Preston glanced off to the side. "And you told me. And we weren't together then. What's the point in bringing that up?"

The two of us had had our dramas, but that night was one humdinger. I'd fallen apart. I said things like I wasn't good enough for him and why was he with me in the first place?

"Arizona, if you don't understand how much I love you, we might as well call it quits. Why else in God's green earth would I be climbing out of bed and stealing out of the house in the middle of the night, barefoot and in my PJ bottoms?"

"I'm sorry, Press. I didn't know where else to go."

"Apologize one time more, and I'm gonna beat your bottom red."

For the first time that night, I grinned.

"Aw hell," Preston said. "Is that what all the crying and whimpering was for? You just buttering me up to spank you, you horny dog?"

He slid his hands around my sides and got me chuckling and feeling warm. Then he turned me a little and found my mouth with his. I sure needed that. Him loving me that way was the only thing that could melt away my worries.

Afterward, he got a clever look on his face. "You think we're going to hell? Making out in a church parking lot?"

I grabbed his mouth for another kiss. I didn't care if I was going to hell as long as it was with him.

10

FOR THE NEXT few weeks, I tried to set my mind to other things besides Dolly and Little Douglas. I told myself I was turning seventeen and soon enough I'd be eighteen, and maybe then I could do right by them. To tell the truth, I think I might've died if I kept wondering and worrying about my little sister and brother. I'd been festering with rage and shame. I would've had a nervous breakdown, and that's no lie.

Meantime, I got into a routine with my internship, and I caught my pal Jonathan on the phone one night. I told him about getting back together with Preston, the terrible situations Dolly and Little Douglas were in, and then we talked about all the fun we were gonna have senior year. Jonathan had his own troubles that summer. His family didn't know about him, which made it hard to keep up with Russell, who lived clear across the country in Scarsdale, New York. Besides that, he was working six days a week from noon to midnight at his uncle's taqueria, sharing his old bedroom with three younger cousins while his aunt was visiting family in Mexico. It was great hearing Jonathan's voice, though I could also hear the chaos in the background, and we had to cut things short. I told him I missed him like crazy and he better stay strong.

My daddy put on a great big party for the Fourth of July. He got the south lawn all done up in flags and a staged tent to hold three hundred people. There was a zydeco band led by none other than John Delafose, a local blues band to lead into his performance, a clambake, pony rides for the little ones, and enough Roman candles to rival the big show at the Moon Walk in New Orleans. The guest list was something else: Governor Edwin Edwards himself, national football players, TV actors and actresses, and all sorts of eccentric artists and personalities from the city. After the fireworks, Preston and I snuck off to the lake and made love under the stars.

Sometime around the end of that month, my daddy was home for supper on a Tuesday night. He'd been traveling every week and working late when he was in town, so I was mighty happy to see him. Unfortunately, my grandmother Virginia was also back from the dude ranch in Montana, which meant the three of us were eating together. But it didn't turn out too bad. Virginia must've had a real good time at that dude ranch. She barely had a coarse word for me, and I kept on my best behavior.

Then, after dinner, Daddy asked me to take a stroll with him down to the stables.

He took off his suit jacket and had his dress shirt open a couple of buttons, which was just about as casual as I ever seen him. Even jetlagged and overworked, my daddy was a handsome man. Maybe even more so when he was tired and a bit unguarded. He got me feeling warm inside no matter how long he'd run off and forgotten about me. We walked down the trail to the stables in the waning daylight, not even speaking at first, just enjoying each other's company.

"How's the internship going?"

"It's fine, Daddy."

"Mr. Rubens's team treating you right?"

I smiled to myself. "I'm mainly working with Miss LaCourt, his secretary. She gives me his assignments, and I do 'em."

"Well, I hear good things. You're learning the ropes. Best way to start is at the bottom and work your way up. That's how you get to understanding how a corporation operates from the chassis to the roof. Now lay on me some of the ideas been percolating in that straight-A brain of yours."

I didn't have much to say. At least not much that would impress my daddy. I told him the few things that had occurred to me.

"It seems to me B&B's main competition is Domino Sugar. They're running neck and neck in terms of price, but Domino is always going to have a bigger share of the market. B&B is beating them in the South and some of the Midwestern markets, but you're getting killed north of Virginia, and you haven't got any distribution west of Texas. For B&B to grow, you've got to get into the big population centers like California, Colorado, Oregon, and Washington. Make B&B a household name in all fifty states."

Daddy got to grinning. "Now you're thinking like a businessman. So, how'd you get B&B on the shelves in Los Angeles and San Francisco?"

I sighed. "I don't know, Daddy. I've only been looking at marketing reports and advertising campaigns."

"Tell me what you think. I've got board members and salespeople lecturing me day and night. I'm looking for a fresh perspective."

"Well. If B&B is going to give Domino a run for the money, I think you need rebranding. One thing Domino's got going for them is they keep things simple. That yellow box of cane sugar is a staple in every kitchen cupboard. It don't make people think where it came from or the history of the sugar industry. B&B, on the other hand, has more of an old-fashioned look. That's a good thing in the Southeastern markets. People like nostalgia and the idea of buying something local. But up north or out west, things are different. They don't like to think about the old days of sugar plantations and the exploitation of slaves. B&B ought to have a more modern look. If you want to do better in the urban markets. It's got to, y'know, blend in more on the shelf."

Daddy nodded along. "That makes good sense, son. But if you blend in too much, how's a new customer supposed to take an interest?"

"I been thinking about that, too. You could expand your products. When people like a brand, they'll buy anything with that brand name on it. Like Levi jeans. Or Hershey's. Most people know Hershey's for their chocolate bars, but when they see Hershey's cocoa or Hershey's chocolate milk, they'll pick up those things too because they like their brand of chocolate."

"You've got a point. So what kind of products you thinking about?"

"You've got a lot of options. B&B lollipops sell well. There's companies putting out all kinds of sugar candies from blow pops to candy cigarettes to pop rocks. Then you've got your sugar drinks."

He stopped and looked at me. "Those are sound ideas. For a fellow who says he's got no interest in business, you're picking things up right quick. Do I presume too much or have you taken a shine to your daddy's company?"

I didn't want to disappoint him, but the truth was, I'd rather be spending my days writing and reading books.

"I don't know, Daddy. I can't see myself doing what you do all the time. With all the business trips and meetings. I think I'm more cut out to be grounded in one place."

"You don't have to do the traveling right away. There's work to be done in the corporate office, and I've got plenty of years left to be the face of B&B."

The conversation was getting me itchy. I didn't want to go to business school, but I didn't want to let down my daddy neither.

"Well, it's a start this summer. Let's leave it at that." He took up walking again and gave me a sidelong smile. "You've got a birthday coming up. You give some thought to what you want for your party?"

I smiled. "I'd sure like Marguerite Francois and her friends to come."

He pointed his finger at me. "You've got good taste."

"I just love her voice." I thought on it some more. "But it don't have to be fancy, Daddy. We could just have hamburgers and hot dogs."

He smirked at me. "You want McDonald's to do the catering? This from a boy who asked for lobster bisque for his homecoming dinner?"

"I'm just saying, it don't have to be so elaborate. Just a few friends and family. The people who're important to me. Preston already put in for the day off work."

Daddy was silent for a while. Something wasn't sitting right with him.

"You and Preston been spending a lot of time together, I hear."

I didn't know what he was getting at so I said nothing.

"He seems like a good fella, but how's that going to work for you?"

I glanced at him. I still wasn't sure what to say.

"I just don't want you getting hurt, son. He know you're going back to school at the end of the summer and off to college after that?"

"We haven't talked about it, yet. Though I was thinking maybe I could go to college some place down here. Louisiana State University has a good writing program. And they got a business school," I added, hoping to warm him up to the idea.

My daddy stopped in his tracks. "Now Arizona, you got the aptitude to go to the best college in the country. You going to fritter away that opportunity for a boy who works at a gas station?"

I think I was red all over. I was still shy talking about being gay with my daddy, and the way he said that last part, well, I'd never thought of Preston like that. But I could picture it now through other people's eyes.

"Look, son. I understand when a man's heart leads him astray. It's a powerful force. I been there myself. I can tell you it hurts like hell, but in the long run, you won't have no regrets calling it quits on something that was never supposed to be."

That was too much for me to let pass. "Preston and I love each other. How you gonna say that's something that was never supposed to be?"

"You're driving in different directions. Son, you're going places, and he's not going farther than Le Moyne Parish."

I turned away from him and stewed.

"Now don't get me wrong. You're turning seventeen, and it's not anybody's business who you're messing around with. But you don't change your life for Preston Montclair," he went on. "I know it's hard to see it now, but you've got your whole life ahead of you. A boy like Preston's only going to slow you down. I know you don't like hearing that, but it's the truth. He's not your equal."

I couldn't hold my tongue any more. "Preston and I grew up in the same town. We went to the same schools. He was there for me when my Mama Lou died, Gus Fanning beat me, and I lost my grandparents. And where were you? Don't go telling me who's my equal." I snorted. "Besides, when was the last time you called it quits on something that was never supposed to be?"

Well, I'd just about dug my own grave with that outburst. I was expecting fiery retribution, maybe a slap across my face. So, I was as pickled as a pig's foot when my daddy stared at me in amusement and coughed out a laugh.

"Son, you've got one hell of a brassy streak. And you're only proving my point. Nobody talks to Gaston Bondurant that way less he's a Bondurant himself. Though just so we're clear, you keep an eye on that temper of yours. I might like it once, but I'm not going to like it twice."

"Daddy, I'm not trying to be brassy, and I'm not being funny. Preston came back into my life for a reason. You think it's easy for me to find someone to love? The world hates me for who I am. That's not your fault, but it's the truth. And you can't understand it's a miracle Preston and I found each other?"

My daddy gently tried to take my shoulder. I shrugged away from him.

"You're right, Arizona. I can't understand completely. It's like I told my brother. It's a tough life you chose for yourself and not just for you. I've gotta worry about you every day for the rest of my life."

"It's not a choice, Daddy. It wasn't for Nicolas and it's not for me. You understand that, don't you?"

"I suppose that was just a figure of speech. I'm still learning, and that's why I need you to teach me. But listen here, you remember what I said when you first told me last year? It don't mean nothing to me, and I couldn't be prouder of you just the way you are."

That was nice to hear, and I'd always felt blessed that my daddy accepted me. But he did have things to learn, never having walked in my shoes.

"So, how you gonna tell me my relationship with Preston isn't special? You think I'm going to find a man to love as easy as you can find a woman?"

He snorted a little laugh. "Son, from what I've seen, I'd be lucky to keep up."

I stared at him blankly.

"You made quite an impression when we had Miss Francois over for dinner. Her friends Curly and Lucius sure took an interest in you."

I turned bright pink again, which only made my daddy rib me more.

"And how about your homecoming party? We all had our suspicions about Steel Linklater's son, Duncan. His eyes were following you around the party all night long. You're a Bondurant. Chip off the ol' block, son."

I barely remembered Duncan, but he made me blush again. The boy looked like he was a couple of years older than me, and he was real quiet, like he didn't want to be there. Anyway, as I recalled, I was too busy watching Daddy at that party to notice anything, and I also spent most of my time with Duncan's younger sister, Fiona.

"Come to think of it, we could arrange a meeting for you boys to get acquainted. Duncan's on the tennis team at Stanford University. Steel's got a tennis court right on his property. What do you say to arranging a lesson?"

I looked at Daddy blearily. "I'm not looking for a boyfriend. I've got Preston. How many times I gotta say he means the world to me?"

"Arizona, I'm going to tell you something that fits in that category of things you're not going to believe at sixteen-years old, but I swear to you, you're going to come around to understand. You can have anything you want in this world. Being gay don't have nothing to do with it. When you're a man like that, you aim high with everything that's out there for you. I'm not talking about being arrogant or selfish about it. It's just in your nature. Like goes with like. I want you to be happy, son."

"What I keep saying but you're not hearing is I'm happy with Preston. Daddy, Preston makes me happy. Why you trying so hard to make me give that up?"

"Look here, I've been sixteen going on seventeen, and I was in love." He grinned to himself. "Annie Longacre. She was my sweetheart all through upper division. She went to Woodland Hall just a few towns over from Middleton."

That got my attention. He never talked about anything so personal.

"There were times I told myself I was going to marry that girl. She was from Dallas. She was pretty. A little feisty, like your grandmother. And like they say, you never forget your first love. She made me happy in all sorts of ways."

I waited for more. Daddy looked like he was caught up in a reminiscence.

"So, what happened?"

"Nothing. And that's the point. I went to Harvard to get the best education I could. Annie, she wanted to go to Bryn Mawr College in Pennsylvania to study psychology. We said we'd stay true. Visit each other on weekends and school breaks. Well, that didn't last through the seventh week of our first semester apart.

There were no hard feelings. I'd made a new life, and she'd made hers. We'd had some good times, and I never had any regrets."

He put his hands into his pockets and glanced at me sidelong. "When you go to college, you're going to meet so many people, a whole new world is going to open up for you. And times are changing, Arizona. There's boys like you at Harvard and any school you want to go to. You're turning into a real charmer, and I think you know you're a young man who turns heads. There's going to be Preston Montclairs and Duncan Steeles and all kinds of men wanting to be with you. You can have your fun with whoever you want, but when it comes to changing your life for that one special person, you aim high. For a fellow who's earned being your number one. And you put to mind, there's going to be plenty after you for your name and all that entails."

"Preston loved me when I was dirt poor."

My daddy sighed. "The way you defend that boy, I know you got deep feelings for him. Just think about your future. I gave you my name, and you're my only son. Think about what you're doing to honor your family and all the generations of Bondurants. I wasn't going to say that, but you're old enough to hear it. You've got privileges few men have in this world, but along with that comes responsibility."

My throat was dry, and I didn't know what to say. Part of me still felt like he didn't understand how important Preston was to me. Another part was wondering if he was giving me good advice. I didn't want to hurt him by the choices I made. Then I got to wondering about following in his footsteps.

"Daddy, you want me to be happy with who I fall in love with. But you can't be happy with my grandmother. You telling me all this about how I should live my life, how I should be looking to the future. But is that the kind of future you want for me? You saying you wouldn't be happier with a woman like Annie Longacre?"

He was quiet for a while, and then he cracked a smile. "You've got a way of cutting to the quick, now don't you? Well, son, happiness is a funny thing. I wish for you something different than I have with your grandmother, but I do love her. I was just twenty-four when I was courting her, and I was aiming high. We were both different back then. It's true, I had an eye out for a woman from a good family, but it wasn't just a high society arrangement. I can see you're a perceptive fellow, Arizona. Your grandmother and I had our problems early on. Things don't always turn out as planned. I strayed with your mama, and I strayed with other women. I know your grandmother done some straying herself, but I'll tell you it's not easy being a Bondurant. I'd never ask you to make any sacrifices I haven't made myself, but there's a responsibility that comes with having power and privilege. The only man who's going to judge you is the good Lord himself. I've always tried to be the best man I can be, and that's all I can expect from you."

We'd reached the stables and went over to Bonnie and Duchess to feed them some alfalfa and brush down their coats. After, Daddy led me along to the locker room. I thought maybe he wanted us to get cleaned up before returning to the house. But after he clicked on the overhead light, he brought me over to a full-length mirror. He stood behind me, clasping my arms and looking me in the eye in my reflection.

"I don't have any regrets about my life, except for you, and I'm fixing it once and for all now. I want you to look yourself in the mirror and see a terrible mistake been made. That you been raised by people who weren't fit to clean your boots. That don't make them bad people, but you're like a thoroughbred stallion abandoned in the wild, taken in by goats. You're not gonna live like that no more. You've gotta be a thoroughbred and graze and race and settle down with other thoroughbreds. You may lose your way sometimes, but I'm always going to be here to set you back on track. You're a Bondurant, son. Now look me in the eye and nod so I know you understand."

I looked at his reflection and did what I was told.

11

A FEW WEEKS later, I had one heck of a swell birthday party out on the south lawn. There was no talking Daddy out of making it a big occasion, but I kept him to ten dozen guests. I wanted everyone to dress in white like an old-fashioned classy affair. For myself, I picked up a new crepe suit with a silk pocket square, and I wore my white fedora. I had Preston come along with me to Rubenstein's gentlemen's clothier, pick out a white cotton suit, and put it on my daddy's account. I ain't lying when I say the two of us looked slick. Things started out real good that night.

I introduced Press to the people I'd been working with at B&B, and a group of us played horseshoes in teams before the band got fired up. For the first time in my life, I was on the winning team. Press had always been real good at that game, and once the men from the office saw that they were dealing with a shark, they took to him like chili to cornbread as my daddy liked to say.

Later, we ran into the Linklaters, and I found myself in a jam. First, there was Fiona, who was looking me up and down flirtatiously. I introduced Preston as my friend and couldn't say more than that.

Fiona wanted to know where my girlfriend was, seeing as I'd

lied to her about having one. Well, I plucked out of my head the oldest excuse in the book. I told Fiona my girl wasn't feeling well. Too much sunburn or something stupid like that. I don't think Fiona bought it for a minute. She fixed on Preston and announced he was going to accompany her to the bar to get some punch, and along the way, she'd be sure to find out exactly what was going on with that girlfriend and me.

I felt bad about putting Press in that situation, and it got me so jumpy, when a group of folks across the lawn waved at me, I took a few steps in that direction, and then I swung back. I was afraid if I didn't stay put, Preston would have a hard time finding me and end up stuck with Fiona. Klutz that I was, I knocked right into somebody. Sent his glass flying from his hand. I looked up and saw I'd collided with Duncan Linklater.

"I'm so sorry," I said. "I'm a damn fool."

Duncan shook out a wet jacket sleeve. Mercifully, most of his draft beer had ended up on the lawn. We both stooped down to pick up his glass and ended up knocking heads.

"Sorry. I ought to have one of them warning labels on me. You all right?"

He was squinting from the bump on the head, but at least he was grinning. "I'm fine. Just as much my mistake as yours. I wasn't looking where I was going."

We exchanged a grin. He was a tall fellow. Easy on the eyes at close range with his thick red hair, green eyes, and strong jaw. We each fumbled with what to say.

"Happy Birthday, Arizona." Duncan stretched out his hand. "I'm Steel Linklater's son. Duncan."

I shook his hand. "Thank you. We been introduced before. At the party after Memorial Day."

"I thought you might've forgot. There were a lot of people at that party." He glanced around. "Kind of like today."

"I don't know half of them," I told him. "I said to my daddy, 'I don't need anything fancy. Just a few close friends. We can have hamburgers and hot dogs.' But that man, he can't do anything small. He'd have the entire city of New Orleans over if he could get the mayor to close up the Superdome for valet parking."

Duncan smiled. Then he narrowed his brow. "Your *daddy*?"

"Oh. He's technically my granddaddy, but seeing as he adopted me, I go back and forth." *Good grief.* That had to be the third time I'd slipped up that night. I hated having to pretend my daddy was my granddaddy. Fortunately, Duncan looked like he'd put it out of mind.

"Gaston Bondurant's an important man. And he throws the best parties in all of Southeastern Louisiana. They call him the Great Gatsby of the South."

I didn't know what to say to that, though I liked him mentioning that F. Scott Fitzgerald book. He was one of my favorite authors.

"I meant that in a complimentary way," Duncan said. "You read *The Great Gatsby*?"

"I have. I'd say that's a fair comparison in more ways than one." Duncan was at a loss for words, and I worried I'd made him uncomfortable. Jay Gatsby had an old mansion where he threw big parties, and he was loose on the issue of marital fidelity. Sometimes I just don't think before the words come spouting out of my mouth. I tried changing the subject.

"I was just talking to your sister Fiona. She's a lovely girl."

Duncan smirked. "Now, you best look out for Fiona. She's been hunting for a boy to take her to the late night drive-in since she got her first training bra."

"Is that so? And what about you?"

Don't ask me why I said it. You put me in the company of a handsome college athlete, and I can't be held liable for what comes out of my mouth. Duncan's eyes popped, and his freckles got freckles. Meantime, one of the cater waiters came over to take Duncan's empty glass and ask if we'd like anything. I told the fellow I'd like some punch, and Duncan said he'd take a beer.

The waiter drifted away, and Duncan looked at me carefully. "Your granddaddy told me you're looking to take tennis lessons this summer. He said if I've got time in my schedule, I ought to talk to you about it and set something up before you go back to boarding school. Am I to suppose you put him up to that with an ulterior motive?"

I coughed out a laugh. "Oh, you got it right about ulterior motives, but you got a small, but critical piece of the puzzle fitting in the wrong place. That'd be my granddaddy who's harboring ulterior motives about tennis lessons. He's hoping to cure me of the boy I've been knocking around with this summer." I glanced across the lawn, wondering if my daddy was watching our conversation, but I didn't see him anywhere. When my glance returned to Duncan, he'd gone stiff as a board.

"Your granddaddy wanted to set us up?"

"Mm-hmm. You all right? You look like you might need a sit-down."

He adjusted his shirt collar for some ventilation. "I'll be fine. I think." His eyes shifted this way and that. "Do other people know about this?"

"I only found out from you, so I'd say the secret's safe. I'm sorry, Duncan. It seems, along with F. Scott Fitzgerald, Gaston Bondurant was feeling a bit Jane Austen when he stepped out in his suit and bowtie to host my birthday party. Well, in this case with a touch of Armistead Maupin thrown in. He'll be getting a piece of my mind. You can bet on that. You sure you're holding up all right?"

He looked like he was running calculations in his head, then trying things on for size. Anyway, he came out of that spell perspiring in the face, but with something of a clever gleam.

"I guess we both know the score now. So long as we keep it to ourselves, we'll be all right, wouldn't you say?"

I nodded along though I wasn't sure what he was driving at. The way he was grinning and peeking here and there, I was beginning to see the family resemblance to his sister Fiona.

"Arizona Bondurant, you're one unusual young man. If I didn't know better, I'd never believe you were only seventeen."

"It's probably the shoes. I always buy 'em with a little extra heel."

"What I mean is you're knocking around with boys, out in the open. You even got your granddaddy working on finding you tricks."

"Now that part's all wrong. I never asked him to." It was high time for a change of subject. "Does your daddy know about you?"

"No, sir. And he never will." He took a cautious look around. "I don't need anyone knowing about my personal life. My teammate and I just broke into the U.S.T.A.'s top forty in doubles. We've got tournaments in the pro circuit this fall. What I do in the bedroom off season every now and then, that's nobody's business."

He gave me a firm look, which reminded me of the bossy jocks back at school.

"Well, Duncan, that's where I'd disagree. If every person like us came out, you know what a difference that'd make? You know how many people like us commit suicide every day? Thinking they're alone and got no future? How about your own future? How you gonna feel when your tennis career is over and you got nobody special in your life?"

The cater waiter came over with our drinks, and Duncan took a healthy sip of his beer. He made sure the man was out of earshot before he replied.

"I don't need to advertise my sex life. You sound like one of them militant gays getting themselves in newspaper photos outside of city hall. There's plenty of them in San Francisco. They make me sick to my stomach, if you want to know the truth." He rolled back on his heels, eyeing me desirously. "The two of us could have some fun though, don't you think? You suppose your boyfriend wouldn't mind loaning you out some afternoons this summer? I've got a house with a tennis court, swimming pool, and a cabana room where we could have some privacy."

Mercifully, I spotted Preston and Fiona walking toward us.

"I'm right flattered by the offer, Duncan, and as it happens, my beau is headed over with Fiona right now. You can ask him yourself how he feels about that cabana room, though I can't promise you'll walk out of here with the same tennis swing. Might need to try out for the Paralympic cycling team."

Duncan took a long sip of his beer and pivoted around to move along in the other direction.

Preston and Fiona joined me, looking puzzled.

"Where'd Duncan run off to in such a hurry?" Fiona asked.

I shrugged. "He might've wanted to work on his tennis swing."

Fiona frowned. "I think he saw me coming and left on purpose. I'm getting a complex. Seems I'm poisonous to boys." She nudged her head toward Preston. "This one says he's got a girl-friend, too. I don't believe either of you. What's wrong with me, Arizona? Is it my hair? My face? You like a girl with more curves? More personality?"

I threw an arm around her and gave her a friendly kiss on the head. "There's nothing wrong with you, Fiona. You're going to find a boy who's head over heels for you."

Preston stepped in and smiled at her. Seemed like he'd become friendly with Fiona right quick.

"Plenty of boys are going to love a girl like you. It's just not going to be me or Arizona."

I shot a glance at him. He wasn't about to…?

"How come? Am I too plain?" Fiona said.

"No. Because Arizona and me, we together."

Preston stepped over and put his arm around me. I was proud of him. A bit shaky in the knees, truth be told, but if I was going to take my own advice about coming out, his declaration was right on time.

Fiona covered her mouth with her hand. Then she looked from one of us to the other. "You gotta be putting me on. You two couldn't be…"

I nodded. Preston nodded, too. The look on Fiona's face made us both crack up. Then she put her hand on her hip, which got us laughing even more.

She waved us off. "Well that doesn't make any kind of sense. The two of you couldn't be…" She whispered, "Queer."

"How come?" I asked her.

"Because you're normal. You're not swishing around like them fellows on St. Ann Street, acting like girls."

"Now Fiona, I take no pleasure in disappointing you, but as a matter of fact, not every gay man—and we prefer to be called gay, not queer—not every one of us is swishy. And what's it to people if some of us are?"

She was flummoxed. Opened her mouth and then closed it again without saying a word. Then, "I just never met a gay person before."

"Glad to be of service. And now you met two, in one fell swoop as my Grandma Tilly used to say."

"Well I just…" Fiona put on a cross face. "I'm never going to find a boy to take me to a dance, am I? The boys I like turn out to prefer dancing with each other."

Just then, the band struck up a lively number that was getting everyone moving into the tent and onto the dance floor.

I offered Fiona my arm. "How'd you like to dance, Fiona?"

She frowned. "Maybe later." She grabbed Preston's arm. "I already danced with you at the beginning of the summer. I can see this is going to be another case of me getting all gussied up and coming up empty, but that doesn't mean I can't have some variety."

I hooted. Preston gave me a shrug, and then Fiona tugged him over to the tent.

LATER THAT NIGHT, when Miss Marguerite Francois took the stage, Preston and I stood in the front row to sway along while she was crooning and jump around and dance when she got into a faster number. Around eleven o'clock, a pair of waiters wheeled out a giant, chocolate-frosted doberge cake, which was seven layers of heaven. Miss Francois led everyone in a round of "Happy Birthday." She and her band kept folks dancing and carrying on while I sat down to eat dessert with Preston at a table some ways off from the stage. It was turning out to be the best birthday party I'd ever had. Until I noticed something shifting with Preston.

"I got you something," he said. He brought out a little velvet box from his pants pocket and placed it in front of me.

I scowled at him, and then I opened it up. It was a silver band for my finger. Part of me was right humbled that he'd spent so much money on me, but I was also breaking a sweat.

"This is too much. Press, what are you doing spending all your hard-earned money? You told me you were saving up for an engine so you can get your uncle's pickup on the road. You could've gotten me a bottle of cologne or a book or a new shirt."

Preston had them stars in his eyes. "I went over to the jewelry store at Lafayette Mall. When I saw it in the men's cabinet, I just knew it's what I wanted to give you. It's an engagement ring, Arizona. If you'll have me. I'd get down on bended knee, but I don't want to ruin your party by drawing funny looks. I can do it later when we're alone. I just couldn't wait."

He clasped my hand under the table. I couldn't look him in the eye. I had some difficult things to tell him. We finished our cake, and I suggested we take a stroll through the grounds. I pointed us in the direction of the main trail to the lake.

When we were a fair distance away from the commotion, I turned to Preston. "Press. You know I love you. But I can't accept that ring. I want to explain to you why, and I'm just hoping it comes out right."

He gone and strangled my heart with the look of disappointment on his face. Then he stopped dead in his tracks. "What're you saying? You breaking up with me?"

I took his arm to pull him along. Guests had spread across all parts of the lawn. I wanted to have some privacy for the conversation I was dreading but knew we needed to have.

"We're gonna walk, and you're gonna hear me out. I didn't say I'm breaking up with you."

He loped along with me. Once we were around the corner in the wooded trail with just the night lamps around us every thirty yards or so, I tried to get the words out of my mouth. As usual, I started with the foul-tasting parts.

"I can't wear that ring. Don't get me wrong, it's beautiful and even more so because you saved up to give it to me. But I'm not ready for all it entails." Preston pulled his arm away. "Now hear me out. I love you, Press. It's not about that." I grinned to myself. "And I'm so damn proud of you, telling Fiona the truth about us."

He kicked a stone down the trail. "I'm starting to think it wasn't the truth after all."

"How we gonna be engaged, Press? In less than three weeks, I'm going back to school. You've got your job and other things you're working on—"

"I knew you'd decide to go back to that school."

I didn't like the tone of his voice. "I did. And what's wrong with that? My education is important to me."

"You can get a high school education in any town, any state. You chose to run off as far away as you can go."

"I'm doing real well at Middleton. I got a straight-A average."

"I heard about your straight-A average. Over and over again."

I halted. "Because it's important to me. Middleton only admits one in ten students. I *made it* in, Press. I didn't just choose it, spinning a globe and pointing a finger."

"Well, congratulations. I hope you and that school will be real happy together. Obviously, it means a lot to you. A lot more than me."

"Preston Montclair, we're seventeen years old. There's got to be a middle ground between splitting up and saying we're going to spend the rest of our lives together."

"Plenty of people make that vow at seventeen. My daddy did. My cousin René is getting married to his girl, and he's the same age as me."

I edged a little closer to him. "You ain't René, and I ain't his girl.

Look at us, Press. We had a real nice summer together, but things are about to get complicated." I took his hand. "If you love me, you're gonna have to love me all the way from here to Massachusetts. I ain't saying it can't be done, but it ain't gonna be easy. We can see each other around Thanksgiving and Christmas, and maybe once or twice, you can come up to me or I can come down to you. But that's not a lot. And if you're gonna make me say wearing that ring means we're together for a lifetime, well, if things don't work out, we're gonna end up hating each other. And I don't ever want you hating me or vice versa."

Preston pulled away from me again and rounded himself.

"It wouldn't have to be complicated if you thought I was worth sticking around for."

Tears burned in my sinuses. It wasn't fair. How was I supposed to make that choice?

"I'm just...stupid." His voice cracked. "Believing you'd come back to me when all along it was just something for you to do between your spring and fall semesters."

He gasped, and tears bled from his eyes. My mouth hung open, and it was like time froze, just watching the boy I loved more than anything in the world with his heart torn open on account of me.

"Press," I croaked. I tried to hold him in my arms, but he shirked away from me. "Now c'mon. That's not fair. I love you. I'm trying..." I hiccupped a sob and breathed in deep to steady myself. "If we're through, that's your fault. I'm saying I'm willing to wait for you."

Preston squatted down, pulled at his hair, and got himself together to come back to me. "I'm done waiting. I waited for you all last year, and it didn't do no good. I gave everything I had. I ain't got no more. And I ain't gonna like it, but for the first time in my life, I'm doing something for me."

He started back toward the house. I grabbed his arm, but he pulled away from me again.

"Press. Please. Don't leave. I ain't got nobody else."

He kept walking and disappeared down the trail. I fell down to my knees and cried into my fists.

I WAS SO low the rest of the summer, I didn't even want to get out of bed. I'd lost Press forever. He wouldn't return my calls, and I was pretty sure he was home when I phoned his house. I tried him in the evening when he'd be back from work and over the weekend. He must've told his mama he didn't want to talk to me.

I considered driving over and catching him at work, but that seemed plain desperate. Don't get me wrong, part of me *was* desperate to make things right with him, but facts were facts. He said he was through with me. It hurt like an incision to my chest, but I had to be a man and try to shake it off. I'd be back to school in a couple of weeks. I'd survive the heartache, and when I could think things over without sobbing, I could say the two of us weren't meant to be. Each day that went by, I felt just a little bit lighter and a little bit stronger. Heartbreak is worse than any physical pain you could imagine, but it heals the same way with time.

A week before I was flying up to Boston, I asked Mr. Wainwright for some nice stationery, and I wrote Preston a letter. There were things I never had a chance to say to him before he stormed off that night, and I'd leave it up to him to write me back. I poured my heart and soul into that letter. I let him know how much he'd meant to me that summer, especially that time I woke him up in the middle of the night after driving over to see my little brother. I said I understood why he left and that I wished I could be the boyfriend he wanted me to be. I told him the two of us been through thick and thin, and when he was ready, I'd be there for him again. I gave him my address up at school and said I'd sure love to hear from him. I signed it: Love, Arizona.

Then I took that letter to the post office myself because I sure as heck wasn't trusting Mr. Wainwright to send it for me.

12

LABOR DAY WEEKEND, I was headed back to Middleton, landing at Boston's Logan Airport and piling into a chauffeured town car for the one-hour drive outside of the city. The summer had been a mess, but now I was excited. For senior year, Jonathan and I were rooming together at Stanton Hall. I couldn't wait to catch up with him and Dale and Russell. I was such a nerd, I couldn't wait to start my classes. In addition to my compulsory courses in calculus, chemistry, and fine arts, I was taking my third term of French, and best of all, creative writing. I just knew it was going to be a great year. When the car pulled into the entrance to campus with its vast, green rolling lawn, my heart lifted outside of my chest.

A proctor Jimmy Leavitt helped me haul my luggage up to the second floor of the dormitory and find room 205. The door was open, and when I saw Jonathan, Dale and Russell inside, my suitcases fell out of my hands.

"Who's ready to start some trouble?" I said.

We all hollered and attacked each other with hugs.

"How was your summ-ah, Arizona?" Dale said.

"Crazy as a bag of raccoons, but I had some fun."

"Pray tell."

Dale was a slip of a boy from Dover, Massachusetts. I knew he came from money since he was one of Middleton's many students who had a car and driver for move-in day. Next to me, he was the loudest of us four musketeers, with his hard, flat New England accent. And while he was short of stature, he was cute as heck with his big brown eyes and dark, handsome features. I called him Chipmunk one day last semester and the nickname stuck.

The four of us sat down on the beds, me and Dale on one, Jonathan and Russell on the other. I told them about reuniting with Preston, all the parties at Whittington Manor that summer, my internship, and the sad story of how things ended with Press and me.

"Well, I'm a single man again. I intend to make the best of it. So you better believe next Saturday, we're catching the train to the South End to round up some boys with loose morals." I looked around at the three of them snickering. "How 'bout all you?" I glanced at Dale who was wearing a pair of Doc Martens in a patchwork of colors. "Chipmunk, you better spill where you got them shoes, or I can't promise you're not going to find them having walked out of your closet."

"I'm nines. You're tens. But you can buy your own pair on Newbury Street. There's a dance next Saturday night at the youth center. What do you say to a shopping spree before we head over to the South End?"

I liked his way of thinking. Dale Knox-Levy had great style, and like me, he had his daddy's credit card to buy whatever he wanted.

"Dale met someone over the summer, too," Russell piped in, looking mischievous. "Multiple someones to be accurate about it."

Dale came back with his dramatic flair. "I can't help that I was popular at Yale's pre-college theater program. I was cast in the part of Eugene Morris in our production of Neil Simon's *Brighton Beach Memoirs*, originally performed on Broadway by Matthew Broderick."

That sounded right impressive to me. Though I could see Russell and Jonathan exchanging glances of amusement.

"I happened to draw the attention of a young understudy from Sioux City, Iowa." Dale sighed wistfully. "Steven Hackett. He was one beautiful, cornfed stud. Well, he was new to, y'know, *this and that*, but once he got the hang of things, that farm boy was sneaking into my room for repeat performances four, five times a week."

I hooted. I was dying to hear more details about that, but Russell wanted to keep giving Dale a ribbing. The two of them had been friends since lower division, and they had a bit of a rivalry.

"And what about the assistant drama coach?"

I raised my eyebrows at Dale.

"Don't be sheisty. Richard and I were in love." Dale clasped my hand and looked deeply into my eyes. "He was tall, handsome, talented, and so sophisticated. Steven was a fun trick for every now and then, but Richard was marriage material. He had a theatre degree from NYU and an MFA from the University of Michigan. We used to stroll through campus and find a sunny spot to lay out in the quad, and he would read me poetry. But the slings and arrows of outrageous fortune tore us apart. Richard got cast in a traveling production of *Nicolas Nickleby*. We had but two months of paradise."

"Sweetheart, that is tragic," I said.

"Richard is twenty-seven years old," Russell said. "I think the better word is prosecutable."

Russell was one of the smartest students in our class. He didn't have Dale's good looks. He was more the kind of fellow you had to spend some time with to appreciate. I wouldn't call Russell overweight. I thought of him as a teddy bear because he was sweet and gentle. But if he had a flaw, he could act like a know-it-all now and again. Having had my own experience with an older man, I swum in to Dale's defense.

"The age of consent is sixteen years old in Massachusetts. Now, I don't know about the laws in Connecticut, but it sounds to me

Dale was fully cognizant and agreeable to having relations with a twenty-seven-year-old man."

"Thank you, Arizona," Dale said. "Russell's just uptight because he had to spend the summer with his family."

I glanced at Russell. That didn't sound so bad considering he'd said they were visiting all kinds of places in Europe. But he was irritable. He and Jonathan had left a gap between each other. Something was going on with the two of them, but it wasn't the right time to pry into it.

"Well, I missed you all something fierce," I said. "And I'm even willing to forgive the fact that out of the three of you, Jonathan was the only one to write back to my letters."

"I'm sorry, Arizona," Dale said. "The summer just went by so fast."

"I only got back home to read your letter two weeks ago," Russell said. "I figured by the time I wrote and sent you something in the mail, you'd be back up here."

I waved them off. "No hard feelings. Now, we gonna have some fun this year?"

"Hell yeah," Dale said.

We stood, and I slapped him five. Then Russell stood up, and we slapped five, too. Jonathan came along, and I pulled us into a group hug, jumping and hollering to raise the roof. It might sound dumb, but we were boys just coursing with the excitement of our freedom and our friendship. And probably in the back of our minds, we realized we'd be splitting off in different directions at the end of the year.

THAT FIRST WEEK at Middleton reminded me of all the reasons I loved that place. I was happy to be back in class, learning things, and I had my pals to goof around with. I started back up with the equestrian club, and Dale and I had a meeting with Dean McGovern to remind him we still wanted to get that Pink Triangle club going for gay students. At night, we four musketeers gathered in the library to study, and then we holed up in me and Jonathan's room to play video games, listen to music, and watch TV. We all had calculus together, and Dale and I were taking chemistry. I had my creative writing class alone, but the instructor was a frequent topic of conversation.

Mr. Wesley Turner was a new teacher at the school. The rumor was he'd only graduated from Columbia University's Teachers College last year. By golly, he was a golden-haired, gorgeous specimen of a man in gold wire eyeglasses. It was like he'd stepped out of my dreams. I'd already been looking forward to creative writing class, and when he showed up in the classroom that first day, I knew for sure it was going to be my favorite class that term. He rolled up the sleeves of his Oxford shirt to read passages from Shirley Jackson and sat on the edge of his desk in his corduroys with his legs spread just enough to cause the eye to wander. I tried to mind my respect and pay attention to everything he said, but I'm telling you, it was hard.

I wasn't the only one who'd taken notice of him. Jonathan confessed he had a crush on Mr. Turner, and Dale could go on for hours talking about how cute Mr. Turner's butt was and how he looked like Christopher Atkins from the movie *The Blue Lagoon*. Dale had a copy of the young actor's photo shoot in *Playgirl* magazine, which the four of us pored over so many times, the pages were smudged from our fingerprints.

It was great rooming with my best friend, and one night that first week, after Russell and Dale had run off, we lay in our beds with the lights off, and I finally asked him how things were going with Russell.

"I think we're drifting apart. Every time we try to talk, we end up fighting."

"You haven't seen each other all summer. What you got to fight about?"

"Russell wanted me to visit before we came back to school. He said I should fly to Scarsdale, and we'd spend some time together, and I could catch a ride with him on move-in day. I told him I'd already booked a ticket to Boston. It would've cost five hundred dollars to change it, and I can't afford that. Russell said if I really wanted to see him, I would've figured out a way."

"Honey, I know something about bull-headed boyfriends. You may recall a certain Cajun who gave me an ultimatum and walked out of my birthday party. But you and Russell, you're together now. Why's he giving you a hard time? You want me to have a talk with him?"

I'd always been protective of Jonathan. We'd met when he was getting shoved around in the hall by a pair of idiots from the hockey team, and I'd called their bluff and sent them packing.

"It's not just that."

I propped myself up on my elbow. "Then what is it?"

"Arizona, I only told him ten times I had to help out at my uncle's restaurant until the end of August. He's having a hard time making his monthly loan payment, and he has to pay a dishwasher twice what he pays me."

"That don't sound fair to you."

"Tell me about it. But he's family. He helped out when my dad got laid off a few years back, so working at his restaurant is more like an obligation than a job. I made a few hundred dollars to buy some new clothes and my books. And I gave a hundred to my sister Gisell. She's having her third kid."

"I'm sorry, darling. Well, if you told Russell all that, he should've been the better man and come see you in California." Russell's family had plenty of money. Last year for spring break, he and Dale had run off to the Virgin Islands. I didn't mention that, though.

I waited for a response from Jonathan in the darkness. I would've slugged Russell if Jonathan wanted me to, though I was starting to worry what I said had come out wrong.

"I didn't tell him all that."

"How come?"

A silence stretched between us again.

"Arizona, I can talk to you about these things, but you know how barrio it sounds?"

"You're going to have explain barrio to me first."

"Ghetto. Low life."

"I see. Where I grew up, they call that padoo. Redneck Cajun. But there's no shame in your situation. What makes you think Russell wouldn't understand that?"

"C'mon, Arizona. You really think Russell is interested in visiting East L.A.? *I* don't want him coming to my neighborhood. It would basically confirm every stereotype he's heard about Mexicans."

I almost told him nonsense, but I remembered then how I felt going back to Le Moyne for the first time that summer.

"I get where you're coming from. But if you two are in a relationship, you're going to have to be honest with him. There's nothing wrong with you, Jonathan. Russell should love you for who you are."

I heard him sigh from across the room. "It's exhausting having to explain. And why should I have to all the time? He knows I'm here on scholarship, and my family's got no money. You *all* know that, so what am I supposed to say when everyone wants to run off to Boston for a shopping trip?"

"That was just an idea Dale and I were floating. We don't have to go to Boston this weekend. We can have some fun right here on campus."

"That's not the point. If you all don't go because I can't afford it, then I'm the busted Mexican who's ruining everyone's fun."

Call me slow, but I only then started to get the picture. It made me feel real guilty.

"I could tell you I'll front you the cash for the trip to Boston and nobody needs to be the wiser, but I'm beginning to think that's not the solution. Listen, if it means going without you, I don't want to go to Boston anyway. I'll just tell Dale and Russell I'd rather stay here."

I listened to the silence, hoping he'd give me a reply.

"You ever feel like you don't know how to be? A week ago, I was washing dishes from noon to midnight and sleeping on a mattress in my old room with my three little cousins on the bunk bed and a cot. I kept a pocketknife in my jeans to walk home at night, and I got chased by a group of boys twice this summer. Now, I'm living in Massachusetts with people whose biggest problem is which pre-college program they should do over the summer or what they can brag about from summer vacation."

That hit me sour at first. "You including me as one of them people?" I didn't wait for him to answer. "Because you know what I went through this summer with my sister and my little brother. You know the agony I went through with Preston."

"Those are things, Arizona. But you had a choice. And when you walk through campus, nobody can see what your life is like. Or what it used to be like. You're another one of them in your nice clothes and shoes. You're another one of them who got a brand new car for his seventeenth birthday and a bank card to buy anything you want."

Jonathan and I had never had a fight, and he'd never given me a reason to be angry at him. But that night, I was fit to be tied.

"You saying you know what it's like to be me? I'd like to hear you elaborate on all the choices I have."

"Arizona—"

"C'mon. Let's hear it. You think I should quit school and move back to John's Island? Get a job and figure out a way to take in my sister and brother in a year when I turn eighteen?"

"Cool down, Arizona. I was just saying what's on my mind."

"I heard it. Now it's my turn. You had choices too. If you care about your family so much, maybe you should be back in Los Angeles helping them out. That's right, Jonathan Gutierrez. We're both finks. Finks who's trying to better ourselves. And I can try to live with that, but you can take your money to the bank I ain't living with my best friend judging me."

I turned over on my side, vaguely aware of Jonathan clicking on a lamp and rustling around. I felt him sitting down on my bed.

I was so hurt and angry, I didn't want to look at him, but gradually I did.

"Arizona, you're the only person in the world I can talk to about these things. I'm not saying we don't have a lot of things in common, but we've got things different, too. You gotta understand that."

I was still a little sore, but slowly, a grin curled up on my face. "I understand. You've got the complexion to pull off pastels while I end up looking like a casting reject from *Miami Vice*."

We exchanged a smirk. Jonathan snuck under the covers, and I threw an arm around his slight body.

"Do you ever wish you were someone else?" he asked.

I laid back and considered his question. "You know what, buttercup? Even when they had me locked up in the loony bin after assaulting my step-daddy, I don't think I ever once dreamt about being anybody else. I might've liked the world different, but you tell me: how many people get to be a queer swamp rat raised by a jacked-up family he ain't even related to?"

"You don't look like a swamp rat anymore."

I turned to look him in the face. "But I'll always be on the inside. And you're a queer Mexican from the barrio. I'd take that any day of the week over these spoiled white boys around here."

Jonathan smiled. Then he got a thoughtful expression on his face. "Now that you're living with your wealthy family, it must be hard to not just *want to* fit in."

Honestly, I'd never thought about it that way, and part of me rebelled against the notion. "Honey, I never had a problem fitting in. It's always been the rest of the world that needed to get used to me."

"You ever wish you weren't gay?"

"Now I'll tell you something about that. I wished and prayed God would make me straight a few times when I was younger, but I come around last year to recognizing there's but one Arizona Bondurant in the world. If I weren't gay, I wouldn't be that man, and that scares me more than any names or threats somebody gonna throw at me to make me feel ashamed. How 'bout you get that nonsense out of your head, too? There's only one Jonathan Gutierrez, and he's somebody I'm right honored to call my best friend."

I knew he was going through something so I pulled him closer to nestle together. After a while, we both fell asleep in my single bed.

13

THE NEXT DAY, Jonathan and I talked things over, and he came around to the idea of me loaning him twenty dollars for our trip to Boston that coming weekend. It would cover his round trip train ticket, the five dollar pass to the dance at the Gay and Lesbian Youth Center, and a cheeseburger and fries at the diner we liked to go to. I said I'd be happy to chip in for any extras that came up, and I left things at that. Jonathan had his pride, and he preferred Russell didn't know I was paying his way.

I also convinced Dale to postpone our shopping trip on Newbury Street until later that month. What were we going to do with our shopping bags anyway when we got to the dance? Dale said he was fine with that, and he and Russell came over Saturday afternoon to get ready for the trip.

I'd picked up a pair of designer jeans for such an occasion when I'd done my back to school shopping in New Orleans. Kids in Boston dressed trendy but casual, so I threw on a sleeveless, patterned T-shirt, my denim jacket, and a pair of black leather boots to go with it. Dale had brought three outfit options for himself, and then he went rifling through my cabinet and closet for more ideas. Russell always wore a polo shirt and jeans when we went out. As for Jonathan, he had gear to fit in better than any of us—one of them Sex Pistols T-shirts, a pair of faded and frayed Levis, and his high-top Converse All Stars.

As usual, we were all good to go while Dale was still flitting around in his Calvin Kleins.

"Chipmunk, we got twenty-five minutes to catch the 6:05," I warned him. "You're going like that unless you put some clothes on in the next five minutes."

"I can't decide." He held up two shirts. "Should I go punk or preppy?"

"Punk," we all answered in unison.

"In that case…" He drifted over to my desk, sat down, and unpacked his little alligator valise. "You give me a hand, Arizona? I've only got a compact mirror."

I had steam coming out of my ears. He was sitting down to put on eye makeup? He'd had an hour and a half to get ready.

"You suppose that's something you could do on the train?"

Dale took out his eyeliner pencil and started on his lower eyebrows. "Oh no. I can't do this with all the motion in the car."

"We miss the 6:05, we're gonna have to take the 6:31, which gives us forty-five minutes to catch the T crosstown, eat dinner, and make it over to the dance."

"Chill out. How long does it take to walk to the train station? Five minutes?"

"Ten. At a good clip. And the four of us got to buy tickets."

Dale kept doing his eyes, unfazed. I tried moving him along, but after squeezing into a tight pair of black jeans, a studded leather belt, and a black cropped T-shirt, he brought out a bottle of gel and hairspray to style his hair in a pompadour. We caught the 6:39 by the skin of our teeth.

After that, things started out all right. We made it to the diner on Tremont Street by 7:30, and Dale got me thinking it wasn't so bad being fashionably late to the dance. Most kids didn't show up until nine anyway. Russell, Jonathan, and I got cheeseburgers while

Dale picked at a Greek salad. The boy didn't have an ounce of fat to lose, but he still made a big deal about watching his weight. I think that ticked off Russell. He was quiet and moody while Dale and I kept conversation going. Then we walked over to the Gay and Lesbian Youth Center around quarter to nine, bought our tickets, and made our entrance.

The basement gymnasium had a dance floor with lights and fog machines, a deejay, and a couple hundred kids inside. I was grinning from ear to ear. I hadn't seen so many people like me in a long time. There were boys around my age, some who looked a little younger or older, and despite what I'd said before, I wasn't looking to meet anyone. I just liked being around my own kind. I grabbed Dale's hand, and we went charging onto the crowded dance floor, claiming a spot right in the middle. The deejay was playing New Wave remixes, which got you jumping around and thrashing. I was so pumped up, I felt like I could dance all night.

Jonathan and Russell joined us for a while, and I can't say at what point I was on my own. Well, not precisely. My friends had scattered, and I was sandwiched between two black fellows who were grinding on me from the front and the back. They were kicking up all kinds of sensations from my body. I might've locked lips with one of them, but I remembered I had three friends I'd come with, and I politely squirmed myself free.

I couldn't spot Jonathan, Russell, or Dale. That dance party had gotten even more crowded, and I had to twist around and squeeze past people, and I can tell you I didn't mind the twisting and squeezing around all them warm, male bodies one bit. But I made it from one end to the other and didn't see my friends anywhere along the way. I decided to take a leak.

There was a long line to the bathroom, but boys were friendly while things inched along. I met a pair of rowdy kids from a Catholic school who offered me some whiskey they'd snuck in. The only gracious thing to do was to toss back a guzzle from their bottle. It burned so much swallowing it down, I near coughed it all back up, but afterward I was warm all over and laughing with those two boys. I think their names were Dave and Ian though it was awfully loud. Gabe and Ian? Gabe or Dave was a tall, curly brown-haired hunk. I wouldn't have minded getting to know him a little better, but after I did my business, I needed to find my other musketeers. My watch read ten o'clock, and we needed to keep an eye on time. If we didn't make the 10:39 back to Middleton, we'd get caught breaking the eleven thirty curfew.

I finally got into the bathroom, and I headed to a stall because all the urinals were taken up. I closed the door behind me, and while I was peeing, I heard intriguing sounds from the stall next door. I looked down and saw a familiar pair of multi-color Doc Martens through the space under the stall. I guessed I'd found Dale getting acquainted with someone new. On his knees.

I didn't feel right about interrupting, so I bumbled out of the bathroom to look for Jonathan and Russell. It wasn't easy with wall-to-wall people and the music pounding, lights flashing, and fog machines pumping. An older kid in an oversized graphic T-shirt tried to delay me with some sweet talk and grabbing me here and there. I pushed past him. I was worried how the heck the four of us were going to make it back to Middleton together.

At last, I found Jonathan and Russell standing in a far corner of the room. Jonathan was sipping from a red Solo cup, and Russell's face was twisted up like his underwear had shrunk in the wash.

I raised my voice over the music. "Where the hell y'all been? I lost you on the dance floor."

Jonathan rolled his eyes. Russell fixed on me.

"I need to talk to you."

That didn't sound like a pleasant conversation, but I followed him to a quieter part of the floor, near the door where people went out to a back lot to smoke. Russell turned to me.

"Why're you giving money to my boyfriend?"

I looked at him blankly.

"You going to deny it? I know Jonathan got the money for his train ticket and the dance from you. Why? Is something going on between you two?"

I was smoked, pickled, and barbecued. I didn't want to create any trouble for Jonathan, but at the same time, I didn't like my integrity being questioned.

"Hold on, Russell. You know Jonathan and I are just friends."

"Do I?"

I snorted. "This sounds like something the two of you need to work out. Why don't you talk to Jonathan about it?"

He glared at me. "I did. He said he couldn't afford to visit me this summer, so I asked him how he could afford to come to Boston this weekend. That's when he told me you gave him the money. Why's he asking you and not me?"

We needed to move along to catch that train and make it back to school before curfew. Meanwhile, Russell wasn't budging. I had to say something to him.

"If you want to know why he asked me and not you, you're talking to the wrong person."

Russell scowled. I don't know what he was expecting, but it wasn't my place to say anything about his relationship with Jonathan. I had my opinions, but it wasn't my place.

I glanced at my watch. "Listen, we gotta head over to the train station if we're going to catch the 10:39. We gotta round up Dale. I think he lost track of time."

Russell relented, and we walked back over to Jonathan. I told them we should mark the spot as home base and scour the room for Dale. We all three headed off in different directions. I went toward the bathroom end where I'd last seen him, and I caught the fool dancing with some older-looking boys. He had his shirt tucked into the back of his jeans.

I tugged him off the dance floor and bored holes into his eyes. "We need to leave now."

Dale's hair was soaked through with sweat, and his face was delirious like he'd been drinking. He nudged me over sloppily and spoke into my ear. "I met some guys from Northeastern.

They invited me to a party at their dorm. You come along with me?"

I shrugged back from him and gave him a look that nonsense deserved.

"C'mon, Arizona." He looked at me pleadingly. "How often we get invited to a college party?" He shrugged his eyebrows. "The guys are wicked cute."

"Dale, I don't care if they're the bisexual division of the Harvard crew team. We're catching the 10:39 and making it back to campus 'fore curfew."

Dale winced and threw back his head wearily. "It's Saturday night. We're seniors. You really want to head back this early?"

"I do."

He glanced back to his new friends. "You guys can run home to tuck in at eleven thirty, but I'm staying out."

He turned to step back to the dance floor, but I caught him by the shoulder.

"Dale, you had your fun. Now it's time for all of us to go home. I'm only trying to look out for you."

Dale eyed me fiercely. "I don't need you looking out for me. Jesus, Arizona. Why you got to be such a prissy faggot?"

That got me burning up. "Is that what I am to you? You low class, bathroom stall cocksucker."

I was seeing red and didn't care that he was flinching like I'd punched him in the gut. "Go on. Have your fun. I hope you get expelled. But if you don't, you best believe you ever speak that way to me again, I'll be swinging for you and knocking the stupid out of your head."

I didn't wait for his reaction. I staggered off to find Jonathan and Russell.

AFTER ALL THAT, Jonathan, Russell, and me caught a taxi, missed the 10:39, and waited a half hour for the 11:10 train back to Middleton. It was a horrible end to the night. Russell wasn't talking to Jonathan or me, and I was too pissed off to play peace-keeper. Truth was, I didn't feel like having a conversation with either of them. We'd gone out to have a fun night, and they'd all ruined it with plain stupidity.

When the train finally came, we sat down in separate aisles. We deboarded at Middleton and walked back to campus single file. At the gates, the security officer had us sign in and made a phone call to our dorm head, Mr. Ruskin, who had to let us in since they locked up the hall at eleven thirty.

Mr. Ruskin met us at the door in his night robe and slip-pers and was none too pleased. I didn't care at that point. I let him have his say, and none of us made any excuses. There'd be disciplinary action, he said, and then he asked about Dale. Russell said we'd lost track of him, but he'd be sure to be coming along. Mr. Ruskin was right miffed about that, but given the late hour, he let us run up to our rooms. I was just glad to strip off my clothes and tuck into my bed with the hope I'd never have to go through a night like that again.

I clicked off my night lamp, and a few seconds later, Jonathan decided to open his mouth.

"Russell and I broke up."

I sighed. "Based on the conversation we had, I'd say that was long overdue."

"I'm sorry, Arizona. I told you not to say you'd given me the money, and then I go and tell him myself like a fink."

"You ever heard the expression honesty's the best policy? Well, it's the last time I'm doing you any favors."

Jonathan didn't reply. Then I heard something like a gasp, followed by something that sounded like crying. I took a deep breath, climbed out of my bed, and sat down next to Jonathan. I was mad at everyone for ruining that night, but I never could stand seeing someone in pain.

"All right Jonathan, I didn't mean it. I know you had your

reasons for not wanting Russell to know about the money. I bet the two of you can smooth things over in the morning."

"He told me he's better off without me," Jonathan said through tears.

"Maybe he just needs some time to cool off."

Jonathan kept sobbing. I lay down and hugged him against me. I was feeling pretty low too. In just one night, we four musketeers had broken up.

14

ON MONDAY, RUSSELL, Jonathan, and I were suspended from classes and had to meet with the Dean of Students, Mr. McGovern. None of us had spoken to Dale, but the rumor running around campus was he'd turned up Sunday morning around six, stumbling to the gates after climbing out of one them white and red Boston taxicabs. Anyway, we sat in Dean McGovern's office for a drubbing. The highlights were he'd have to inform our parents about breaking curfew, and a further infraction of the code of conduct could result in expulsion from school. We filed out of the office, and Russell ran off without saying a word. I don't know what crawled up that boy's ass.

In the end, the whole thing wasn't such a big deal. I called my daddy that night and told him exactly what happened. He said I best stay on the straight and narrow for the rest of the year, but he didn't sound too sore about it. Jonathan got off even easier. His parents didn't speak English too well, so they had no idea what Dean McGovern told them. Jonathan cleaned things up by saying it was a routine progress report for parents, and he was doing just fine. We had a good chuckle over that. It's not that Jonathan liked lying to his parents, but they'd have skinned him alive for jeopardizing his scholarship, and we'd tried our darndest that night to make it back by curfew. Anyway, Jonathan and I went right back to being best friends like nothing had happened.

We were sure Dale was in for much worse trouble. The proctor on our floor, Jimmy Leavitt, had a loose tongue, and he said Dale came back that night stinking of liquor, and he puked right at Mr. Ruskin's feet. But Dale showed up for all his classes on Tuesday. I wasn't keen on having a conversation with him, and I sped by when we passed each other in the halls. Then some boys I knew in the equestrian club told me Dale's daddy took things up with the school president after Dean McGovern gave him the news. Mr. Knox-Levy was an alumnus and a big donor to the school. The boys said he threatened to destroy Middleton's reputation if they tried to sanction his son. Dale didn't get into a lick of trouble.

That didn't sit well with me at first, but considering what Dale had said to me and done that night, I decided to leave things be and let him jog ahead like I always said. I had my schoolwork to focus on, including Mr. Turner's creative writing class, which excited me for all kinds of reasons.

I'd hoped my crush on him would wear off like the flu, but every time I stepped into his classroom, I had butterflies in my stomach. Mr. Turner was so intelligent, so kind and gentle in his demeanor, and I was fascinated by everything about him from his deep, sincere blue eyes, his long, wheat-colored hair, his hands, which had a dusting of light hair on the back, and his big smile when we were talking about something funny. He gave me back my first writing assignment, where we had to cut out pictures from magazines and tell a story based on the photos of characters we chose. His handwritten comments and the big A on my paper made me feel so special, I put that paper in a plastic sleeve to hold on to for the rest of my life.

I could've gone on that term without thinking about Dale Knox-Levy again. Then one day in our chemistry class, when Mr. Schroeder stepped out of the classroom to grab some supplies from his office, a pair of dumb jocks shoved Dale's textbooks and notes off his desk and called him a fairy cocksucker.

Brad Ellis and Tom Zimmer. The two biggest dopes in the entire school, if not the state of Massachusetts. They were always picking on somebody to show off how much bigger and better they were.

Most of the students broke out in laughter, and that made me snap. I stood up from my desk and stepped over to the ignorant jerks.

"You gonna pick that up?"

Brad and Tom looked at one another, and Brad came back to me with a sneer.

"Who do you think you're talking to, Scarlett O'Hara?"

"I'm talking to the two boys with the tiniest pricks in the classroom." I glanced around the room. "Well, ain't I?" I wagged my pinkie finger. "We all seen them in the shower."

It took a beat or two, then everyone started laughing. Brad and Tom turned beet red. They looked like they couldn't decide if they wanted to storm away in shame or murder me.

"That's not true," Tom said.

"At least we don't *suck* pricks," Brad said.

"Why're you looking anyway?"

"Believe me, I regret it. I seen newborns packing more down there. And as a matter of fact, I do suck prick. But I'd have more fun with one of Mr. Schroeder's eye droppers than either of you." I looked down at the floor. "Now you gonna clean up the mess you made?"

Brad got on his feet, charged at me, and balled up my shirt collar in his fist. I was ready to go out fighting. But just then, Mr. Schroeder came back into the classroom and dropped the crate of supplies he was carrying on his desk.

"Brad Ellis, what the hell are you doing?"

He unhanded me and stepped back, trying to act blameless. "Arizona started it."

Mr. Schroeder rolled his eyes. "I bet he did. C'mon. You're going to Dean McGovern's office for the rest of the afternoon. Arizona, you okay?"

"Yes, sir. But Mr. Schroeder, Brad and Tom didn't pick up Dale's stuff they threw off his desk."

Mr. Schroeder looked around the room. "Is that true?"

Boys slowly nodded their heads.

"Let's go, Tom." Mr. Schroeder waved the two along, and they swaggered out of the classroom giving me the middle finger on their way out.

After class, I headed to the library. I had a free period, and I wanted to get started on my next paper for Mr. Turner's class. Then Dale caught up to me.

"Arizona?"

I really wanted to ignore him, but Dale kept plodding along beside me. I was only halfway to the library, but I stopped because I couldn't take it anymore.

"I just wanted to thank you for what you said to Brad and Tom."

"Dale, let's get something clear. What I did, I'd do for any stranger getting picked on. It don't make us friends."

I tried to move along again, but Dale traipsed after me. "You want me to say I'm sorry? I will. I'm sorry, Arizona. I was a real a-hole Saturday night."

"Why?" I shook my head and scowled to myself. "You know, there's no shortage of people in the world who'd like to call me a faggot. But coming from you?" I looked him in the eye. "I don't have time for friends like that."

His eyes bulged. "I called you…?"

"Mm-hmm."

"Damn, Arizona. Those guys from Northeastern…we'd been drinking. I don't even remember half the night."

I wasn't sure I believed him. "Well, I do. And so does Jonathan. And Russell. We would've made it back by curfew if it wasn't for you."

Dale looked at me with his eyes so big and pained, he was either sincere or on his way to a very successful acting career. "I'm sorry. I'll do anything to make it up to you. I miss us four musketeers. I miss *you*, Arizona. You're my best friend." He glanced off to the side, and then his face brightened. "What about that shopping trip on Newbury Street? I'll buy you anything you want. And take you out for ice cream afterward at J.P. Licks."

I drew him over to a little alcove in the hall where we'd have some privacy.

"Dale, I'll be honest with you. I said some things to you that night I'm not proud of either, so I'm fine calling things square on that matter. But how about having some self-respect? What're you doing running off with a group of boys you just met?"

His face flushed, and he skirted my gaze. "I was just having some fun." A smile crept up his face. "There was this cute boy Peter I was dancing with. We really liked each other, and he introduced me to his friends. They were cool. Then it turned out Peter's friend Victor liked me, so we fooled around. A little. Then we went to a party at the dorms, and I'd never been to a Northeastern party. You would've loved it, Arizona. I know you would've."

I thought about what I'd observed in the bathroom stalls that night. Now don't get me wrong. I'm not gonna claim to be a prude. But Dale's decision-making was concerning me.

"Chipmunk, you know I'm all for gay liberation. But how about taking boys one at a time? There's a virus out there killing people like us. You using protection?"

He gawped at me. "You make it sound like I'm some kind of skeezer. I only go with boys who're clean."

I could've said this or that about how he made that determination. But I was wore out by the conversation. Truth was, I missed his friendship too.

Dale gave me a playful nudge. "You run lines with me tonight? I've got my audition tomorrow for the fall play. We're doing *Bye, Bye Birdie* with the Woodland Hall Girls School."

He looked real excited about that. Though it felt like too much, too soon. "How 'bout we meet up for dinner instead? Get the whole gang together to mend some fences."

His eyes lit up. "That's a great idea. I've barely seen Russell and Jonathan this week."

"Well Jonathan probably won't be a problem, but Russell…" I told him about Jonathan and Russell splitting up.

"I'll talk to him after dance class." Dale grinned. "Russell can be a little stubborn, but I'll bring him around."

Well, I didn't seem the harm in him giving Russell a try, but I told him I ought to make sure Jonathan was on board. We said we'd meet up at the dining hall at six thirty, tentatively.

JONATHAN DIDN'T LIKE the idea at first. It wasn't so much Dale as Russell, which stood to reason since the boy had gone and broke his heart. I told him I'd gladly cancel plans with Dale, and then Jonathan spun around to say he wasn't going to be the cause of us four not making up. I asked him twice if he was sure he wanted to go through with it, and he insisted. So, around six fifteen, we headed across campus to the dining hall.

We grabbed our usual table in the corner of the noisy, hard-wood-paneled room. Dale came along, and to give the devil his due, he'd dredged up Russell, who loped behind him, still looking sour. Nothing more than "hi" passed between any of us at first. We went to the buffet line to heap our plates with turkey, mashed potatoes, corn, and creamed spinach.

Back at the table, Dale filled the silence, going on and on about the school play and debating out loud whether he should be trying out for the part of Albert Peterson, who was traditionally considered the lead, or Conrad Birdie, who got the most laughs. I don't think any of us were paying much attention. That boy could talk all day and night all by himself.

"What do you think, Arizona?"

"Personally, I prefer *Oklahoma*. Now that's a musical with numbers a fella can sure have fun singing along to. And Mr. Gordon MacRae from the old movie version." I wriggled my eyebrows at Jonathan. "I'd take a ride on his surrey with the fringe on top any night of the week."

Russell spit out his diet cola. Jonathan cracked up.

"Wouldn't it be the fringe on the bottom?" Jonathan said.

"I suppose that's a matter of perspective. And personal grooming. Now according to Dale's collection of *Honcho* magazines, it seems shaved on the bottom with just a trim to the top is *de rigeur* these days."

That got Jonathan and Russell red faced and grinning. Dale didn't look too happy. I turned to him.

"Seeing as we're talking 'bout *Oklahoma*, come to think of it, Chipmunk, you'd be perfect for the role of Ado Annie, being a girl who cain't say no."

Dale frowned at me, and then his eyes shifted cleverly. In a blink, he jumped up on the table, and we three stared at him while he unbuttoned the top of his shirt and rolled up his sleeves. Then, after some thumps of his shoe to pick up the meter, he started belting out "Oklahoma" right there in the dining hall.

Russell just about slid under the table. I gave Dale a whistle, and Jonathan and I stood and clapped and sang along. Boys around the dining hall jeered, but pretty soon the better half of them got to picking up the tune and singing. The proctors looked at each other, but they came up empty in terms of what to do about all the commotion. That dining hall was roaring with our big, rowdy chorus.

I'll say this about Dale, he had a great voice and put on one heck of a show. When he finished, he took his bows to a roomful of clapping, cheers, and hollers.

15

ALL I CAN say about being gay at Middleton Academy is it was complicated. That night, nobody cared four queer boys whipped up a Broadway singalong at dinner. People slapped us five, and they talked about it all week, even saying we should do things like that more often. I can't say I ever caught much guff since I stood up to Christopher Watts-Jennings last year. Boys had an unspoken kind of respect for me. Could be because I had a loud mouth. It wasn't so easy for Jonathan, Dale, and Russell.

All last year, Jonathan had gotten tripped and knocked around carrying his tray from the breakfast line. It always happened when I was looking the other way. I never had a chance to pick out the idiots who did it. And Dale, well, things were always up and down for him. A few days after his big performance at the dining hall, the cast for the fall play was announced. Dale got the lead part of Albert Peterson. Kids congratulated him. I think his talent roused up a sense of school pride. But the next day, somebody spray painted his bedroom door with the word "Faggot" in bright pink letters.

I went with Dale to report it to Dean McGovern, and I told him Brad Ellis and Tom Zimmer had been messing with Dale in chemistry class, which made them persons of interest. I also brought up we were still waiting on an answer about the Pink Triangle Club, and I made the point that incidents like this were precisely why we needed an organization to fight homophobia on campus. Dean McGovern was real careful with us. He said there'd be an investigation about the graffiti, and our request was still being considered by the Board of Trustees. I was pretty sure he was stretching things out until the two of us graduated.

As for Russell, he hadn't told anyone he was gay, but one night when we were studying at the library, he confessed his roommate Carl, who he'd been friends with since seventh grade, confronted him about why he was hanging out with the three of us, wondering if he was queer, too. Russell denied it, but Carl started hanging out with a group of boys from the hockey team, and they were all giving Russell dirty looks around school. I had a theory that was the reason he'd broken up with Jonathan. It ate at me he'd made that decision, but he and Jonathan were getting along all right, so I chose to shut my mouth. Like I said, it was complicated being gay at that school.

Autumn came with its nip in the air, and the forested grounds turned brilliant reds and yellows. I had a meeting with my academic advisor, Mr. Toomey, and I started on my applications to Columbia and Brown. I also started one for Harvard to please my daddy. I'd done well on the SATs, and Mr. Toomey said I had good prospects anywhere I applied if I could put together a strong essay. I suppose I ought've been excited, but I got light-headed and tight in the chest a lot that term. For all my big talk about not caring about fitting in, I was scared to make a new start at a college where I didn't know anybody. Jonathan was applying to Brown as well, but he was also putting in applications to the University of Iowa and the University of Michigan. Dale was applying to Yale University on early decision. Russell had his sights on Cornell where his father and older brother had gone.

The next day, on a crisp and sunny afternoon, the four of us staked out a spot on the lawn to study outside. We had our textbooks and notebooks, but I was having a hard time focusing on my

classes. I had a restless feeling torturing me, and I didn't know how
to scare it away.

We'd chosen a spot by the Humanities Building. Everyone got
quiet all of sudden. Jonathan nudged me and pointed out Mr.
Turner had come out of the building en route to the parking lot. I
looked over at that handsome man in his tweed jacket and leather
briefcase.

Dale sighed. "He has to be the best looking teacher in the
entire history of the school."

Russell twitched his nose. "What about our dance instructor
Mr. Bernadetti?"

"He's good looking," Dale said. "But Mr. Turner, he's got that
classic look. Like he could be a *GQ* model."

I couldn't agree with him more. Eager feelings stirred inside
me just watching Mr. Turner from fifty yards away. I didn't even
hear Dale asking me a question until he repeated it a second
time.

"Earth to Arizona. This is Houston calling. You think Mr.
Turner could be gay?"

I tightened my shoelaces, got up on my feet, and grabbed my
book bag. "I don't know. But there's only one way to find out." I
smoothed out my school jacket and went jogging over to the
parking lot.

Dale and Jonathan hollered like fools. They must've thought
I'd lost my mind, and I wouldn't have argued the point. But I'd
been pining for Mr. Turner for so long, and my daddy had told me
I could have anything I wanted and should always aim for the best.
There wasn't a man alive any better than Mr. Wesley Turner in my
estimation, and he was going to be mine. I just needed to summon
my daddy's charm. He never let a pretty woman pass by without
putting out some feelers.

I made it over to Mr. Turner just as he was opening the door of
his forest green Volkswagen GTI. He stopped short when he heard
my voice.

"How do you do?" I halted a few paces from him for fear I'd

scare him off. He did look puzzled. I prayed my friends would cool it with the catcalls and laughter.

"Hi Arizona. What can I do for you?"

"A couple of things, actually." I scratched my ear. "I have a question about the paper due on Friday." I swallowed down a big gulp of courage. "And I could really use a ride into town." I jostled my knapsack. "I've got a package for my grandma I need to send special delivery. Her birthday is this Saturday, and I'm gonna catch it good if I don't make it to the post office 'fore five o'clock."

Mr. Turner shrank up his brow. "Don't they have a mail room on campus?"

"They sure do. But this package would just be sitting in the storeroom until Mr. Sawyer takes things over to the post office in the morning."

He looked around. "Don't they have a shuttle into town?"

"Yes, sir. On the quarter hour. I just missed the 4:15. But if you happen to be headed into town, I can catch the shuttle coming back to campus at five o'clock."

I tried to hide the flood of anticipation inside me. I could feel a drop of sweat sprouting at my temple and rolling down my face. Meanwhile, Mr. Turner hesitated in a bemused sort of way. I don't know if it was against the rules for teachers to drive students in their personal cars, but he looked a bit put off by the suggestion.

"All right Arizona. Hop in. I am headed that way."

"Thank you, Mr. Turner. You saved my skin."

I hurried over to the passenger side door and jumped into his Volkswagen.

I'D DONE A lot of bold things in my seventeen-year-old life, but making up a fib to spend time with Mr. Turner had to rank in the top five. Well, make that the top three. I was sitting in his cozy, little car, admiring how he worked his stick shift and gunned the engine when we got on the country road into town. He looked sexy driving. I'd never been so up close to that strong, clean-shaven jaw of his or gotten to peek at places on him here and there while he was looking straight ahead to the road. He sure liked driving fast, and he looked totally in control of his vehicle.

"You live in town?"

"Yes. The school rents apartments for junior faculty. Over by the Middleton Pond Conservancy."

"It just you?" He didn't wear a wedding ring, though I supposed he could have someone special in his life.

"Yep. Just me. And that's a good thing. Those faculty apartments aren't exactly spacious." He smiled at me.

"How you liking Middleton?" I wriggled my eyebrows. "I bet it's a whole lot different than New York City."

"That it is. But I only lived in New York for two years."

"While you were studying at Columbia?"

He nodded.

I'd seen his faculty profile, which was on the wall in a glass display case in the administrative hall. He had a bachelor's degree from the University of Buffalo.

"Where'd you live before you went to college?"

"Undergraduate?"

"Mm-hmm."

"I stayed in town. I was born and raised in Buffalo. But I moved out of the house to live in the dorms." He turned to me. "So, what's your question about the assignment?"

I blinked and searched my head. I'd already written a first draft. "Well. This is supposed to be an autobiographical paper about a moment in our lives when we were at a crossroads and had to make a decision, right?"

"That's right. The goal is to tap into personal experiences. That'll help you whether you've got an interest in writing memoirs or writing fiction. We're studying Hemingway's *A Moveable Feast* to understand how a writer's life influences his work."

I had a good understanding of all that. I spent more time studying for Mr. Turner's class than any other, and I'd written six pages about the time I was living in foster care and decided to move in with my birth daddy. I reached for something to keep conversation going.

"I'm having trouble getting started. You ever been at a crossroads yourself? What would you write about?"

Mr. Turner pushed back his hair, which was a cute little tell I'd hit on a subject that made him nervous.

"Well, Arizona, life is full of crossroads. I suppose for me, a big one was deciding on a career. My father's a doctor. My grandfather's an engineer who worked for the military in World War II. My older brother is a chemical engineer for Standard Oil. Just about my entire family chose a career in the sciences, so I had to decide whether to pursue that or follow my dream to teach and write."

That had me all sorts of interested. I told him about my daddy wanting me to go to business school while I wanted to be a writer.

"Sounds like you've got good material on your hands. And you're a good writer, Arizona. I'm sure you'll do a great job with that assignment."

I was warm in the face from his praise. But I wanted to take things farther than just talking about careers.

"I suppose there *are* all kinds of crossroads. You ever experienced something more personal?"

"How do you mean?"

I pieced together a response in my head, and then I decided to be gutsy and say what was on my mind. "I been thinking about writing something else. You mind if I run it by you?"

He shrugged.

"Well, Mr. Turner, about this time last year, I had a choice to pretend to live a conventional life or to be true to who I am. I guess I'm wondering about your opinion. You think it's better to live your life closeted or to come out and say you're gay?"

I peeked at him. His face had darkened, and he'd gone a little stiff all of the sudden.

"I don't think I'm qualified to give you advice on that sort of question. But you could talk to one of the school counselors."

"What do you think makes a fella qualified to answer that sort of question?"

He wrinkled his brow thoughtfully. "I suppose someone who has a degree in human development or psychology."

"Do you subscribe to the view that being gay is a psychological disease?"

Don't ask me why I was giving my English teacher such a hard time. If I had a lick of sense, I wouldn't have, but something takes over inside me when I'm around a man I've got feelings for. It was the same thing with Nicolas, giving him lip right from the start. Thinking about it, a lot of what I did that day had to do with Nicolas. I missed the attention of an older man, that gentle affection which made me feel special. Mr. Turner got me feeling the same way.

Meantime, he was burning up in the face again. "I didn't say that." He gave me a nervous grin. "This is an unorthodox conversation to be having with your creative writing teacher, don't you think?"

"I don't think it's unorthodox at all. You've been teaching us how a man's life experience shapes his world view and leads him into the subjects he decides to write about. You know Truman Capote never once wrote explicitly about gay people and their relationships, though everyone knows he was gay? Oscar Wilde, too. But then there's writers like James Baldwin and John Rechy who write about it openly. I'm trying to decide what kind of writer I should be."

Mr. Turner nodded along. "There's also Thomas Mann. Walt Whitman. Gore Vidal."

I stretched my hands behind the neckrest of my seat. "Somerset Maugham, Edmund White, Tennessee Williams. I read them all. On my own time. So maybe you can answer me this: how come they don't make us read one gay story in any of the English classes at Middleton?"

"I'm in my first year of teaching. I don't have any say about the curriculum."

"Suppose you did. What would you have to say about it then?"

He glanced at me twice before saying anything. "I believe representation is important in literature. We've made some progress with giving women authors more attention. Black authors like Maya Angelou as well. Literature and the arts have always led the way to greater social equality. Consider the impact of George Orwell's *Animal Farm*, which is taught in just about every high school in the country. It was written as a commentary on the state of society post World War Two and as an argument against the spread of totalitarian ideologies and the exploitation of minorities."

"I read *Animal Farm* in eighth grade. What's that got to do with gay representation?"

"Well, it doesn't. Directly. But even *Animal Farm* faced resistance and challenges in the academy. In the 1940s, it was considered too radical for any of the big publishing houses to publish, and in the 1950s, it inspired book burnings. What I'm saying, Arizona, is the philosophy of social equality has always had its ebbs and flows in popular society, and that includes, as you say gay rights. Martin Luther King said 'The arc of the moral universe is long, but it bends toward justice.'"

He smiled at me in a smug, teacherly way.

"I don't mean any disrespect, Mr. Turner, but I think that's a wagonload of horseshit. I don't see social equality ebbing and flowing or bending in any direction so long as people don't get to read about folks who are different than them. And in order for that to happen, it takes gay people in charge having the courage to do what's right."

That wiped the grin right off Mr. Turner's face. He stared straight ahead, and after a while, he muttered, "Arizona, I'm beginning to think you didn't ask for a ride into town to send your grandmother a birthday present special delivery."

I leaned over on one side to face him with a playful smirk. "Well, there, Mr. Turner, you might be right. But I'll see you that and raise you one. I'm beginning to think you might've figured that out before you told me to hop into your car."

Mr. Turner slowed down and pulled over to the curb. I hadn't even noticed we'd made it to Meadow Drive, which was the town's main drag. Mr. Turner muttered stiffly, "I don't know what you're implying, but I can assure you, you're mistaken."

Send me to blazes, but looking at his face all twisted and out of sorts, I laughed. "I'm sorry. It's just, your face looks kind of funny."

The man was pink with indignation. I tried to smooth it over, but then he told me to get out of his car.

"I said I'm sorry. Look here, I think I know what the problem is. You never been in the company of an avowed homosexual before."

"Arizona, we can't talk about that."

"I didn't read that anywhere in the Middleton Academy Code of Conduct. And if it is in there, that's a violation of my constitutional rights. Freedom of speech." I tried to catch his glance again, but he was staring out the windshield, looking grim. "Isn't that right, Mr. Turner?"

"What do you want? A guaranteed A? Money?" He shook his head like he couldn't believe his bad luck. "I'm not wealthy, but I'll settle on any terms you have in mind."

I drew back in my seat, feeling sick to my stomach. He thought I was blackmailing him?

"Mr. Turner, I admire you. I'd never try to get you in trouble. You haven't done anything wrong."

"Then open the door. Go on your way." He looked me in the eyes. "Could you *please* not mention this happened to anyone?"

The pained look on his face made me feel like steaming pile of horse manure. I looked at him one last time, and I stepped out of his car. I stood on the curb and watched him drive off in a hurry.

I KNEW I'D done wrong. I hadn't meant to, but I did. I wanted Mr. Turner to like me, and though I couldn't say what it was that happened in his car, all my teasing and challenging had scared the living daylights out of him. Made him think I was some no-good troublemaker trying to get him fired.

Dazed, I walked a couple blocks in town, trying to make sense of it. Did he think I was threatening to out him? That I was planning on making up a story that he'd touched me inappropriately? Nothing could be farther from the truth, but I'd seen with my own eyes, he dreaded me now. What an idiot I was! I'd made an enemy of Mr. Turner, the man of my dreams. I'd just been trying to get to know him. That's what I told myself. My feelings for him and I suppose my pride suppressed any reckoning that I'd been up to trouble from the start.

I took the shuttle back to campus and drifted along to my room to change for dinner. It was after six o'clock, but Jonathan had waited for me. Well, I shouldn't have been surprised. He was dying to know what happened as soon as I walked through the door.

I slunk over to my bed. I fully intended to honor Mr. Turner's plea, but I knew I could trust Jonathan with a secret so long as he understood how important it was to me.

"You swear on your life you won't breathe a word to Russell or Dale?"

Jonathan gaped, and he nodded vigorously. So, I told him everything, and then I collapsed on my side, wishing I was dead.

I felt the bounce of my mattress from Jonathan jumping aboard. "Arizona, you think he thought you knew he was gay?"

"I don't know."

"Well, why else would he say that? He must've thought you were threatening to out him. Which is crazy. I mean, you don't have proof that he's gay. Do you? What did he think you were going to do? Tell Dean McGovern that you have a hunch?"

I sat up limply. "All I know is I just ruined my favorite class and got the poor man scared for his life. I gotta make it up to him somehow. Y'know, this is another reason we need that Pink Triangle Club. There's students and teachers terrified of just being accused of being gay. You tell me that's fair."

Jonathan watched me like a hawk. I'd sure perked his interest.

"He was really that scared?" he said.

I nodded.

"You shouldn't have asked him for a ride into town. And he shouldn't have agreed to it. He is a teacher, after all."

"What's that got to do with anything? Mr. Banner is always taking the hockey team for ski trips in his minivan. He has them over for private dinners at his house."

"The difference is, you've got a crush on Mr. Turner."

"So? Hang me for it. It's not like I was forcing myself on him. Just because I'm gay don't mean I can't conduct myself appropriately. And vice versa. Look at the two of us. We're gay and sharing a room, and there's nothing going on between us. What you're talking about is a double standard."

I studied Jonathan while he took that in. He had something else on his mind, and I was starting to think I wasn't going to like hearing it.

"There's nothing going on because we're not attracted to each other. But you and Mr. Turner...well, I think there's something there. And he could get fired if that got out."

I heard the words, but the shameful truth is he set my spirits soaring. Jonathan thought what happened that day was because Mr. Turner was attracted to me? I'd felt it myself, and that set my mind and body to thinking I had to pursue where that was leading. I kept it to myself. When we went down to the dining hall to meet Dale and Russell, I nipped things in the bud by saying Mr. Turner told me he had a girlfriend. Then that night, I couldn't sleep, wondering what I could do to earn back Mr. Turner's trust and show him how much I cared about him. It felt like my whole world depended on it.

16

THAT WEEK, I wrote a new essay about being at a crossroads. I took the experience I'd shared with Mr. Turner and laid bare all the feelings I'd been having. I poured out my heart, expressing my desires and my guilt and shame about how things turned out. I think it was the best paper I'd ever written because it was raw and honest. So raw and honest, I near had a cardiac arrest when it came time to pass it along to the front of the classroom. I just prayed Mr. Turner would see I never meant him any bad will, and he shouldn't count me out as someone with whom he could have a special relationship.

On Saturday, Dale and I finally took that shopping trip to Boston. Jonathan and Russell weren't interested, and a curious thing—they seemed right pleased to have some time together on their own. Those two were on again, off again, and let anyone try to keep up. Anyway, Dale and I took the train and then a cab over to Newbury Street.

It was crowded with college students and tourists, and we loped along from shoe stores to men's boutiques to record stores to vintage clothing shops. I bought myself a new pair of bucks, a suede jacket, a pair of jeans, and two button down shirts. Dale picked up twice as much, and we were both wore out from lugging shopping bags up and down the street.

Then we came to a jeweler, and while we eyed the display cases, Dale decided he was getting his ear pierced and that I should do the same. Lots of boys were getting their ears pierced back then, so I said why the heck not? It hurt like blazes, but we both got little platinum studs in our right ears, which signified we were gay. I felt exhilarated, but then the woman who pierced my ear told me I had to leave the stud in for six weeks or the hole would close up.

After we paid and walked out of the store, I shot a glance at Dale. "Were you aware of that?"

He snickered. "I think I heard something about it. But all you have to do is wear a beanie around school for a few weeks."

I was incensed for more than one reason. "You seen me in a beanie? Maybe you can pull it off, but I look like a turtle. Especially if I've got to pull it down over my ears." I shook my head and realized something else. "Wearing a hat's against the dress code too."

"I don't think a knit cap is."

"You want to find out? Have Mr. Ruskin pull it off in front of everyone and haul us over to Dean McGovern's office?"

"Just chill. We got our ears pierced, Arizona. It's a bonding moment. Don't ruin it."

I felt like swatting him, but I let it go for now. We found a café to have some lunch, and Dale said he was paying, reminding me he owed me for that night he'd been such a jerk earlier in the term. I didn't argue with him, and we chowed down on sandwiches in baguettes, french fries, and chocolate Coca-Colas. When we were done, I pulled out the train schedule from my back pocket. If we found a cab right quick, we could make the 4:44 back to Middleton. I told that to Dale, and search me why it got him grinning.

"Or, we could head over here." He brought out of his leather jacket pocket a postcard sized flyer and handed it to me.

I near turned it face down. That café was crowded, and we

were practically elbow-to-elbow with an elderly couple at the table next door. The flyer was mainly comprised of some fellow's naked torso and his unbuttoned jeans.

"It's a tea dance at a club in the South End," Dale said.

I noticed the lettering at the bottom. Jack's. A Columbus Avenue address. "Why I got a feeling they ain't serving tea?"

Dale guffawed. "Peter and Victor told me about it." He leaned over the table and spoke a little softer. "They also told me about a sex club on Stuart Avenue."

I slid the flyer back to him, face-down, and gave him a glare. "Don't tell me you got a flyer for that."

He smiled. "No. But I've got an address. C'mon. Doesn't it sound like fun?"

"Chipmunk, I prefer to get my sex the old-fashioned way." I took a pull from my straw.

"How? At a highway rest stop?"

"No. I mean by getting to know a fella. Having a little romance before the britches come off."

Dale rolled his eyes. "We're single. What's wrong with getting some action? No strings attached."

"I'm about to tie some strings on you. Make it a lasso." I pointed a finger at him. "You're getting home by curfew, young man."

Dale got that scheming look on his face. "It's early. Forget about the sex club if you're too high and mighty for it. We'll just run over to the tea dance for a little while. If it's lame, I've got an invite to a house party at Northeastern." He beamed at me. "Tell me that's not going to be a wicked good time? And don't worry. We'll catch the 10:39 and be back at the dorm before Mr. Ruskin locks up."

I'm not going to say I wasn't intrigued, but Dale was the last person to have in charge of an itinerary. "And what're we supposed to do with all this loot? They got a coat check at this tea dance?"

"I don't know. But they've got lockers at the train station."

"Hmm. I see you been premeditating. You premeditate how we're going to get into a club that's twenty-one and over?"

Dale reached into his pants pocket, brought out his leather wallet and scrounged out a driver's license. I looked it over. He'd somehow knocked back his date of birth by five years. I giggled. Dale could barely pass for his own age let alone twenty-two.

I gave him back his ID. "You can take your chances with that, but I ain't got anything. I'm catching the 4:44, and you should too."

"C'mon, Arizona. We're in Boston. Just come with me to the tea dance. I heard they don't check IDs. We can just stay for an hour or so if that's all you want. How often do we get the chance to hang out with college boys?"

He had a point. A few weeks back, I would've been all for it. But I knew Dale Knox-Levy. He'd be needling me from the tea dance to that house party to Lord knows where else? I couldn't afford to break curfew again. We could get arrested for underage drinking for all I knew. Besides, we were supposed to be getting together with Jonathan and Russell that night to watch dirty movies on HBO.

"You're on your own. And you've been advised." I stood and sorted out my shopping bags.

"Arizona, when am I gonna get you to have a night out on the town with me?"

"You figure out a way to stay out past curfew without getting expelled, and we can talk."

The little devil got a clever gleam on his face. "They let you stay out overnight if you've got a note from your parents."

I looked at him twice. "You got parents who'll write you a note so you can stay out drinking and carousing with boys?"

"No. You forge it. You say you're going home for the weekend. Then you get a room at the motor lodge over on Mass Ave. If you don't find better sleeping arrangements, that is. My older brother Louis used to do it all the time. You can write a letter saying you're going home with me."

"And Dean McGovern don't call your parents to confirm they wrote the note?"

"Arizona, with all the money our parents give the school, they don't bother checking."

It still sounded risky to me. Especially in the fall semester of our senior year when we were sending in college applications and counting on letters of recommendation.

"Did you give Dean McGovern a letter for tonight?"

"No."

I heaved a breath. "Then Dale, please be back before curfew. We'll be up in my room until lights out. I expect to see you there."

I got all my bag handles gripped in my hands and was fixing to leave, but Dale delayed me.

"Since you're going back, you think you could take my stuff with you?"

That boy was lucky he was cute. Otherwise, I might've beat him with my shopping bags right there in the café.

IT WAS REAL fun lugging eight shopping bags into a cab, through the train station, onto a train and then hiking from the train station to campus. I must've looked like I bought out a department store or I was some kind of crazy bag lady. I could've been mugged. I cursed Dale all the way home.

Back at the dorm, I met up with Jonathan and Russell. Of course, they wanted to know what happened to Dale, and I told them this and that. That led to more aggravation.

Jonathan said I shouldn't have let Dale go to the tea dance by himself, and he pointed out my earring broke the dress code, which I already knew. Russell called Dale a no-good punk who'd never learn his lesson so long as his parents let him do whatever he pleased. Russell was still sore from the previous incident. He'd been the only one of the four of us who caught it bad from his parents. They'd called off his Vermont ski trip with Dale over winter break and put a block on his bank account so he couldn't take out money without their permission. I tried to defuse the two of them.

"Number one, I told Dale ten times he needed to come home with me, and as far as keeping an eye on him, you tell me how that works with a horny seventeen-year-old whose parents couldn't care less that he's crawling home at six o'clock in the morning?" I turned to Russell, "Number two, Dale's a genuine, blue ribbon winning pain in the ass, but he's been a good friend to all three of us and don't deserve to be called a no-good punk."

Russell looked like he wanted to go at me again, but when I looked him the eye, he backed off. I was one grumpy badger that night. I couldn't see any solution other than taking out my earring. It stung something awful, and it was going to close up. I'd gotten to wear it all of four hours and wasted thirty-five dollars.

Jonathan came over while I was holding my earlobe with tissues. "Aren't you worried about Dale? He's going home with older guys and drinking and doing God knows what else. Can't you talk to him?"

"Why's it always gotta be me having to talk to him? You've got a mouth, don't you? And Russell, you've known Dale longer than either of us."

"Because he listens to you. He looks up to you," Russell said.

"That boy looks up to everybody. He's only five foot five."

"Russell's right. We all listen to you." Jonathan smirked. "Because we know if we don't, we're never gonna hear the end of it."

"Well, clearly Dale doesn't feel the same way. I'm tired of talking about it. Now what happened to one of you getting on the phone to order us a goddamn pepperoni pizza? Half hot peppers. And those cheapskates better not be out of cream soda again."

After that conversation, the three of us had a real good time that night. I got my cream soda and ate three slices of pizza while we watched a movie about Patsy Cline on HBO. Jonathan snuggled up with Russell, and I was glad to see the two of them back together. Later, they were playing a really dumb skin flick called

The Happy Hooker Goes Hollywood, but we laughed until our bellies burst making fun of it.

Eleven thirty rolled around, and Dale didn't show up. Then twelve, then twelve thirty, and by the time Russell had to go back to his room for lights out at one, Dale was still nowhere to be found.

17

THE FOLLOWING MONDAY, I spent the whole day on edge, waiting for Mr. Turner's 1:10 class to come along. He'd said he'd have our papers back to us, and I was both eager and scared to death to find out what he had to say about mine. I couldn't pay attention in my morning classes, and when I met up with Jonathan and Russell for lunch, I let the two of them banter back and forth about the midterm exam they'd just taken in American History.

To back up a few clicks, our prodigal son did make it back to campus Sunday morning. Russell came by around ten o'clock with the news. He'd heard from Jimmy Leavitt that Dale's roommate Greg Polk reported him to Mr. Ruskin. Apparently, Dale had snuck onto campus early in the morning and thought he could escape detection when they opened up the doors to the dorm at seven a.m.

We all rushed over to Dale's room like the busybodies we were. Dale was lights out, but when I poked him in the behind, he turned over, covered his head with his pillow and told us to fuck off. So, that's what we did. He didn't come looking for us all day, and we didn't go looking for him.

I got to Mr. Turner's class at 1:05 and sat restlessly at my desk.

Students filed in, and Mr. Turner arrived and took attendance. He hadn't looked me at me since I'd stepped out of his car almost a week ago, and that day wasn't any different.

He passed back our papers, and my heart started doing skips. When the student in front of me passed mine back, I had a cowardly impulse to just tuck it into my book bag. I forced myself to take a look. I leafed through my six-page paper three times and couldn't find anything but the red ballpoint A written in the top right corner of the cover page. That stung worse than if Mr. Turner tore apart my essay with corrections and given me an F. He couldn't have bothered to come up with a single comment?

I wondered if he'd even read my paper. I'm not bragging, but it was an attention-grabbing essay. I'd not only told him my regrets about my behavior, I'd confessed I sometimes felt like an imposter at school, having grown up poor with a different way of talking than everybody else, along with being one of very few gay students. I wrote how much I admired him, and that I wanted to be a great teacher like him. Mr. Turner had nothing to say about any of that? He either had a heart of stone or he thought I was a disease.

When class was over, I stormed out, not wanting to talk to nobody. Instead of going to chemistry, I went to the infirmary and told the nurse my stomach was acting up, which was basically the truth. It's just that the cause wasn't physical. Mrs. Callahan had me lie down on one of her cots and gave me two Pepto Bismol tablets, which I snuck into my pocket when she stepped away.

Thirty minutes later, I told her I was feeling a better and would be going to my room to rest. But I headed straight over to the humanities building and found Mr. Turner's office on the second floor. Nobody treats Arizona Bondurant like yesterday's news.

He'd mentioned our creative writing class was the last one he taught on Mondays, and he had office hours until three thirty. It was about a quarter to three. I knocked on his big wooden door.

The door opened, and we were face to face. I brought out, breathlessly, "I need to talk to you."

He didn't look happy about that, but he took a quick gander down both sides of the hall and stepped aside to let me in. I was too keyed up to sit down at the chair in front of his desk. Mr. Turner closed the door behind him.

"What can I do for you, Arizona?"

I pointed a finger at him. "Did you read my essay?"

He nodded. For a moment, I felt like I'd lost my marbles. He was acting so routine.

"You didn't have anything to say about it?"

He folded his arms in front of him. "I can check my grade book, but I believe I gave you an A."

I fixed on him. My hand was trembling at my side. "I didn't write that paper looking for a grade. I…" I had to wipe my eyes because they were tearing. "I was trying to tell you how I feel."

"Arizona, I'm going to sit down, and I think you should too."

"I don't want to sit down."

"All right." He glanced at his desk chair but remained standing. "I'm glad you came to see me about that paper. Some things are better expressed verbally."

I glanced at him expectantly. By the look on his face, I was suddenly regretting coming to his office.

"I made a copy, and I'm going to give it to Dean McGovern."

"Huh? Why?"

"Because I think it's best that you transfer into Mr. Harper's class." I must've looked as crushed as I felt inside. He turned stricken. "Arizona, it's not your fault. This happens sometimes with students and a teacher. There's nothing for you to be ashamed about."

"I'm not ashamed. I stopped being ashamed one year ago when Christopher Watts-Jennings called me a faggot, and I let him know where to stick it. What about you? Are you ashamed?"

He shifted nervously and pushed back his hair. "What would I have to be ashamed about?"

I frowned thoughtfully. "Maybe offering me a ride in your car?"

"That was a misjudgment on my part but entirely innocent." He bent his arm at his side. "You made up a story to get a ride into town. I'm prepared to tell Dean McGovern everything."

I had hot needles and cold needles piercing my chest. I gazed at him in disbelief. "I poured all the contents of my heart into that essay. And you're going to kick me out of your class?"

"You're a very talented writer." He heaved a breath. "But it's the best thing for both of us. Your feelings aren't wrong, Arizona. They're just misplaced. I'm your teacher. You have to understand that, don't you?"

"I was wrong about you. You're not a role model. You're a coward. You're afraid of somebody loving you. I pray I don't become that kind of man."

He glanced nervously at the door, showing me how cowardly he was. Like most of the buildings at Middleton, the humanities hall had to go back one hundred years or more when they made buildings with plaster walls and doors four inches thick. We weren't even talking loud. Nobody could overhear us.

He lowered his voice. "I could get fired. All right? You know, it's easy when you're seventeen years old with a rich family to fall back on. You can do anything you want and make mistakes. People will forgive and forget, and you've still got your whole life ahead of you." His face turned ashy like he'd aged ten years in a split second. "This job is all I have, and if I were to lose it because of an inappropriate relationship with a student, there wouldn't be any second chances. No school in the country would hire me."

"I'm not dumb. I understand all that. Now how 'bout you listen to me? I'm not going to hurt you, Mr. Turner. I'm trying to tell you how I feel." I took a half step closer to him. "What if this —you and me—was meant to be? I think there's something happening here that goes both ways. I'm not your average seventeen-year-old. I been with a man a lot older than you, and it wasn't just fooling around."

"Arizona, I'm your teacher."

"I thought about that. I don't think it matters. You've been teaching us to not think conventionally."

He sighed impatiently. I went on. "What kind of rules do gay people have to follow anyway? The world's gonna hate us whether we're the same age or not. Whether we're supposed to be together or not. We can make our own rules. We can follow our hearts."

He swiped his face, stepped behind his desk, faced the wall, and came back to me, grave and pained. "I can't give you what you want. Can you please just leave this be?"

I couldn't. In an instant, I pressed up on him, held his face, and grabbed his mouth with mine. It was one of them pent up, forceful kisses. I just wanted him to love me.

Mr. Turner was struck to stone at first, then he backed away a little, and then he kissed me back as passionately as I'd kissed him. He stretched his arms around me and crushed our bodies together. It was ecstasy for at least a count of twenty. Then he broke things off, and we awakened to each other.

"I don't think that was misplaced," I said. "Do you?" I snuck my hands around his sides. He was warm and firm, and his chest was heaving. I kissed his neck and found his mouth again. He tasted like spearmint chewing gum, and I loved the scent of his woodsy cologne, his starched shirt, the heavenly manly odors seeping through his clothes.

He spoke quietly in my ear. "No one can know. You understand?"

I nodded. He stepped away and locked the door.

THE THING ABOUT secrets people don't talk about too often is they're awfully exciting. I know I probably sound like a hypocrite, preaching all the time that gay people ought to be out in the open, but my relationship with Mr. Turner was different. At least that's how I thought back then. I was doing something I wasn't supposed to do, and it was dangerous and could get me in a heap of trouble. But it was something of my own like how my daddy had his mistress in Chattanooga. I hadn't realized how much I needed that sense of rebellion till I found it. Things been pressing in on me for a long time, from not being able to help Dolly and Little Douglas to losing Preston to everything about my life changing so quickly. I never had a chance to settle anywhere. Soon enough I'd be starting all over again in college. I know now none of that made my choices right, but I'm telling you, nothing felt righter for me at the time.

My head was miles above my body the rest of that day. I met up with Jonathan and Russell for dinner, but I only paid attention to bits and pieces while we went through the food line and they got to talking about their classes and what was going on with Dale. I was wrapped up in happy memories, and all I really wanted to do was write about them in my journal. I was already pining to be with Mr. Turner again real bad. Then I noticed Jonathan's raised voice.

"You okay, Arizona? You're acting like you got run over by a bus."

I swiped my face. "I'm fine. What were we talking about?"

Jonathan and Russell stared at me.

"You got a fever or something?" Russell said.

"We asked if you talked to Dale?"

I shook my head and speared some pot roast onto my fork. I chewed it down while the two of them looked at me blankly. "What's going on with Dale?"

Jonathan rolled his eyes. "We were talking about the rumor he's been cut out of the fall play."

"Oh. Well. Where's he at?"

"Nobody knows," Russell said. "He must've been suspended from classes."

I took a sip from my Coca-Cola and shrugged.

After dinner, Russell came up to our room to study, and he and Jonathan worked on calculus while I tried getting interested in my

French workbook but mostly scribbled. Around eleven, Russell said goodnight, and Jonathan and I got into our sleeping togs and tucked into our beds. When we turned off the lights, I played over moving pictures in my head. Mr. Turner shucking his shirt and tie. His mouth attacking my neck and chest. My slacks and briefs sliding down my legs. His swollen, sultry manhood in my hand.

18

I KEPT MEETING up with Mr. Wesley Turner in his office around three o'clock every day. We were careful with each other during class, him not calling on me too much, and me not asking too many questions. But when we were alone in his office, we were off to the races. Like I said, secrets are exciting, and we were all pent up and urgent when we were together. We only had an hour, and less than that if someone happened to knock on his door.

Sometimes, we'd talk a bit while we were warming up, and after, while we cozied up together in his desk chair. Mostly, he did the talking. In his office, he wanted me to call him Wes. He told me he'd never had a boyfriend before, but I teased out of him he'd been with men in bookstores in New York City, which sounded more like the sex club Dale had mentioned. He didn't like the city and preferred a place like Middleton where it was safe and clean and full of nature. He told me he'd been mugged on the subway, and there'd been a lot of heroin addicts in the neighborhood where he lived by Columbia University.

He'd never said he was gay to a single person, but he had a roommate at Columbia who caught him looking at a dirty magazine. That roommate stopped talking to him and found other places to sleep at night. I felt real bad for him. Wes said he got along with other faculty members, but he couldn't be completely himself around them. Now that we'd broken the ice, he was a real chatterbox and more like someone my age than an adult. You'd never know it looking at Mr. Wesley Turner. He was handsome, well-dressed, and real intelligent, but he was one of the loneliest people I'd ever known.

Now and then, he slowed me down and talked to me real sweet, saying what a miracle it was he'd found me and I was beautiful and smart, and he thought my Louisiana accent was sexy. I felt beautiful and sexy around him, and mainly I just wanted to get down to business when we were alone. Life outside his office was plenty complicated, but when I stepped in and he closed his door, I could escape from all that.

It was hard not telling Jonathan or Russell what I was up to, and we drifted apart a little because of that. We saw each other at mealtimes, and Russell was always in our room at night, but my head was someplace else. I'd dug myself into a double life, and as good as it felt being with Wes, I was feeling things I didn't like to feel, almost like I was on my lonesome again at that school. Now that's the downside of secrets. I just nodded along with whatever Jonathan and Russell wanted to do, and sometimes the two of them ran off and did things by themselves.

Then, one night at dinner, a big commotion broke out that shook me out of my funk.

A group of boys from drama club were passing around leaflets in the dining hall. They were chanting, "Bring back Dale," and they wore black T-shirts they'd gotten silk screened with that slogan. One of them stopped by our table and passed us a flyer.

Russell read it aloud. "No justice, no peace. Dean McGovern wrongfully removed Dale Knox-Levy from the drama club's fall production of *Bye, Bye Birdie*. The drama club asserts its authority to assign students to roles based on a fair and democratic process. Join us in standing up for Dale and all students' rights at Middleton. Walk out of class at fourth period on Friday, October 20th and assemble on the steps of the administrative hall for a peaceful protest."

The three of us glanced at each other, and grins crept up our faces.

"I'm in," I said. "Either of you talked to Dale?"

Jonathan looked at me like I was an airhead. "He went home. He got two weeks suspension, remember?"

Russell thwapped the flyer with his fingers. "I bet he's coming back for this."

I felt a little bad about not keeping up with Dale. He'd pulled one hell of a stunt, but we were friends. We were supposed to look out for each other.

I skipped over to one of the students wearing a black T-shirt and asked how I could get one. He said they were selling them for fifteen dollars, and I handed him two twenties and a ten for T-shirts for the three of us. I came back to our dining table and tossed the shirts to Jonathan and Russell.

"You boys ready for a strike tomorrow?"

FOURTH PERIOD THE next day, nearly every senior skipped class and converged on the administrative building, along with groups of juniors and lower division students. I marched along with Jonathan and Russell, and we were all hopped up, hollering for justice. One of the boys from the drama club, Michael Townes, brought a bullhorn and climbed up on the statue of Middleton Academy's founder Ezra Farthington.

He riled us up, telling us Dale had been the club's unanimous choice for the lead role in the play, earning the faculty directors' votes as well, and he'd already put in three weeks of rehearsal. Then he'd been suspended for breaking curfew, but he was only supposed to be banned from classes and school activities for two weeks.

Michael said the school had overstepped its authority in removing Dale from a school program he had a right to participate in, and they'd denied Dale his due process. He led a chant of, "Bring back Dale." Some students had made a banner, others held up signs, and we all turned to the administrative building shouting for them to make things right.

Dean McGovern finally came out of the front door with his assistant dean and a security officer. We gave him a chorus of boos, and he had to raise his voice real loud to be heard. He told us the school was taking Dale's matter into consideration. Meanwhile, classes were in session and we were all expected to return or we'd be marked absent for the day. There must've been two hundred of us so he got drowned out by our response. "No Dale, no class." I was so charged up, I squeezed my way through the crowd to climb up that statue with Michael. I had to speak my mind.

It was a moment I'll never forget. Students clapped and hollered my name, encouraging me to speak. Well, I took that bullhorn from Michael, and that's what I did.

"Dean McGovern, we're tired of hearing about you taking matters into consideration. What about Dale's door being spray-painted with the word faggot? It's been a month, and what did you do about that? The boy's being harassed for being gay, and what do you do? You punish him and not the ones harassing him? We're students, and we've got a right to dignity and safety. I'll say it right here and now. I'm a student, I'm Dale's friend, and I'm on strike until he returns to the school play and Middleton takes up a policy to prohibit discrimination against gay students."

Students cheered and took up chanting, "Strike." I raised my fist in the air and stared challengingly at Dean McGovern. He was pretty well nonplussed and looked like he was ready to give up any hope of breaking up our demonstration. Then a new commotion broke out. Someone shouted, "Dale's back," and heads turned to the other end of the quad.

I had a good view from that raised statue so when I looked in that direction, I spotted Dale dressed up in a jacket and tie. He was accompanied by two men in business suits, one of whom must've been his father. The other fellow was carrying a briefcase, so he probably was a lawyer.

Things got even louder with people chanting Dale's name and screeching triumphantly. I learned that day life can be one big paradox. That school had plenty of lugheads who looked down their noses at boys like Dale and me, and it sure wasn't a friendly place to be gay. But the situation with Dale roused up something everybody could relate to whether you want to call it distrust of authority or a sense of personal injustice. And we all wanted the best of the best representing Middleton at the school play.

Anyhow, that day, a sea of students filled the quad to demand that a five foot five, theater-loving gay boy have a right to sing and dance on stage and, furthermore, that gay students get treated equally. It was our own Stonewall Riot.

MOST EVERYONE STUCK around the quad while Dale, his father, and their lawyer went into the administrative hall to meet with the school bigwigs. Friday classes were over for all intents and purposes, and some of the teachers came out to watch in quiet solidarity. I didn't see Wes. I figured things hit too close to home for him, though I was a little disappointed. I sat on the lawn with Jonathan and Russell to wait things out.

A little over an hour later, Dale emerged from the big columned doors of the hall. Everybody quieted in anticipation while he stood at the top of the stairs with an inscrutable expression. He looked down at his shoes, and then, with a jazzy flourish, he broke into "Put on a Happy Face" from that damn musical. That boy loved a dramatic moment. The quad roared, and we all ran over to swarm on him. Michael and I lifted Dale on our shoulders and paraded him around like the king of Mardi Gras.

Dale got his part back in the school play, and the school expunged the academic suspension from his record. It all got negotiated when Dale's lawyer threatened to sue the school for negligence, educational malpractice, emotional distress, and retaliation after Dale's complaint about harassment. I'd like to think our demonstration had some influence, but knowing that school's administration, it was probably all about the potential lawsuit. No matter. We all celebrated that night like the home team had won the Rose Bowl.

Later, when the proctors told us we had to move along from the common room to our bedrooms, I caught up to Dale and drew him aside to talk.

"How's it feel being a celebrity?"

Dale grinned. "Not bad. But I missed hanging out with you, Russell, and Jonathan."

"You catch it from your daddy?"

"Yep. He took away my credit card and cut my allowance in half."

"Well, I think you'll survive."

I noticed for the first time he'd taken out his earring. Dale said his father made him. I told him about removing mine as soon as I'd come back to my room that infamous Saturday. We exchanged woeful grins.

"How 'bout this?" Dale said. "We get them re-pierced right before graduation. They can't take our diplomas away for doing it."

"Boy, you haven't found a line in the sand you didn't want to cross, have you?" I scratched my chin. "This might be a conversation for another time, but I'd sure like to hear what happened to you that Saturday night."

"You should've come with me. You could've seen for yourself."

"That right?"

We took the stairs and at the second floor landing where I'd be heading to my room on one side and he'd be going to the other, Dale stopped and got a clever look on his face.

"Come to my room, and I'll tell you the whole story."

I studied him. He looked like he had mischief on his mind. Then he opened one side of his jacket a little and gave me a peek of a shoulder bottle of whiskey in his inside pocket.

I drew up close and spoke real low. "What about your roommate?"

"I got a new room. A single. My dad's lawyer worked it into the deal since Greg and I weren't getting along."

That boy lived a charmed life, and that's no lie. I had no reason to turn down the invitation. In fact, it gave me an idea. Jonathan and Russell could have some alone time in our room. I got Dale's new room number and told him I'd be over after I gave Jonathan and Russell the good news.

OVER AT DALE's room, I kicked off my tennis shoes and sat down with him on his bed. He twisted off the cap of his whiskey bottle, and we alternated taking slugs. I can't say I'd developed a taste for whiskey, but I did like how it got me feeling warm and loose.

"All right Chipmunk. You gonna spill? Because it won't take too many draws on that bottle 'fore I either pass out or puke."

"It was a real good night. But you should've come with me." He gave me a scowl and tipped back another gulp. "I met a boy, Ethan, at the tea dance. He was cute. A redhead. He lives right over in the South End, working as a waiter." An adorable beam came over his face. "He asked me to come home with him, but I told him I was meeting some people so we just went to the bathroom to fool around a little."

"Now that there is plain good manners," I told him. "A fellow gives you an invitation, the right thing to do is to be gracious in turning him down."

Dale giggled. "Then I ran into Joe and Arnie at the bar. They were going to a club in Cambridge and told me to come with."

I quirked an eyebrow. "I thought their names were Peter and Victor?"

"Who?"

"Your friends from Northeastern you said you were meeting."

"Oh. I forgot all about them. They might've showed up later. Joe and Arnie are Harvard boys."

"I see. So, you were trading up. What year?"

Dale screwed up his brow. "You know, I don't remember. PhD of something or the other."

"Graduate students?"

Dale shrugged. "Something like that. Anyway, we went to this rippah dance club in Cambridge. The place was so packed, I lost track of Joe and Arnie. But I met Sam." He peeked at me. "Arizona, he was *fine*. Half Persian and half Caucasian. He had beautiful amber eyes I just wanted to swim in."

"Now what school was *he* from?"

"I didn't ask. I think he graduated a while ago. He said he worked in real estate. He bought me some drinks, and we danced for a while. Then he showed me his car. A black beamer. And Arizona, we did cocaine. Right off his dashboard."

I took the whiskey bottle from him and threw back a guzzle. "I got a feeling I'm gonna need a few more of these. So, how far along are we that night? Nine o'clock?"

Dale threw back his head and laughed. "I don't know. But when I went back into the club, I felt like I could dance all night. I was flirting with some kid who looked like Simon LeBon from Duran Duran. I think we made out on the dance floor. Then they announced last call, and I tagged along with some guys who were going to a house party in Somerville."

He took a drink from the whiskey bottle. "Now, this I remember. They were from Tufts. The party was at one of those old, rundown rowhouses, and it was mixed, gay and straight." He snickered. "It was pretty rowdy. Everyone was trashed or stoned. I made out with this boy Dennis then another guy Henry came along, and all three of us started fooling around.

We ended up in someone's bedroom, and I don't know what happened after that."

I cocked a glance at him. "I think I need to check into the Betty Ford clinic just hearing that story. And get a shot of penicillin."

He jabbed me with his elbow. "Be nice. That's why you should've come along with me. You would've helped me stay out of trouble."

"Dale, the secret service and a belly chain couldn't stop you from getting into trouble." I grinned at him. "You just let me know if you miss your next period. I know a Louisiana remedy for that."

Dale elbowed me again. "You think I'm a slut?"

"I didn't say that."

"I just like feeling desirable. Like someone wants me. Even if it only lasts for ten or fifteen minutes. You ever feel that way?"

"I do." I tossed back some more whiskey. We were nearly done with that shoulder bottle.

"Then come out with me sometime," he pleaded. "I know you'd meet somebody. You're real attractive. And you've got that cute Suth-an accent everybody loves."

I thought on it for a couple of seconds, and then I blurted it out. "I'm seeing someone."

I'd stepped in it for sure. There was no way Dale was letting me out of the room without elaborating on that confession. I could blame the whiskey, but I'd been dying to tell somebody about my relationship with Wesley Turner. So, I told Dale. Just about everything. It felt good, and I knew he wouldn't judge me. Though I hadn't been prepared for him to stand up, jump on the bed, and holler like a lunatic.

"I knew it. You lying bastard. You're fucking Mr. Turner."

I grabbed his legs and wrestled him down on the bed. "Dale Knox-Levy, I'm not being funny. You can't tell nobody. Not Russell or Jonathan or anybody else. You swear it to me."

"Okay, I swear."

I eyed him carefully. "Raise your right hand."

He did as he was told, and I curled my pinky finger around his.

"This is an oath what for you take it to the grave."

Dale joggled his head.

I released him and sat up on the bed. I loved Dale dearly, but I was worried sick I'd made a terrible mistake.

19

I DIDN'T DARE tell Wes I'd broken my promise to him, and after a few days, my guilt kinda faded away. Wes and I kept meeting up at his office after classes. Nobody seemed to be the wiser, and with all my homework, college applications, the equestrian club, and my friends, I didn't even think about it much.

Thanksgiving break was coming up, and the Wednesday prior, Wes surprised me. He said there was a creative writing conference that weekend at Amherst College, and he'd talked to the chair of the English department and gotten the okay to take a student along with him. There were two days of workshops with a special track for select high school students, and the school would pay for two hotel rooms for the two of us.

I was mighty excited about that. I just needed to call my daddy to change my plane ticket from Saturday to Monday and tell Mr. Ruskin about the conference so he knew I'd be leaving school the Friday before Thanksgiving. Then I started packing up my big suitcase. Wes said he'd drive me to Logan airport for my Monday morning flight, so I needed a nine days worth of clothes.

Thursday night, while I was getting my gear together, I explained things to Jonathan, Russell, and Dale.

"Arizona, that's amazing," Jonathan said. "I read about that

Amherst College conference. They only admit twenty high school students across the country. You'll be going to workshops with college students and famous authors. They've got James Michener and John Irving as keynote speakers."

"And he's going with Mr. Turner," Dale added.

I gave Dale a quick peek. He wouldn't, would he? Fortunately, it didn't seem like Jonathan or Russell were reading into things.

"Way to pad your college applications and make the rest of us look like bums," Russell said. "I'll be spending Thanksgiving break working on my early decision application to Cornell."

I had my own early decision application to do. Just for Columbia. I hadn't told my daddy about that yet.

Dale came over and patted my back. "Well, congratulations Arizona. You're going to be the next William Faulkner."

"Now he's from Mississippi, but I don't hold it against him. Thanks. What're you doing for Thanksgiving?"

He rolled his eyes. "I'll be imprisoned at my grandparents' house on St. Simons Island."

That didn't sound so bad to me. He'd shown me pictures. It was on one of them barrier islands on the Georgia coast, and his grandparents had a big house on the beach.

"At least you might get a tan."

"I might die from boredom. Louis is spending the holiday with his girlfriend's family. I won't have anyone to go with to Savannah, which is the nearest semblance of civilization down there."

"Might do you some good to get some R & R, don't you think? You've got the school play coming up."

We all quieted. Everyone had noticed Dale had been hitting the whiskey bottle pretty frequently, and the Saturday prior, he'd disappeared again, probably run off to Boston for an all-nighter.

I let that be, and meanwhile it hit me I hadn't asked Jonathan what he was doing.

"I'm staying here. Y'know, the flight to L.A. is kind of expensive."

I glanced at Russell. He stepped over and rested a hand on

Jonathan's shoulder. "I asked my dad if Jonathan could stay with us. But I'm still on punishment until January 1st."

"Nobody should be alone for Thanksgiving. If Russell doesn't mind, Jonathan, I say you come down to Louisiana with me."

Russell turned to Jonathan. "I don't mind. I'd rather you weren't alone."

"I don't want to be a burden, Arizona. You've got your family and friends back home. I'll be fine. I've got a lot of schoolwork to do anyway."

"It ain't a burden. We only have to get you on my flight Monday morning. I'd much rather have you along, darling. Dale's not the only one with a complicated family situation." A great thought occurred to me. "We can whoop it up in New Orleans, boy."

That got Jonathan glancing at me.

"I want to go to New Orleans," Dale said with a pout.

"Chipmunk, you ain't ready for New Orleans. Them Creoles invented trouble. A Yankee boy like you would get eaten up for supper. Don't get me wrong, you'll have some fun, but I'm not spending my Thanksgiving break rounding up divers to fish you out of the Mississippi River."

We all laughed. I looked at Jonathan. "So what do you say?"

"All right."

I hollered and gave him a big hug.

ON FRIDAY AFTERNOON, we loaded my luggage into Wes's VW GTI, and we zipped off to Amherst, which was across state, about a two-hour drive. The campus was gorgeous. Amherst College wasn't part of the Ivy League, but it had that look, and it was real prestigious. Kind of a bigger version of Middleton with all its nineteenth century brick buildings, treed lawns, and paved walkways through campus.

We checked into a Holiday Inn by the thruway and got two

rooms with one of them adjoining doors. That was so Wes could monitor me as his student, but while the fella at the reception desk was getting the keys, Wes and I exchanged a little grin, knowing we'd both be sleeping in one room or the other.

Once we went up to our rooms, Wes couldn't wait until after dinner. He knocked on that adjoining door, and when I opened it, he was standing with his shirt unbuttoned and a flirtatious grin. I took up the invitation, and we were out of our clothes in no time flat, wrestling around on his bed. The sly devil had picked up lubricant and condoms for the trip so he could have me the way we'd never been bold enough to try in his office. He was real gentle and loving, holding me and kissing my neck and ear while he entered me. I told him he did just fine for his first time.

After, Wes was cuddlier than ever. I think losing his virginity blew his mind. He held me like he never wanted to let me go. While he was nuzzling against my neck, he told me, "How about we stay in bed all weekend?"

I chuckled. "Now, I'm not saying that's the worst idea in the world, but don't you think we ought to make an appearance or two at the conference? We're here on the school's dollar, after all."

Truth was, I was looking forward to seeing famous authors and meeting students from across the country, not to mention learning a thing or two about becoming a better writer.

"These conferences are overrated." Wes laid his thigh over mine and squeezed me tighter. "This is all I want this weekend. We can go to the programs during the day, but after five o'clock, you're all mine."

The conference started the next morning, and I was dizzy when we walked into the lobby of the academic hall where all the lectures and workshops were happening. We got our name tags and programs at a crowded registration table. There was a keynote speaker for everyone in a big lecture hall, and then I went off to sessions for the high school students.

I was right inspired being around students who loved writing as much as me. Like Jonathan had said, there were just twenty of us. In our first session, we went around the room with introductions. The other students were real friendly and came from other private schools in New England and farther places like California, Oregon, Illinois, and North Carolina, to name a few. The instructors were published authors. They talked about the craft of writing and gave us exercises to do. We'd write for a while, and then we'd read our work aloud and give each other feedback. I was nervous at first because everyone seemed so talented. But people said they liked what I wrote, and we were all there to encourage each other.

We ate lunch together, and I hit it off with a boy from Philadelphia named Ray and another fellow from San Diego named Anthony. Ray was Black, and he was also applying to Columbia. Anthony was Filipino. It was his first time traveling to the East Coast. I'd never had a Black or a Filipino friend, and neither one of them had ever met someone from Louisiana. But it was real easy talking to both of them. We'd read a lot of the same books, and Anthony was cute and funny while Ray had a real lyrical style of prose that I admired. We sat together at the afternoon sessions. At the end of the day, everyone was going to dinner together, and then there was a youth open mic where people were reading their poetry and essays.

I felt bad telling Ray and Anthony I couldn't go. Wes had said to meet him in the lobby at five-thirty, and he was taking me to dinner. It didn't feel right saying that, so I made up a story about having some friends in town. To tell the truth, I would've preferred spending time with the students in my cohort, but I didn't want to hurt Wes's feelings. I wouldn't have had the opportunity to go to the conference if it hadn't been for him.

Wes took me out to an Irish pub, and afterward, he was raring to go in the bedroom. He treated me like a prince, and I didn't feel like I had a right to complain. But I have to admit, I couldn't help thinking about the fun I could be having with the other students at the conference.

We had another full day of sessions on Sunday, and then Wes

just wanted to order in room service and cuddle up in bed. After we made love, we snuggled up together and watched TV.

"Did you have a good time?" Wes asked me.

"Mm-hmm."

He turned to me with his head resting on his pillow. "I'm going to miss you this week. Are you going to miss me?"

He devoured me with his deep blue eyes. It feels funny to say, but things had started out with me chasing after him, and now it felt like he was chasing me. I can't explain, but our relationship was shifting. Wes was one heck of an attractive man, and I still admired how smart he was and felt right honored he had taken such an interest in me. But I was starting to feel pinned down, and at the same time, I felt guilty for thinking that way.

I brushed the tips of his hair on his forehead. "I'm going to miss you, too."

"I love you, Arizona." He clasped my face. "I never thought I'd find someone to love. But you showed me it was possible."

"You're sweet." I couldn't bring myself to say I loved him back. "And I'm not going anywhere. I'll be back at school next Sunday."

"You know, Amherst has a top ten writing program. With your grades and SAT scores, you're a shoo-in for admissions. We could see each other on weekends. It's an easy drive."

I skirted his gaze.

"There's also Williams College right here in Massachusetts."

"Wes, I've got my mind set on Columbia. I want to live in New York City. Experience something different."

He closed his palm over my chest. "Just think about it, all right? We've got something really special. It doesn't have to end when you graduate."

I guess that's when I knew for sure things were headed south with our relationship. I didn't want to carry on with him after graduation. I was feeling like it might be best if we split up when I came back from break.

I couldn't spoil our weekend saying any of that aloud. I gave Wes a kiss and turned over on my side.

20

A FEW DAYS later, I was back at Whittington Manor with Jonathan. I had to wait out his initial shock at the size and grandeur of the estate, but once he stopped gaping and freezing up around the servants as though they might grab him and escort him out, the two of us had a blast.

Jonathan was scared of horses, so I just took him on walks through the grounds to show him the woods, the lake, the gazebo, and the cemetery. During the day, it was warm enough to hike around in jeans and polo shirts, and the woods were dry with leaves crinkling under our sneakers. We hopped in my Corvette one day to take a drive down River Road with all its wooded scenery, plantation mansions, and the endless bank of the big Mississippi River along the side. Later, I showed him how to play croquet on the south lawn.

At Thanksgiving dinner, he met my daddy and Virginia. Daddy was gracious and charming, and Virginia spared Jonathan her worst behavior. She asked him if he'd ever had turkey before, like he was a foreign exchange student, but besides that, she just chain-smoked her cigarettes and swilled her martinis while the rest of us talked about school.

I asked Mrs. Laroche to set up a cot in my room so Jonathan

and I could spend more time together during our short visit, and we ended up sharing my big bed anyway. After Thanksgiving dinner, we stayed up late. Jonathan read a poem he'd written about being brown-skinned at a white boy's school. It was real good. Then he told me about Chicano poets like Marcela Christine Lucero-Trujillo, who wrote about machismo and sexism, and LeRoy Quintana who wrote about white people's hostile attitudes toward Mexicans. I was right impressed. I'd never thought about those things exactly, but I agreed there were a lot of problems with how society treated femininity and people from different cultures.

"I didn't tell you, I've been hanging out with Gladys Lopez from Woodland Hall. She's a junior. From San Antonio, Texas. We met at the co-ed conference day earlier this semester, and we've been getting together to study on Thursdays at the coffeeshop in town. She's mad cool. She's a feminist, and I think she's warming up to tell me she's a lesbian."

"Sounds like my kind of people."

Jonathan giggled.

"What's funny?"

"Arizona, I don't think *your* kind of people would've liked Mexicans. They must've owned a couple hundred African slaves to work this size of sugar plantation."

I stiffened up. "Whittington Manor has only been in my daddy's family since the late 1800s. My great grandfather bought it for a song. It'd been out of use for years."

Jonathan still had a silly smile on his face. "I'm sorry. I didn't mean to suggest your family were slave owners. But they probably were, weren't they?"

I'd never asked my daddy those particulars, though I'd thought about them from time to time. I also remembered something I heard him talking about with his friends.

"Well, here's something you might not have known about French Creoles. Long before the Civil War, the Louisiana Purchase, and the American Revolution, the French established some of the most liberal laws in the continent with regard to Blacks. We had more freed Black people than any state in the South."

Jonathan kept looking at me funny. "I'm sure they appreciated that. While Louisiana joined in to secede from the union so they could keep their slave labor."

I was feeling real stupid and getting red in the face. "All right. I get your point."

Jonathan cracked up.

"It ain't my fault. And listen here, up until a year ago, I thought my family was Irish."

"It's okay, Arizona. I'm not saying you're a racist." He grinned. "But I'm pretty sure your ancestors were."

I elbowed him.

He laughed. "Now you're going to take it out on a Mexican?"

"Y'know, you can be a real pain in the ass."

He curled up close and took my hand, looking like he was trying to make amends. "I'm sorry, Master Arizona. I won't do it again. Just please don't whip me."

I stared flames at him. "Cool it. You got me having an identity crisis."

"'Not everything that can be faced can be changed. But nothing can be changed until it is faced.' That's James Baldwin."

"Hmm. That's wisdom all right." Things percolated in my brain. "I'm sorry if my daddy's home makes you uncomfortable. I should've asked you about it before."

He cuddled up to me again. "Arizona, I had a pretty good idea what to expect. And the legacy of American racism isn't exactly new to me. I live it every day at Middleton."

I laid my arm around his shoulder. "But it shouldn't be that way. And I'm still learning. Probably make mistakes sometimes."

"You might. But guess what? You also could be stuck with me a little longer. I decided to apply to Columbia."

I think I hurt him a little jolting with excitement. "Get out. We gonna be college roomies too?"

"I have to get in first. But I think I want to live in New York

City. Gladys told me about the Nuyorican Poet's Café where a lot of Latin writers got their start."

"You shouldn't have any problem getting in." He'd scored ten points higher than me on his SATs. I looked at him with a scheming smile. "We gonna have some fun at Columbia. They got a big gay student organization. First one in the country. I done my research." A thought occurred to me. "Did you tell Russell?"

"No." Jonathan shifted around. "It's hard talking to him about that kind of thing. He'll find some way to criticize me. Call me a flake for changing my mind or say I'm planning on cheating on him."

"Hmm. He's got one of them type-A personalities. But that don't make no sense. Why's he thinking you're the one who's going to cheat? He's going to have equal opportunity at Cornell."

"Because that's the way he thinks. Honestly, it's stupid. It's not like he's got to worry about guys lining up to be my boyfriend."

I could sense where that line of conversation was going. Jonathan had one big insecurity complex. Funny, it made me think of Fiona Linklater. I steered things in another direction, and we kept talking into the early morning about all the things we wanted to do in New York City.

THE NEXT DAY, we had our big trip to New Orleans, and we did it in style, having Buck chauffeur us around to the Garden District, Bourbon Street, and City Park. We even took one of them river cruises on a paddleboat. Before we headed home, I asked Buck to take us over to that gay bar Preston and I had gone to over the summer. We ordered beers and sat out on the porch. Two older gentlemen asked if they could join us, and one of them had an eye on Jonathan, which might've been the highlight of his day. It was just some innocent flirting, but Jonathan made me swear not to tell Russell about it.

"I told you Creoles invented trouble, and I'll have you know we also invented discretion." I gave Jonathan a wink.

We left our schoolwork and college applications for Saturday, which might not have been the best of ideas. We both had a lot of assignments to get a move on, and around midnight, my brain was fried from taking notes on two chapters from chemistry and typing up my essay for Columbia. I told Jonathan I was calling it a night and we could get some work done on our flight back to Middleton on Sunday.

We changed into our pajamas and each used my bathroom to brush our teeth, and then we climbed into bed and had our usual chat about this or that. I was telling him about the dormitory options at Columbia, and then I said I had a short story due for Mr. Turner's class. That led into a question I wasn't ready for.

"I never asked you about the conference at Amherst College. How was it?"

I hesitated. It felt like that had happened ages ago even though it had only been a week. And I'd been enjoying not having to think about my relationship with Wes, which made me squirmy. But it didn't feel right hiding things from Jonathan. Before I could talk myself out of it, I told him everything.

I didn't expect that to turn into a disaster. Jonathan sat up on the bed and stared at me like I'd given him a murder confession.

"Arizona, you're gonna get the man fired."

"How you figure that? The only people who know are Wes and me and now you." I didn't mention Dale. The temperature in the room was hot enough already.

"People find out about these things. Someone could see you leaving his office. Or if the two of you have a fight or split up, it could just come out."

"I told you we been careful."

"You shouldn't have to be careful. You shouldn't have slept with him in the first place." He glanced at me twice. "How long has this been going on? Were you lying when you said he asked you to get out of his car that day?"

"No, I wasn't lying."

"So, he told you to leave him alone, and you pursued him?" He shook his head. "I can't believe you've been doing this on the sly all this time. It's crazy."

A rash of defenses rose up in me. "I guess I pegged you wrong. I thought you had an open mind. I'm seventeen years old, and he's only twenty-four. It's not a crime. You know I been with older men before, so what's the big deal?"

"I have an open mind. It's not about him being twenty-four years old. And as a matter of fact, it is a crime, for him. Teachers aren't supposed to have sex with students."

I didn't know what to say to that. I sure wasn't in the mood to cop to being in the wrong when I'd told him about the affair to get some moral support, not the third degree.

"I'm sorry, Arizona. You asked me what I thought, and I think it's selfish. You got this man to fall in love with you, and now you're saying you don't even know if you want to be with him? You're going to break his heart, ruin his career, possibly get him in legal trouble. And anybody who finds out is obligated to report it."

Now he'd really gotten my adrenalin pumping. "We're two consenting adults, so don't go making it out like I lured him into anything he wasn't driving for already. It's just...I wasn't counting on him getting ideas about being in love and wanting something long-term."

"You lied to get into his car, and then you wrote him that love letter for your paper." He eyed me like I was a criminal again. "You know what wigs me out the most? You could have anyone you want. Why go after a man whose career depends on being trust-worthy around students? Did you do it so you could go to the conference at Amherst?"

I sucked my teeth. "No, I didn't do it to go to the conference. I didn't know about the conference till he told me the week before." I was furious. "You know what? I think I understand now why you're getting bent out of shape. You've always been jealous. You had a crush on Mr. Turner since the first day of the semester, and now you're mad I had him instead of you."

"Straight up, Arizona? You're going to take things there?"

I caught myself. It was a mean thing to say. He just got me so upset criticizing my character.

"All right. I'm sorry. Maybe that came out wrong."

Jonathan kept glaring at me. "I'm just your poor, ugly Mexican friend who you like being around because it makes you look better. Who you like showing off so people think you're worldly and sophisticated."

"Now, hold on. Ain't none of that is true, and you know it." I heaved a breath. "I said something that was out of line, and I'm apologizing. You telling me you think our friendship always been fake?"

Jonathan said nothing.

"Listen, Jonathan. You hurt my feelings real bad, saying I led Wes on to get into that conference. That's why I said something out of spite. But if you truly, really, genuinely believe I'm the kind of person who would lead *you* on, pretending to be your friend all last year and this one, I guess I'm the one who misjudged our friendship."

Neither one of us spoke up again for a while.

"How'd we go from talking about being college roommates to fighting like mortal enemies?" Jonathan said.

"I don't know. Feels like you started it."

"Arizona, if you really feel in your heart there's nothing wrong with what you're doing with Mr. Turner, I'm not going to say you're right, but I can agree to disagree."

"That's fine with me, too. And I'm sorting things out with him as soon as I get back to school."

"And I'm *not* jealous you're sleeping with him."

"Fair enough."

We were quiet for a while, and I thought we might be done with the subject. Then Jonathan laid into me again.

"It must be nice for you and Dale to be able to do whatever you want."

I cocked a glance at him. "What do you mean?"

"Can you picture what would happen to me if *I* broke curfew again? It's like Gladys says. We can't afford not to be perfect. People are constantly looking for a reason to confirm we don't belong at a private school. And if I slept with a teacher?" He threw back a bitter laugh. "You can bet it would be all my fault, and they wouldn't blame the teacher."

I took a deep breath before saying anything because he was getting my blood boiling again. "I got a good idea how it feels to be under scrutiny, and I think Dale does too. Jonathan, we all gay, and we got plenty of people who'd like us out of that school. Why you think I keep pushing for that Pink Triangle club?" Jonathan hadn't once come with me to advocate to Dean McGovern about it.

"It's not just about being gay. That's something you can turn on or turn off when you want to."

I scowled at him. "Oh I can turn it on or turn it off. Turn it on if I want to risk getting beat up like I did last year. Turn it off if I wanna suffer in silence and feel so lonely I might as well kill myself. I choose to be open, for myself and for other gay people." *Would you have preferred I turned it off and not stood up for you last year?* I didn't say it, but I was thinking it.

"I'm not saying it's easy for anyone being gay. But you've also got a lot of entitlements to fall back on that brown-skinned people don't have."

I was trying to be understanding. I really was. But I was feeling indignant about him saying these things when I'd invited him to my home for the holiday. Paid for his business class flight and every one of outings.

"I asked you to come home with me for Thanksgiving because you're my best friend. But I guess you shouldn't have come if my lifestyle offends you so much."

"That's not what I mean. Arizona, we've been through a lot

together, and I'm grateful for all you've done for me. I'm telling you this because you *are* my best friend. I just feel so angry, all the time. It's not your fault, but I wish you could understand sometimes. I always have to be the person who doesn't disappoint other people. My parents. My teachers. The Mexican community. My friends. Even you."

"That sounds like weight you're putting on your own shoulders. And I always supported you. Hasn't always felt like that went both ways, but you tell me one time I put pressure on you to be a certain way."

"This conversation kinda feels like an example of that."

"How? I listened to you speak your mind. I'm not arguing with you."

"Maybe we should just drop it."

"No. If you've got something to say, I think I deserve to hear it."

He sighed. "Every time I say it's hard for me being in a relationship with Russell, you turn things around like it's just my problem to figure out. And it's not easy for me being around white, good-looking guys from wealthy families all the time. It's this constant reminder I don't fit in."

"Jonathan, we, *I* done everything to include you. Now I don't what it's like to be in your shoes, but as for you saying you're less attractive than anyone else, I think that's on you. And if you want to know how I feel about you and Russell, I think you should break up with him if he makes you feel so lousy. I didn't want to say that before because you're both my friends."

He didn't have anything else to say about that, and neither did I. We said goodnight and turned on our sides away from each other.

THE LAST WEEKS of the fall semester always seemed to go real fast. I had lots of studying to do for final exams and final papers, and the Middleton Academy-Woodland Hall production of *Bye, Bye Birdie* was a big to-do with lots of people talking about Dale's scene-stealing performance. Meanwhile, I finished my application for Columbia. I wouldn't get an early decision until early March, and I decided I'd tell my daddy about it and deal with the consequences then if I got the big acceptance packet.

I also had consequences to deal with concerning Mr. Wesley Turner. He was after me about applying to Amherst College so we'd be close, and I couldn't bring myself to tell him how I was feeling. Truth was, that conversation with Jonathan had gotten me all turned around and confused. I didn't want to get Mr. Turner in trouble or break his heart. I knew I'd come on to him strong without thinking things through, and I sure didn't want anybody thinking I'd gotten him to like me just so I could go to that writing conference. The rest of the semester, I tried showing him who I really was, thinking that might help to break things off gently. But that didn't work out so well.

I kept finding things about him I wasn't crazy about. He was needy. I'd say he was also a little bit pretentious, always dropping into conversation how well-read he was and how dumb his students were. He was real hung up about being gay, and I couldn't talk to him about a lot of things. Whenever I wanted to say something about what was going on with AIDS and that I wanted to be part of that ACT-UP group, Wes always said I was cute, like I was a five-year-old. He wanted us to be together after I graduated, but really, he wanted to turn me into someone he could have a hidden relationship with, someone who'd be happy just spending time with him. I don't think he was interested in who I really was, and nothing could get me angrier than someone arguing against being gay and proud. That topic came to a head one afternoon in his office during finals week. Wes had given me a novel manuscript he was working on, and he wanted to hear my opinion.

It was a beautifully written story, and far be it from me, a high school student, to criticize the work of a man with a master's degree. The main character, Johnnie, was a fellow in his twenties who was coming back to his hometown for the funeral of the father of his best friend from school. There were flashbacks from the two boys' childhood, and Wes spent a lot of time depicting their close relationship. Then it got into how Johnnie was in love with his best friend's sister, Alexandra, and to me, it just felt like that wasn't the direction Wes had in mind.

I should've kept my mouth shut. I was stepping into quicksand criticizing Wes's work. He was definitely the sensitive artist type. But words slipped out, and things got tense.

"I just think what you have here is a love story between Johnnie and Thomas. I mean, you have that scene where Johnnie finally asks Alexandra out for a drink, and he's thinking about Thomas the whole time and even talking about how much he and his sister look alike."

"I know you'd like it to be a gay love story. But it's more complex than that. Johnnie's not gay, and Thomas certainly isn't. They have an intense emotional bond from the events they experienced when they were younger."

"Well, you know your own story. I'm just saying how I feel since you asked. And what's wrong with liking a gay love story?"

"There's nothing wrong with it. It's just a bit pedestrian. There's more to life than just being gay, you know?"

That ticked me off. "How many gay love stories you read? There's not many of them. Doesn't something have to be common in order to be considered pedestrian?"

"I'm not looking to be the next Gordon Merrick or Patricia Nell Warren. A good story should be about people and say something about human nature in a universal sense."

"You think a gay character can't get across a sense of humanity?"

"No, but there's a lot more to being human than one's sexual preference."

"Hmm. So, you think writers ought to make their characters asexual? Seems to me love figures into just about every classic story. A man pining over a woman. A woman pining over a man. You're always going on about that book *Gravity's Rainbow* by Thomas Pynchon. There's plenty of sex and love in that novel. Would you call that book pedestrian?"

Wes scowled. "*Gravity's Rainbow* was a groundbreaking novel. I don't think you're helping your argument with that example."

"Would it have been groundbreaking if the main character was having sex with men instead of women? I mean, in your personal view."

"If it was about that, it wouldn't have been Pynchon's story to tell."

"I see. So, a writer should write what he knows."

Wes looked at me, hesitating to speak. "Why are you getting so hostile? If you don't like what I wrote, maybe it's just not for you."

"Wes, I said I liked it. You know I think you're real talented. And I'm getting it now. You wouldn't be true to yourself writing an openly gay story. You don't know anything about it."

I hadn't meant it to come out sharp, or I don't know, maybe I did. It got Wes flustered again.

"I don't need to be pigeonholed as a person *or* as an author."

"What should I think of you then? You don't want to be pigeonholed as gay? Did we just happen to start screwing because you liked me as a person and not a man? You suppose we'd be screwing if I had tits and a vagina?"

"Arizona, you're getting really irritating. I'm tired of questions you already have answers for."

I'd been sitting on his desk, facing him at his chair, while he was running his hands up and down my legs. That sounded like a cue, so I hopped down and told him I had to get a move on to meet my study group for chemistry in the library. Wes took my arm and stopped me.

"Hey, I love you. You understand that, don't you? Just because I don't need to put a label on myself doesn't mean that my feelings for you are any less than if I walked around wearing a gay pride button."

The funny thing was, what I was getting out of our conversation was I really didn't like Wes as a person. I was wishing I hadn't gone after him in the first place, and I ended up saying something rude.

"I guess that's why you didn't have nothing to say when we were all rallying around Dale Knox-Levy."

Wes screwed up his face. "Is that what this is about? I'm sorry I didn't feel a sense of solidarity with a young man who feels entitled to run off to college parties every weekend and sleep with everyone he meets."

I yanked my arm away. "Dale's my friend. He's not some slut. What's he supposed to do? People are so afraid to come out, he's not finding anyone to date at school."

"You're going to have a hard time getting my sympathy on this one. Dale gets away with murder, and his father is so entitled, he clears the way for Dale to behave however he pleases."

"And why do you think his father does that? It's because he's ashamed of Dale. He can't face who his own son is."

"Arizona, not every problem stems from homophobia. He's not the only boy who has a strained relationship with his family. And there's plenty of boys with family issues who don't go home with different men every weekend."

"And how many boys are meeting up with girls from Woodland Hall on the weekends? Bragging about all the sex they having? Y'know, you got a lot of issues, and a big one is double standards."

He stood in front of me, trying to cool things down with a grin. "Hey, let's just drop it. I'm sorry I insulted your friend. I don't even understand why we're arguing." He put his hands on my waist and drew me into a hug. "Don't get so worked up about these things. I love you, even when we disagree."

I hugged him back a little. But I was good and done with him talking down to me. It was past time to call things quits. I was wishing I could come up with an easy way to do it.

TWO DAYS BEFORE winter break, I came back to the dorm after my French final and found Jonathan curled up in his bed. He'd been crying, and he told me he and Russell had split up again. Seemed they'd had a talk before the two week break and come to the conclusion they were better off as friends.

I comforted Jonathan, and he wasn't as torn up about it as he'd been earlier in the semester. He and Russell just had too many trust issues as a couple, and I was glad they still wanted to be friends. All four of us musketeers had had a heck of a tumultuous semester, and I was praying we'd have less drama in our final term.

Wes dropped hints he'd like it if I came back from break a few days early, and we could spend a night or two in a hotel room. I told him I didn't see that flying with my daddy, though the truth was, I could've made up a story to get my return ticket moved up. Wes gave me his home phone number and said I should give him a call on New Year's Day. I threw that scrap of notebook paper in the trash.

21

WINTER IN LOUISIANA was nothing like in New England. It got colder, but I'd only seen it snow once in my life, when I was ten years old. I remember they announced it on the radio. Schools were closed, and Mama Lou let Duke and me run out to the backyard to try to catch snowflakes on our tongues. We chased each other around the muddy yard, slipping in our yellow rubber boots, and then we locked arms, back-to-back, and spun around, thinking we could make it snow harder, enough to build a snowman if we did it fast enough. Two boys spinning around and gazing at the sky, laughing, not having one care in the world besides making it snow.

It was warm enough to wear my light fall jacket over my shirt and trousers. I had nothing in mind to do those two weeks but sleep in and take Bonnie out on the trails in the afternoon. I got to do that my first few days, but like everything in my life, my winter break didn't go as planned.

First thing was I got an invitation to a birthday party for Fiona Linklater. It was on December 23rd, 8:00 p.m. I couldn't very well turn her down seeing as she'd come to my birthday party. I picked out a shirt and tie, slacks and a blazer, got dressed and drove over to the jewelry store in town to pick up a birthday present. A nice saleslady suggested a charm bracelet, which she said any eighteen-year-old girl would like. I picked out a little angel bangle that she could wear on it for starters. I got it boxed and wrapped up in a bow, and then I headed to the Linklater's house in Metairie.

Cars were parked up and down the street. I was a little nervous, not knowing anyone besides Fiona and her brother, Duncan, who I wasn't looking forward to seeing after our last conversation. I was let in by a house staffer who also took my duster. I stepped very gradually down the hall toward the noisy room where everyone was gathered.

An elegantly dressed lady came over to greet me. Mrs. Linklater. I introduced myself and thanked her for the invitation. She pointed out where Fiona was sitting with her friends. As I crossed the room, my gaze landed on Duncan. His gaze landed on mine at the same time, and we both quickly glanced in the other direction. I forged along to say hello to Fiona and give her the present.

Fiona was dressed to the nines in a burgundy sweetheart evening gown with layered tulle skirting. I thought I'd never get her attention while she was chatting away with a group of girls. Then her glance strayed, and she spotted me. Fiona squealed and came over to grab my arm.

"Arizona Bondurant, you made it."

"How do you do, Fiona? Happy birthday." I showed her my wrapped gift.

"Aren't you the sweetest thing? And I do much better now that you're here." She got the attention of a waiter who took my present over to the gift table. Then she clasped my hand and led me over to her friends. "Girls, I want you to meet my boyfriend Arizona Bondurant. He goes to Middleton Academy. That's an elite boarding school up in Boston."

My face paled like a corpse. Eight high school girls in fancy dresses stared at me and smiled. Fiona introduced me around and whispered in my ear, "If anyone asks, we've been going steady since last May."

I took a dry gulp.

I hoped to blend in and stay on the periphery of conversation, but Fiona's friends had dozens of questions for me. I told them about school, said I was eyeing Columbia for college next year, and mentioned I wanted to be a writer. The girls all went to Our Lady of the Immaculate Conception, and they were staring at me like I was something else, a prep school boy with the Bondurant family name. Later, a band struck up a tune, and when they got into an upbeat number, people rushed onto the dance floor. Boys and girls bounced around and shimmied in that freestyle way. I found myself bopping along with Fiona and her friends.

They brought out Fiona's cake, and we all sang happy birthday. While Fiona was doing her rounds, I met some fellows from St. Bartholomew's Academy, which was the boys' Catholic school in town. It was nice being back with Louisiana folk who were a lot more friendly than people up North. You could walk up to anybody and strike up a conversation. I was having a good time talking to two boys Tommy and Carter and trying not to let on I wouldn't have minded if one of them wanted to get acquainted more privately.

The band eased into a slow song that was getting couples on the dance floor, and in a blink, Fiona found me and pulled me along to dance. My shock had passed, and I didn't really mind her lying about the two of us being together. I thought it was funny. But I gave her some grief anyway while I led her in a slow step with her hand on my shoulder.

"Anything else I should know about the two of us since I been out of town?"

"We've only kissed, and last summer at your birthday party, I let you touch my breasts over my bra."

I laughed. "Fiona Linklater, you're one strange girl. You could've given me fair warning about this ruse of yours."

"Oh, be quiet. I told you I'm poisonous to boys. All you have to do is act like you're my boyfriend for one night."

I scowled at her. She'd made up quite an elaborate lie, and I had a feeling she was fixing to draw me into it for more than one night.

"How's Preston?"

"As a matter of fact, the two of us split up. He wasn't keen on me going back up North for school."

"Why, that's terrible. I'm sorry, Arizona. I liked Preston a lot. Did he break your heart?"

"Preston's a good man. But I've moved past it."

"So, you're single. I guess I have a chance with you after all."

I looked at her squarely. "I don't know how many times I've gotta tell you, you're barking up the wrong tree." I glanced around the room. "You've got plenty of boys here to choose from. You telling me you can't find anyone to date?"

"There's plenty of them to date if a girl wants to get herself a bad reputation. Boys from New Orleans move too fast."

"Fiona, you understand a boy like me don't move at all when it comes to girls?"

"You're a gentleman, which is the perfect kind of boy to be my beau."

"I suppose I don't mind helping out. But it's just this one night, you hear?"

"Just make sure you give me a kiss on the lips before you leave. I'll make sure people are watching."

I chuckled. It was a strange night, but not a bad night, if you know what I mean. I had some fun, and before I left, I did give Fiona that kiss on the lips while her girlfriends were standing around staring at us. It wasn't such a big thing to pretend for her sake. She was my only friend in town, and she sure could make me laugh.

ON CHRISTMAS EVE, we had our traditions. Daddy and I went to midnight mass at St. Anthony's Cathedral in town, and afterward, Daddy had some friends come over to the house for Réveillon, which is a Creole celebration I'd only participated in for the first time last year. I didn't even know I was one hundred percent Creole until Gaston Bondurant confessed to me he was my daddy. Come to find out we Creoles have all kinds of strange traditions. For Réveillon, you stay up all night Christmas Eve eating, drinking, and dancing until you pass out somewhere around seven o'clock in the morning.

That year, it was a low-key affair by my daddy's standards. Three dozen people and a big buffet set up in the Fontainebleau ballroom with a jazz band alternating with a piano player. There was enough food to feed an army: seafood gumbo, roast duck, daube glacé, candied fruits and jelly roll cakes, among a thousand other things. Most people drank wine or eggnog with rum, and Daddy said it would be okay for me to drink beer.

The whole thing was still kind of surreal to me, all them grown-ups carrying on in the wee hours of the morning, but I'm not going to say I minded. I chatted here and there with businessmen I'd worked with over the summer. Virginia showed off in a marigold, stretch velvet wrap dress, and we stayed out of each other's way. Around four in the morning, we all went up to the second floor balcony to watch the bonfires on the levee along River Road. All up and down the bank of the Mississippi River, giant pyres of wood burned like the world had gone back to colonial times. That was so Papa Noel could find his way delivering presents to children.

On Christmas Day, everybody slept in till noon or later. When I came downstairs to the gentlemen's parlor, I saw they'd wheeled in a glazed ham, eggs benedict, grillades, fried potatoes, and sweet rolls. I swear if I'd have lived at Whittington Manor year round, I'd have weighed three hundred pounds.

Daddy and Virginia had beat me there, and we were all three groggy. We exchanged gifts. I'd bought my daddy a backgammon set from a boutique in Boston, and I had a pair of pearl earrings for Virginia. Daddy gone and bought me a dozen gifts or more: clothes and shoes and roller blades and new headphones for my stereo system and a new Nintendo video game system. After brunch, he told me to suit up to go riding with him.

I hadn't seen much of my daddy since the summer. It was nice to be in his company, just the two of us for a change. Once we got Bonnie and Duchess out on the trail, we walked the girls side by side. Like I said, we were all a little groggy, which is a nice way to say wore out and hungover.

"You have a good term at Middleton?"

"Yes, sir. How're things going with the company?"

"I'd say they're going just fine. Y'know, we took some of your ideas from the summer. We've got product development working on some sugar drinks. We're just testing them out for now, but I think they've got good potential."

He winked at me. Call me a lousy son, but I'd completely forgotten any conversation we'd had about my daddy's company. I had a good idea what he was easing into talking about.

"How're them college applications coming along?"

"Fine, Daddy."

"Well, tell me. What's your top choice?"

I drew in a deep breath through my nose. "Daddy, it hasn't changed. I want to go to Columbia. I'm applying to Harvard and Brown to keep my options open, but I already lived in New England. I want to see New York City. It's the biggest, most exciting city in the country."

"I always found it loud and filthy. It's not the safest place in the world, son."

I didn't want to have a fight with him on Christmas Day, but it felt like there was no way out of it. "Daddy, there's got to be tens of thousands of students going to college in New York every year. It's not like I'd be moving to Beirut."

"Pardon me for having some concern. You are my only son."

"I understand that, Daddy. But I got to live my life. I'll be eighteen this summer. I know how to take care of myself."

He was quiet for a spell while we walked the girls down the trail.

"You've got the family business to consider, too. I'm not going to be around forever. I'd like to know I'm leaving it in good hands."

I scowled. He was only forty-two years old. It seemed to me he had plenty of time to figure things out.

"Well, it's Christmas Day. We best change the subject. You've got time to decide one way or the other anyway."

"Thank you, Daddy. You know, wherever I go, I'm gonna make you proud."

He smiled at me. "No doubt about it. And I haven't gotten any phone calls from Dean McGovern lately. You either been staying out of trouble or staying out of sight."

I chuckled. Then something pinched my stomach. I guess it was my guilt. I'd been getting into trouble and staying out of sight with Wes. There was no way I could tell my daddy about that. Though I could use his advice in a general way.

"You remember telling me I should always set my sights on the best?"

Daddy nodded.

"What do you do when you thought you had your sights set on the best, but it turns out the scope on your rifle was a little off?"

A quiet grin passed over his face. "You talking about a fellow?"

"I am. He likes me a lot, and I don't want to hurt his feelings. I never let somebody down easy. I don't know how to go about it."

I watched him gathering his thoughts. "Son, the truth is, there's never anything easy about letting somebody down. You can be as gentle as handling a newborn, but you're going to take your lashes. And you're going to feel like a villain for a while. No way around it. But that guilty feeling don't last forever. If you know in your heart it's not meant to be, the manly thing to do is to let her know." He caught himself and got an amused expression on his face. "Let *him* know."

"I don't know if I can do it, Daddy. It hurts my heart just thinking about it."

"You've got a big heart. Nothing wrong with that. Now you

just be brave and tell him how you're feeling. Don't be a coward. Do it face to face. That shows you're a man of integrity. What happens from there, you can't control, but you'll walk away knowing you did the honorable thing."

It sounded like good advice. I just needed to find the courage to do it.

LATER THAT WEEK, Fiona Linklater rang me up to say it was a good day for me to take her shopping and out to lunch in the Vieux Carré. I told her I'd pick her up about eleven o'clock. I'd wanted to buy gifts for Jonathan, Dale, and Russell, and I was never opposed to browsing for a few things for myself.

I drove over to her house, and she came downstairs. She'd gotten her hair all done up in pins and curls, and she was dressed up in a pink, collared, short-sleeve dress like we were headed to a society affair. I shook my head. In town, we stopped by Weinstein's for her and Rosenstein's for me and a couple of boutiques Fiona had in mind. Then we went for lunch at the Hotel Monteleone. Fiona wore the charm bracelet I'd bought her, and she thanked me for it. I reminded her it was a gift of friendship, and she glanced away.

"All right, Fiona. How long am I supposed to be putting on this façade about the two of us?"

"At least through my first term at college," she said. "I'm counting on college boys being more mature. I'll let you know if I find one to take me on a date. But you're not off the hook until I get a dozen roses. And I'll never get them as a single gal. Boys like a girl who's already committed. I need to find a man who's willing to fight for me."

I snickered. "You want me to be your beard? You know, typically, it's the other way around."

She sipped her ginger beer lemonade through her straw. "Don't be cruel, Arizona. You owe it to me for breaking my heart."

"I never broke your heart." I waved her off and changed the subject. "Where you going for college next year?"

"Barnard."

I gulped. It was the women's college right across the street from Columbia.

Fiona scowled. "You should see the look on your face. I was kidding. You don't have to worry about me slowing you down. My daddy would never let me go to school in New York City. He says it's teeming with criminals and perverts. I've got a choice between Newcomb College here in New Orleans or L.S.U. But I'd rather get married and forgo any of that. Between our families, we could have a real nice wedding, don't you think? They'd help us out with a beautiful house in the Garden District. Wouldn't that be something else?"

I stopped picking at my french fries. "I don't understand you, Fiona. Let's just say I was the closeted type looking for a marriage of convenience. Is that the kind of husband you want? A man who's got no interest in you physically?"

"I've never been physical. You can't miss something you never had."

I looked at her squarely. "Believe me, the first time you have it, you're gonna want some more. Besides, you're real smart. Don't you want a college education? I bet you could do anything you put your mind to."

"I don't want to be a woman with a career. Some dowdy schoolteacher? A nurse?"

She said it with such distaste, it made me laugh. "Why, you could be a doctor. An astronaut. Or if you've got an artistic flair, you could be a fashion designer or an architect."

Fiona sighed. "I'm only going to college to meet a husband."

I smirked and went back to picking at my fries. "I wouldn't mind that, either. But he's going to have to accept I want a career as a writer."

Fiona frowned at me. Then she frowned some more as I watched a handsome, Italian-looking waiter passing by our table. I wriggled my eyebrows and got her laughing. We had some good fun the rest of the afternoon.

I tried to reach Dolly that week and come to find out she'd left that home in Mississippi back in August. That dreadful woman Mrs. Witt would only say Dolly had run off with some boy, and she had no idea where they'd ended up. Then I tried calling Little Douglas, and his adoptive mother was even more curt with me. I felt real blue for a while, thinking I might never see my siblings again. Then, on New Year's Eve, I got the surprise of my life.

I was trying on some clothes I'd bought at Rosenstein's, working on putting together an outfit for a dinner party that night at Glen Oaks Country Club. Fiona had invited me, and it was a good thing. My daddy had left on a "business trip" to Atlanta, though I was pretty sure he was taking that mistress of his from Chattanooga on some getaway. I'd overheard him asking Mrs. Laroche to pack him a couple pair of Bermuda shorts and one of his linen suits. He was leaving me on my lonesome, and if it hadn't been for Fiona, I'd be ringing in the new year with Virginia. While I was tucking in the shirttails of my new pink checkered Oxford, Mr. Wainwright barged into my room, shifty-eyed, like he had some delicate news to deliver.

"You have a visitor."

I was stumped. Besides Fiona, I didn't have any friends within a six hundred mile radius. The nearest one was Dale, and if he had stolen his grandparents' car to drive over from Georgia, I would've thought he'd have the sense to call ahead.

"Mr. Preston Montclair."

I know it sounds dramatic, but I thought I might faint. I rushed to my bathroom to splash my face with cold water. *Holey Moley.* Well, I gave my hair a quick smoothing over in the mirror, and I scooted along to follow Mr. Wainwright down to the first floor. He led me to one of the white-curtained salons off of the entrance hall.

Standing by the window, checking out the view, was the fellow who'd walked out on me at my seventeenth birthday party, saying we were through. Preston swung around when he heard me step into the room. We looked at each other and said nothing at first. I was worried he'd come by to curse me out some more.

"This is the last place I'd expect you to lose your manners. How do you do, Arizona?"

He had a warm grin on his face. I stumbled over to him. "How do you do? I know they raised the price, but it only costs a quarter to use a pay phone. Y'know, to give a person a heads up you coming over?" I glanced over my shoulder to make sure Mr. Wainwright had moved along. "Or you could've written. Did you get my letter? Postmarked August 13th. I still have the receipt for it."

"I know you're sore." He sighed. "That's why I didn't call ahead. I said to myself, I'll take my chances and drive over, and if it's meant to be, I'll catch you at home." He waved me closer to where he'd pulled back the curtain to look out to the front of the house. "I drove, Arizona. Got that engine, fixed up my uncle's pickup, and got her back on the road."

I spotted the truck parked by the fountain in the circular driveway. It looked like it had a new coat of black paint.

"She looks real nice. I'm happy for you, Press." I took him in, up and down. He looked real nice too in his plaid shirt, jeans, and leather work boots. "Well, I'm surprised, but I'm not mad. You suppose we should both have a beer?"

"Not for me. I can't be drinking and driving." He took account of my clothes. "You headed out somewhere special?"

"It's New Year's Eve. But I've got some time." I glanced at my watch. "The party doesn't start till eight."

"Your daddy having something here at the house?"

"No. He's out of town."

"Y'know, I made it here in less than an hour and thirty minutes. Took the state highway instead of Route 70."

"Why'd you come, Press?"

He shifted his gaze. "I was warming up to say. You mind sitting down?"

I stepped over to a divan and took a seat. Preston came along and sat a respectful distance away.

"You've got every right to wonder. I could've replied to your letter and sent it to your address at school. But you know I'm not so good at writing. Not like you." He wrung his hands, antsy as a gambler at confession. "That letter you wrote, it broke my heart. All over again."

I scowled at him. "You beat me to it when it comes to breaking hearts."

He drew a breath. "I'm not here to argue with you. I was hoping maybe we could put the past aside."

"So, what is it you came to say?"

I watched him fussing, picking out his words. I was starting not to mind him showing up out of the blue. With Preston, it always felt like we picked up where we left off, high note or low note. Press crossed and uncrossed his legs. He was looking breathless. I almost felt bad for him, but he had a lot of explaining to do.

"I didn't think it would be so hard. I practiced on the drive over." He looked at me soberly. "Arizona, I had a lot of time to think about things. I would've liked for you to give me another answer when I gave you that ring on your birthday. It hurt me. Deep. Like I'd never been hurt before. I didn't see it coming, but I think I seen the signs now. I just had this picture in my head 'bout how things with you and me were gonna be, and it was so clear, so perfect, I didn't think it was possible it wouldn't come true. You call that an illusion, don't you?"

I nodded.

"I had an illusion, and you shattered it." He hid his gaze. "I spent plenty of nights stewing over what you said. I even thought I hated you for turning me down." He peeked at me. "But I don't want to hate you, Arizona. You were right about that. The two of us, we got too much history. You're always going to be a part of me, and I'm hoping I'll always be a part of you. What I came to say is, I don't want to lose you, Arizona. It don't matter if you're going to college up North. I'll always love you, and I just hope we can still be friends."

My heart was bursting. I'd missed him real bad. "You drove all the way from Le Moyne to say that to me?"

"Mm-hmm."

"Thought it all up by yourself?"

He nodded.

"I'm glad you did. Press, that's the sweetest thing anybody ever said to me. And I'm sorry I hurt you. I had a lot of time to think myself. I don't want to lose you, either." I scooted over a little closer on the divan. "We been up and down and sideways. I don't know where we're gonna land, but you can bet I'll be your friend."

I breathed in because I was tearing up. "How 'bout we get you something to drink and eat after coming such a long way?"

He nodded, and I led him toward the back quarters to see if I could pester Mrs. Gundy to throw together something for Press.

LATER, I TOLD Press he was taking me for a spin in his pickup. I wanted to see the truck he'd put together with his own hands. It was a 1970 Ford F-100, and it was old and nothing luxurious. But that truck had style with its flareside bed and silver strips. The fresh coat of paint made it look brand new, and Preston had fixed up the upholstery in the cab.

I got a kick out of watching him drive. I knew how proud he was, and I was mighty proud of him too. I only told him once he drove like an old lady. Well, he loved that pickup, and he didn't watch a scratch on her.

We parked down at the overlook to the river, off River Road. I told Press about some of my capers up at school, and he got me all caught up about the Montclair family drama. His brother Earl had started hanging out with some boys who skipped school to go boozing and smoking. He was working his way to have to repeat tenth grade, and now he was saying he wanted to quit school like

Preston had done. Preston's cousin Francine was pregnant again by another boy, and she'd been kicked out by her daddy, so she and her one-year-old were squeezed into Preston's house. He was real keen to move out on his own.

"They still talking about you," he said. "I had to lie and say we was keeping in touch. Otherwise, I think it'd break my pere's heart."

I wished I had more time. I would've gone over to Le Moyne and visited his family. But it was Friday, and I was flying back to Massachusetts on Sunday. I told Press that.

"You seeing anyone up there?"

My chest tightened. "Kinda sorta. But it's nothing serious. How 'bout you?"

He quirked an eyebrow at me. "Now who am I gonna see?"

I was happy he hadn't moved on to someone else. That was probably selfish of me. I felt like I could get used to spending time with him again.

"I'm hoping to go to Columbia next year. That's in New York City. But I'll be home at the end of May."

Preston glanced out the window. I placed my hand on his shoulder. "I really missed you, Press. You suppose I could give you a kiss?"

"I don't think that's such a good idea."

"How come?"

"Because I'm stuck on you, Arizona, and I'm trying not to be."

"It's just a kiss."

He turned to me. "It'll feel nice while we're doing it, but what's it mean? In the long run, it'll only make things harder. 'Sides, you seeing someone."

I wanted to say I was fixing to break up with that someone. I stopped myself. I could've tried sweet-talking and cajoling him into it, but I owed Preston some respect.

"I wanna do right by you, Preston Montclair. You tell me how?"

"You could write me another letter. Follow it up with a phone call sometime."

"Done and done." I heaved a breath. "Press, I'm gonna tell you something. They don't have boys like you up North."

He kicked on the ignition of his truck. "You damn right about that."

22

I RETURNED TO Middleton with a lot of things on my mind. Maybe I should've told Press I loved him, and if our love was strong enough, it didn't matter we weren't living in the same place. We could figure out a way to work things out. I could come down to him some weekends. We had the summer to look forward to. We could take things step by step, and who knew? Maybe he'd want to live in New York City while I was going to Columbia. We were right for each other in so many ways, it was worth giving it a try, wasn't it?

I told Jonathan all that when we were having one of our late night talks. I was hoping he could give me some advice, but the conversation ended up getting his horns twisted again.

"You've got so many boys chasing after you, there's no one left for the rest of us."

"What's that supposed to mean?"

"It means I'd sure like to have the kind of problems you have. A boyfriend at school. A boyfriend back home. Doesn't sound so bad to me."

"If you were listening, I don't have neither."

"Whatever, Arizona. I'm going to bed. I've got a physics quiz tomorrow morning. I should get some sleep."

I listened to him turn over on his side, and I stared at the ceiling, wondering what the hell I'd done wrong.

That January in Massachusetts was bitter cold. We'd gotten a two foot snowstorm at the start of the month, and the campus looked like an arctic wonderland. Snowball fights broke out in the quad, and boys went cross-country skiing during free time or over to Middleton Pond to ice skate. I'd never been one for those activities. It was cold enough just having to cross campus, let alone staying outdoors for hours playing sports.

Our old gang had plenty of fun indoors, gathering together in me and Jonathan's room most nights. Everyone was excited about that new Nintendo system I'd gotten for Christmas, and we had trouble tearing ourselves away from that. And we had a fifth. Wally Alhomaizi, an international student from Saudi Arabia, came out that term.

Jonathan had gotten over Russell, and he had one heck of a painful crush on Wally, who was a good looking fellow with bright brown eyes, and he was real sweet, too. I was really hoping something would happen with the two of them. Then one Saturday night, Dale came up with the bad idea of playing truth or dare, and he proceeded to ask Wally in front of all of us who he'd most like to kiss at school. Wally peeked at me and answered, "Arizona."

I hadn't seen that coming. Dale rolled over himself laughing. Russell, who'd been a grump since we got back from break, said he'd had enough of the stupid game and went to his room. I caught a glance of the shattered look on Jonathan's face and felt like Benedict Arnold. The party broke up soon after that.

Alone with Jonathan, I tried smoothing things over. He'd buried himself in his bed and turned away from me.

"I'm sorry. I had no idea. If you want, I'll talk to Wally and tell him I'm not interested. It was probably just something he said in the heat of the moment, y'know?"

"*Dale* obviously knew."

He was awfully alert for someone who was acting like he was ready for bed. "How you figure?"

"He asked Wally the question. And it was his idea to play truth or dare."

"Dale's always getting crazy ideas. I don't think he knew, Jonathan. He only talks to Wally when he comes over here."

"Dale knew how I felt about Wally. And so did you."

I snorted. "Like my Grandma Tilly used to say, that and a penny'll buy you a gumball over at the Dollar General. None of us knew how Wally was gonna answer."

"Did you and Dale plan it? To embarrass me? Because I'm brown-skinned?"

"For Pete's sake, now you're getting paranoid. Why the hell would I do that to you?"

Jonathan said nothing.

"Listen here, maybe it wasn't the best choice on Dale's part, but you know how he is. He don't think too much before he blurts things out, but he means well."

I heard sniffling.

"Jonathan—"

"Save your breath. I hope you and Wally will be real happy together. Just leave me alone."

"I've got no interest in Wally, so don't be putting this on me."

"Yeah. You don't even have to try. Guys just drop at your feet."

"C'mon now."

I couldn't get another word out of Jonathan that night. I might've tried harder, but he hadn't been very nice to me ever since we came back from winter break.

WITH JONATHAN GIVING me the cold shoulder, I started spending more time with Dale those first few weeks of the term. Dale was a little wild and a bit of a flake, but we sure could have some fun. Meantime, I think Wally was embarrassed after that game of truth or dare. He steered clear of me whenever our paths crossed around campus, and he started sitting with another group of boys at the dining hall. Sometimes Russell would join Dale and me for breakfast or supper, though something was bugging him. Any time Dale and I talked about boys or getting that Pink Triangle club started, Russell excused himself, saying he had this or that to do. I was feeling blue. It seemed the four musketeers were breaking up again, and this time for no good reason.

Anyway, I had lots of schoolwork on my hands. For my final term, I had another semester of chemistry, French IV, contemporary English literature, an introduction to psychology class, and Philosophy I. I was aiming to maintain my straight A average, so I was going from my classes to the library most days. Then one morning on my way to second period, I happened to pass by Wes.

He was talking to a student in the doorway of a classroom. I didn't duck my head fast enough. Wes looked straight at me, and I think his eyes followed me all the way down the hall. I remembered what my daddy had told me about being a man and calling things off face to face. So that afternoon around three thirty, I went to Wes's office in the humanities building.

I caught him alone. He let me in and closed the door. My heart was thumping in my chest. Wes looked pretty steamed.

"How do you do, Wes?"

"What brings you here? You decided you weren't going to punish me anymore?"

"Wes, I haven't been punishing you."

"Isolation is a form of punishment. It's like you sent me into exile. I didn't realize you could be so cruel."

He had me feeling small. I was forgetting what I planned to say to him.

"You know I was home for two weeks."

"And you didn't call me on New Year's Day like you said you would."

He's the one who told me to call him, which I never intended to do. I kept that to myself.

"Well, I been busy."

He stared at me in disbelief. "Arizona, you can't lie to me. I don't deserve to be treated like that."

I was recognizing things that made me jumpy. The widening of his stance and shoulders. The cold rage on his face. It was the way Gus Fanning looked when he was getting ready to push me around or take a swing. That office felt like tight quarters for the two of us.

Could be Wes noticed I'd gone pale. His voice and posture softened. He shook his head in self-reproach and spread his arms. "Come over here."

I didn't budge.

He looked at me with a lopsided grin, like I was taking things too seriously. "Come here, Arizona."

I didn't want to. He was like one of them split personalities, like Two-Face in *Batman* comic books. But I did as I was told because I was scared of what would happen if I didn't. Wes encircled me in his arms and kissed me on the head.

I maneuvered a little so my face was turned away from him. He held me really firmly, and though I'd planned on saying what was on my mind, I couldn't reckon how to get around to that.

"I forgive you." I felt his chest rise and fall as he sighed. "You gave me quite a scare, but I understand what's going on. I know this is hard for you, Arizona. It's hard for me, too. But I'm willing to risk everything for this." He chuckled. "Did you think I was going to break up with you? That's why you've been avoiding me, isn't it? You don't have to worry about that. Don't make this harder by playing childish games."

He eased off from that hug and clasped my face, making me look at him.

"Say you won't do it again, Arizona."

I gulped and nodded.

He crushed our lips together and kissed me wet and deep. I was wincing on the inside, and eventually, I found the guts to break things off.

"I just wanted to stop by for a minute. I gotta get to an appointment with my advisor. About my college applications."

Thank God he laid off after that. He told me to stop by that Thursday, and I gave him a nod. I stepped out of his office feeling like I'd just sprung free from a cage set over hot coals.

Then I locked eyes with Jonathan. I guess he'd come up to that second floor corridor for an appointment with one of his professors. I'm sure I looked shocked to see him and couldn't help feel like I'd done something wrong, though I hadn't. Jonathan looked at the nameplate on the door, and he smirked a little in a not so friendly way. He moved along without a word.

23

I TOLD DALE about my troubles with Wesley Turner, and he didn't have a lot to say about it, but he always had some Irish whiskey to drink, and he got me developing a taste for Lucky Strike cigarettes.

I was antsy about my application to Columbia, and Dale was just as antsy about getting a decision from Yale. He'd also been cast as the lead, George Gibbs, in the spring production of *Our Town.* Some nights, he pestered me to run through lines with him. On weekends, he pestered me to come along with him to Boston, and I gave in one Saturday. I went to my first tea dance, and Dale was right—we walked right into the bar without anyone asking us our age. I paced myself drinking my Bud Lites and keeping an eye on my watch, and we had a heck of a good time that night.

At the tea dance, we met some cute fellows from Boston College, and we all trekked over to another club in the South End. I cut a rug on the dance floor, and one of them college boys, Charlie, got a bit frisky with me. To tell the truth, I didn't mind. I was feeling frisky too, but when I saw it was ten o'clock, I told Charlie I had to say goodnight and went to look around for Dale.

Naturally, he was nowhere to be found. I wasn't gonna have a repeat of that night last term. I told our new friends to let Dale know I'd headed back to campus, and I grabbed a cab on the street and made it over to the train station to catch the 10:39. I loved Dale dearly, but that boy could give you high blood pressure and gray hairs at seventeen years old.

I woke him up the next morning around eleven, and he said he'd only been asleep since nine. I didn't ask any questions, but I dragged him down to the dining hall before they closed up the breakfast buffet.

In February, the big to-do was the Valentine's Day dance. It was an especially big deal for us seniors, and while all our class-mates were scheming to find a girl from Woodland Hall to take to the dance, Dale and I came up with the idea of going together. We told Russell at supper one night, and he got all bent out of shape.

"I'm sorry, but I think that's the stupidest thing I ever heard."

I glanced at Dale, and then I cocked an eyebrow at Russell. "What's stupid 'bout it?"

"A Valentine's dance is for boys and girls. You're just looking to make a cause out of it."

"Valentine's Day is about love. A boy and a girl or a boy and a boy."

"The two of you aren't in love. You just like drawing attention."

"We love each other as friends," Dale said.

"That's not the same."

"Why you got a problem with it?" I said. "If you and Jonathan hadn't split up, don't you think you should've had a right to go to the dance together?"

Russell burned up in the face. "We're not together, so I don't see the point in answering."

I stared at him while he went back to finishing his linguine alfredo. "Russell Thorne, I been wanting to ask you this since we got back from break. What the hell happened to you? You just been one continuous bad mood since term started."

I was going to soften that by saying I was concerned. But he snapped back at me right quick.

"I'm not like the two of you, all right? I'm sick of talking all the time about boys and clothes and Broadway and the South End. I decided I'm going to be normal. I like girls now."

I coughed and exchanged an eyeroll with Dale.

"Normal you say? You got a girl to go with to the dance?"

"I do."

"Who?"

"Cindy Abington. We met at the co-ed ski trip a few weeks ago. She goes to Woodland Hall."

I was stunned. I thought I'd called his bluff.

"Well if that's what you want…" I raised my glass of diet soda. "Here, here. Don't forget to include us on the invitation list for your engagement party. Though just because you're heterosexual all of a sudden don't mean you gotta be a bigot."

Russell lowered his voice. "I'm not a bigot. I don't care if the two of you want to walk around campus being out and proud. That's just not me."

"Excuse me? I'm having a little trouble hearing you. You catch that Dale?"

Dale smirked and shook his head.

"Something about being a bigot?" I said.

"Does this mean you're finally going to return my *Honcho* magazines?" Dale asked.

Russell threw down his napkin and stood. "You two can fuck off. I've got some real friends to meet up with."

He rushed out of the dining hall. Dale and I had a good laugh over it, though the truth was it was starting to feel lonely all over again being gay at that school.

DALE AND I went to that Valentine's Day dance together. We got snooty looks, but we had some fun on our own. It helped that we tossed back some whiskey before going. We got ourselves a photo together and hammed it up for a slow dance, with a big kiss at the end for the crowd. Some people cheered, a lot of them laughed, and one asshole called out, "I hope you both get AIDS." Then the phys ed teacher Mr. Phelps came over to say kissing was not permitted at the dance and we ought to move along.

I squinted at him. "We got a right to dance. How 'bout you do something about the fool who told us to get a disease and die?"

"You're not ruining the dance for everyone else. Let's go."

I had a few more choice words for him, but Dale tugged me along, being the steadier of the two of us for the first time. He told me we'd go back to his room and keep the party going.

Dale was a heck of a bad influence. I woke up the next morning feeling like I'd gone through the tumble cycle of the dryer and had hair growing on my tongue. I was a bit concerned about Dale's drinking. But I was also going through some things that made getting blitzed appealing.

I missed my friendship with Jonathan. Even though we shared a room, we barely spoke or even saw each other. I tried talking to him about it when we were together in the room one Sunday. We were both waiting on decisions from Columbia, so I thought that would make for a good conversation starter.

"I also applied to U.C.L.A.," Jonathan told me. "My parents can't afford Columbia unless I get a full scholarship. U.C.L.A. is in-state, so financial aid will cover the tuition. And I can live at home and save my parents a lot of money."

That sounded disappointing. He'd been so excited to go to school in New York City. I didn't know what to say to him.

"Why do *you* look upset? Now you can be roomies with Dale."

He knew Dale was dead set on going to Yale. I decided not to correct him. For the life of me, I didn't know what I'd done to turn Jonathan against me. Now he was sounding jealous of my friendship with Dale on top of being pissed about what happened with Wally.

"I wish the four of us could hang out like we used to. You know Russell's saying he's straight now? He's got his 'new friends,' and he told Dale and me being gay is abnormal."

Jonathan took off his necktie and school jacket. "It's not my fault."

"I wasn't saying it is."

"Russell has always been insecure. He's trying to live up to his father's expectations, and he never will. That's a big part of the reason we split up."

"You never told me that."

Jonathan shrugged and threw on his denim jacket. "Now you know. I've got to catch the shuttle to meet Gladys in town."

He'd grown out his hair and been wearing that denim jacket with its big Chicano Power patch just about every day. I suspected his new style was Gladys's influence. They'd been hanging out three, four times a week.

"Jonathan, before you leave, I want to ask you something. Ever since we came back from winter break, you've done nothing but treat me like dirt. Don't I deserve to know the reason?"

"I'm just staying out of your way so I don't cramp your style."

"You going to explain what the hell that means?"

"I'm tired of being a sidekick in the Arizona and Dale show. It's time I accept who I am. I'm a broke-ass, nerdy Mexican. I just want to get through the year at this lousy school and move on."

"You saying we're not friends anymore?"

"Friends stand up for each other."

"When haven't I stood up for you?"

"You took Dale's side when he wanted to play truth or dare that night. You're obviously better friends with him."

"You still hanging on to that? Well, I'm gonna tell you something, Jonathan. Maybe if you hadn't made such a big deal out of that night, the four of us would be friends like we were last term. The whole thing scared off Wally, too."

Jonathan coughed out a laugh. "That's my fault? I got my heart broken, but it's my fault."

I sighed. "You had a crush on that boy, and it turns out he's not interested. That's not the same thing as having your heart broken, darling."

"You'd be the expert, *darling*. You broke Wally's heart and Preston's heart, and you're still screwing Mr. Turner, who you said you were breaking up with. I guess you'll break his heart too, along with getting him fired. But not before you get a letter of recommendation from him for your college applications, huh?"

"I'm not screwing Mr. Turner any more, and anyone who says I am is a liar."

"Whatever, Arizona."

With that, he left the room.

I WAS REELING after that conversation. I'd thought Jonathan and I were best friends to the end, but if he was going to treat me that way, I wasn't sure I wanted to be friends with him at all. Anyway, he'd hit on something I was overdue dealing with. Wes. I knew I had to end things with him, but after the last time I tried, I hadn't been in a hurry to try again.

I avoided him for another week or so, then one day, I shored up the courage and went over to his office after class.

He closed the door behind me, and I could tell something was off with him from the start. Before I could say a word, he motioned for me to sit down in the chair facing his desk, and he took a seat on the other side, acting very formal.

"Arizona, I've given our relationship a lot of thought, and I need to tell you it's over between us. You don't have the maturity I'm looking for. Your behavior lately has shown me that. You're a young man of poor moral character. An ethical course of action would be to rescind the letters of recommendation I wrote for you. But out of respect for your feelings, I'm not going to do that. Instead, I ask that you stop coming by my office. Our relationship is over."

I looked down at my lap, guarding an impulse to tell him I'd only stopped by to say the same thing. I didn't like him criticizing me, but I was also starting to get the picture Wes was one mixed up fella. It was like he'd switched personalities again, and beneath his arrogant veneer, I was pretty sure he was hurt. I felt a little bad for him, but you can bet I was happy to be free.

"I'm sorry, Arizona. I know this must be difficult to hear. But with time, I hope you'll understand."

I nodded along. "I'll try, Wes. And I'll be sure to stay out of your way. I wish you all the best." I stood up from my chair.

He put on a forced smile. "I wish you all the best, too. I'm glad we've reached an understanding. Everything that happened in the fall term was an error on both our parts. We can chalk it up as a bad decision and forget it ever happened."

"Sounds good to me."

"And one more thing, Arizona. I can rescind those recommendations at any time. And I still have a copy of that essay you wrote last semester, which I can give to Dean McGovern. But I won't as long as you don't give me any cause to take those steps."

I glanced at him and nodded, and then I let myself out of his office for what I hoped would be the last time.

I DECIDED TO write Preston a letter that week. I was hankering for his company, and with everything going on that term, I could sure use a friendly ear. But when I took pen to paper, I had a hard time working out what to say.

I couldn't tell him about Wes. That was a story to confess face to face without any written documentation. Then, I wasn't sure how well it would come out if I told Preston about the problems I'd had with Jonathan. In the end, I wrote about a page and a half on lined notebook paper about winter in New England and the Valentine's Day dance, and I told him I missed him and was looking forward to seeing him when I came home in late May.

The next day, Dale didn't show up for breakfast, and he didn't make it to our third period philosophy class. I skipped French to run over to his room to check on him. After pounding on the door, he finally opened up.

Dale looked kind of washed out, and he was still wearing his pajamas. I pushed into his room to find out what was going on.

Dale retreated to his bed and crumbled. "I don't feel so well. My glands are swollen, and it hurt so much going to the bathroom this morning, I was in tears."

I'd paid attention in seventh grade health class so I was pretty sure what was going on. "You notice a discharge when you peed?"

"It wasn't peeing. It was out the other end."

I bit down on my lip.

Dale threw off his bed sheet. "You take a look?"

"Hell no."

"Please, Arizona. I can't look myself."

"I'm not a doctor. And I like my eyeballs the way they are. A sight like that is liable to turn me cross-eyed and make me blind. You need to get yourself over to Mrs. Callahan so she can take a look."

Dale stood. "I can't. She'll have to inform my parents."

I'd never seen such terror in Dale's eyes, and believe you me, I was right there with him. If I'd picked up a sexual infection in my caboose and had to tell my daddy, I might choose to live out the rest of my days in a leper colony instead. Then I remembered I'd held on to a leaflet from a community health center when we'd been at that tea dance. It had a phone number for a clinic in Boston. The flier had the word confidential all over it. I told Dale about it.

"You come with me?"

Dale's face was desperate and pleading. I couldn't tell him no. I hustled him along to get dressed, and then we hurried over to my room so I could get that clinic phone number. Dale was too torn up to make the phone call, so I called for him. A lady told me we could come straight away. We hoofed it over to the train station.

LATER THAT AFTERNOON, I was sitting in a bucket seat in the basement waiting room of a public health clinic, paging through a trifold brochure about hepatitis for a third time. I wished I'd thought of taking one of my school books with me. We'd sprung out of campus like we were leaving a burning building. I hadn't thought out how I was going to explain missing my classes either.

I was getting jittery. Dean McGovern had told me last term there'd be serious consequences if I broke rules again. I glanced at the hallway. We'd passed a phone booth down the street. I could call my daddy and explain things to him. He'd probably help me out with an excuse seeing as I was doing a good deed in regard to a very delicate matter. Before I could stand up to give it a try, Dale came out of the clinic.

He picked up some papers from a receptionist, strolled over to me, and nudged me along out the door.

When we got outside, he showed me a prescription note. "They said I could fill it at the pharmacy down the block. It'll clear me up in a few days."

He looked relieved. I was too, for the most part.

"Which one was it?"

"Gonorrhea." He grimaced. "They wanted to know everybody I had sex with in the past two weeks."

That sounded like it stood to reason. "Did you tell 'em?"

Dale scowled. "No. They need full names and a phone number and an address."

We walked along to the pharmacy. Fifteen minutes later, we walked out with Dale's prescription and two cherry Cokes. Dale washed down his first pill, and then we grabbed a taxi to the train station.

"Thanks," Dale told me on the train ride back to school.

"Don't mention it." I considered saying what was on my mind, and as usual, it came out before I'd run over how to put it. "You think this might be one of them wake-up calls?"

"Wake up for what?"

I gave him a lopsided glance. "To slow things down. Take a break from staying out all night every Saturday. Sleeping with guys you only know by first name."

"Are you calling me promiscuous?"

By the look on his face, I was scared of giving him a yes.

He fixed on me, deadpan. "Because I'm not promiscuous. I'm a straight up slut. You get that right from now on."

A grin crept up his face. The fool was practicing his acting on me. I couldn't help chuckling so loud, people were shushing me in the car.

"Dale Knox-Levy, you're one classy fella."

He pantomimed wiping the corner of his mouth like he'd just swallowed down something juicy. "You think I'm catching a bad reputation?"

"Well, let's see. You could be with Harvard. Northeastern. Boston College." I counted on my fingers. "Boston University. Tufts. St. Francis Preparatory Academy for Boys, if I'm not mistaken?"

"I'm a people person. And St. Francis barely counts. Those Catholic boys bust their nuts before they can stick it in."

"Ain't that the worst? But hold on. *I'm* Catholic."

"Which proves my point. You're a big ol' bottom. Don't even try to pretend you're not."

"I ain't pretending, but I ain't advertising, neither."

"It's not like I took out an advertisement in the *Boston Globe*." He scratched his chin. "You think I should? It would help widen my range."

"It would widen something, all right."

We laughed and got cheeky with each other like that for a while. You could say this or that about Dale's flaws, but no one could make me laugh like him. We were both tearing up. Then, out of the blue, Dale quieted.

"Seriously, you think I'm gross?"

I frowned and waved him closer in our three-seater so I could stretch an arm around his shoulder. "Dale, all kidding aside, I'm worried about you."

"Y'know, I go through every day feeling like a freak. Most days, I don't want to look at myself in the mirror. My dad can't look me in the face. I'm sure he hopes one of these days I'll get sick and die so he won't have to be embarrassed by me anymore."

I gave him a squeeze. The man who'd raised me, Gus Fanning, had made me feel the same way.

"But, Arizona, when I'm out at a bar, surrounded by guys, I forget feeling that way," Dale went on. "And guys actually want to be with me." He lowered his gaze. "I know it's just for sex, but it makes me feel like someone special. For a change. Why does that feeling have to come with VD?"

"Chipmunk, you *are* someone special. I just know if you slowed down, got to know one of them guys you're meeting instead of running off to a bathroom stall with them, you'd find yourself a fellow who likes you for who you are."

He looked up at me. "The way Mr. Turner likes you?"

I screwed up my face. "We split up. I thought I told you. You be careful not to be talking about that around anyone else."

I was a little worried about the grin on his face. I clopped him on the side. "You didn't mention it to anybody, did you?"

"No."

"Let's keep it that way."

"He got a big dick?"

I looked at him twice. Then I cracked up. "Darling, you got enough problems without messing around with Mr. Turner."

"You said it was over between you."

I shook my head. "I don't know if you're putting me on or being serious, but I'll say this. Me and Mr. Turner's dick had some real good times. Until the man it was attached to showed me who he was."

Dale's eyes widened. "He *is* big."

I gave him a swat. "What I'm trying tell you, fool, is it ain't always a good idea to mess around with someone just because they're good looking."

Dale scowled. "You bagged the hottest teacher in the entire school. And you said it wasn't just sex. He said he loved you." Dale gazed out the window of the car. "I wouldn't mind trading places with you."

That ticked me off. "I'm trying to explain, Mr. Turner was a big mistake. Why'd you want to trade places with me? I screwed up every relationship I ever been in. There's a boy back in Louisiana who really loved me, and I gone and ruined things with him."

"At least you had someone fall in love with you. I don't think I'll ever find someone like that."

"Chipmunk, you got looks and talent and one hell of a personality. Like they say down South, you just got to stop giving away the milk for free."

"You think that works with gay men? There's so many places to get the milk for free, they're moving through the dairy section pretty quickly."

I chuckled. "Well, you might have a point about that. But how 'bout taking a sniff before you open your mouth? Make sure things aren't past their expiration date."

Dale elbowed me. We cut it up all the way back to school like we'd just had a day out on the town rather than getting Dale's clap fixed up.

24

OUR ABSENCE FROM school that day appeared to go unnoticed beyond our teachers. I prayed that was the case, and then the next day I got one of them big envelopes from Columbia in my mailbox.

I raced up to my room to open it up in privacy. Inside, I ripped it open and then I read a cover letter I'd been dreaming about for over a year. *Welcome to the Class of 1990.* I jumped around and hollered like a country boy. Then I ran over to the phone booth in the hall and rung up my daddy.

I was so excited and talking so fast, he wasn't following what I was saying.

"Slow down now, son, and tell me what the heck is going on."

"I got into Columbia, Daddy. Please, can I go?"

I thought I heard him chuckle. "Well that's real nice, but you still have Harvard and Brown considering your applications."

"I want to go to Columbia. They've got the best writing program in the country. They graduated Jack Kerouac and J.D. Salinger. Allen Ginsburg, too."

"I know you've got your sights set on that school. When do they need to hear back?"

"I applied early decision. The letter says they need my deposit right away." I scratched my ear. "Please Daddy, don't be sore at me. Early decision means I've got to withdraw my applications to other schools. It's what I want to do. You said I should aim for the best of the best, and you can't do any better than Columbia if you want to be a writer. I just know it's the place where I belong."

I waited out the silence on the other end of the line. Nerves were eating me alive. I couldn't do anything without my daddy's support.

"If that's what you want, I guess you're going to Columbia."

I burst into tears. They were happy tears, but they had me heaving and garbling my words for a while before I could get anything out.

"Thank you, Daddy. That means everything to me."

"Well, we're going to have to have a celebration. I have a trip up to Boston the week after next. What do you say to spending the weekend with me? I'll get us a suite at the Ritz-Carlton. Take you to dinner at a nice Italian restaurant in the North End."

I wiped my eyes. "That sounds great. Thank you."

"Son, I was going to wait on telling you this, but I've got a graduation present coming your way. I booked you a trip to Europe this summer. I'm going to join you for a week, but it's a full month. So, if you've got a friend you want to tag along, you start thinking about it."

In the state I was in, I couldn't wrap my brain around that development. But I thanked him, probably a half dozen times. We said goodbye, and I stumbled off to find Dale and tell him the news.

I was on cloud nine for a little over twelve hours. But the next morning, right after I'd cleaned up in the shower and gotten into my shirt and tie, Mr. Ruskin came by my room to say I was to report to Dean McGovern before my first period class.

Walking over to the administrative hall, my mind went to a lot of places. Had Dean McGovern found out I'd skipped classes that day? On a brighter side, I wondered if he might finally have some news about the Pink Triangle club I'd been pushing. In my heart, I was feeling it was probably the former and not the latter. I sat outside the dean's fancy office and couldn't stop my knee from bouncing.

Mrs. Woolsey let me in, and I sat down at a chair in front of Dean McGovern's desk. He had his assistant dean, Mr. Armitage, with him. My balls were pretty well burrowed inside me.

"Thank you for coming, Arizona. I'm afraid we have a very serious matter to discuss with you. I asked Mr. Armitage to be here in order to have proper documentation of this meeting. It's protocol for the school, but I want to assure you that your confidentiality will be protected."

At that point, the blood had drained from all my extremities.

"Tell us about your relationship with Mr. Turner."

I looked down at my lap.

"Arizona?"

I cleared my throat and raised my head. "Mr. Turner was my teacher for creative writing last term."

"Yes, we're aware. He also took you to a conference at Amherst College in November."

I joggled my head.

"Did you spend time with Mr. Turner outside of class?"

Options scurried through my brain. I didn't know how much Dean McGovern knew, and I didn't want to get Wes in trouble.

"A few times. During his office hours. I asked him for some feedback on one of my papers."

"When you were alone with Mr. Turner, did anything else transpire?"

I did my best to look like I hadn't a clue what he was talking about. "I'm not sure what you mean."

He leaned closer in his chair and knit his hands together. "Was there physical contact between the two of you?"

I shook my head. "No."

"Did Mr. Turner make you feel uncomfortable? Did he express a sexual interest in you?"

"No. He was my teacher."

Dean McGovern exchanged a glance with Mr. Armitage.

"Arizona, I understand it might feel wrong to suggest one of your teachers did something improper. Especially if you had a close bond, or perhaps had romantic feelings for that teacher."

"I don't have romantic feelings for Mr. Turner."

Mr. Armitage scratched down something on his notebook. I felt like I was having an out-of-body experience. I didn't want to be in that office, and I didn't want to talk about Mr. Turner no more.

"It's been reported you had a physical relationship with Mr. Turner."

"That's not true."

"Arizona, this is a very serious allegation. Is there anything that happened between the two of you that might have caused someone to believe Mr. Turner pushed an inappropriate relationship on you? You said you went to his office hours. It sounds like the two of you were close."

"He was my teacher."

Dean McGovern looked down at his yellow legal pad, picking out something.

"He chose you, out of all the students in the school, to attend the writing conference at Amherst College. Did he mention to you why?"

Jesus. I was under cross examination.

"He knew I was keen on going. I was doing well in his class. I want to be a writer after college."

"Did Mr. Turner ask you to do anything in exchange for taking you to the conference?"

"No."

"What happened that weekend?"

I managed to exhale a breath. "I went to workshops. I was in the high school track. I met students from all over the country."

"Did you spend time alone with Mr. Turner?"

"Not much. He went to sessions on his own." I shrugged. "The two of us had dinner one night."

"Did you spend time with him in his hotel room?"

"No. I had my own room."

"Did you sleep in Mr. Turner's room?"

"No."

"Did Mr. Turner make advances toward you that weekend?"

"No."

Dean McGovern cocked his head. "Can you think of a reason why someone would make allegations to the contrary?"

I shifted in my seat. "I wish I knew." I eyed him hopefully. "This sounds like one big mix-up."

Dean McGovern exchanged another glance with Mr. Armitage. He seemed to have run out of questions and looked a bit bothered by it. Then he turned back to me.

"Arizona, I imagine it would be embarrassing for you to report having engaged in sexual acts with Mr. Turner. But I promise you, anything you say will be kept in strict confidence. Are you certain everything you told me is the truth?"

"Yes, sir."

"Because if you're protecting Mr. Turner, I'd like you to think about something. You're graduating from Middleton in a few weeks. Your high school days will soon be in the past. But Mr. Turner will remain here, and if he's the sort of man who has the proclivities which were reported to us, he could take advantage of another student. That would be a very harmful thing, both for our students and the school."

I didn't know what to say to that. I just looked up at him and nothing came out of my mouth.

"All right. That's all. But if something occurs to you later about the times you were alone with Mr. Turner, I want you to check back in with me. You needn't make an appointment."

I stood and strolled out of his office, picking up the pace as I went.

WALKING AROUND CAMPUS that day, I could've been paranoid, but it felt like everybody was looking at me. I'd only told two people about me and Wes, and I had sworn them both to secrecy. Still, somebody had to have reported our relationship to Dean McGovern. I felt like I was falling apart. The whole school was going to find out. Wes was going to lose his job, and like he'd warned me, it was going to ruin his career when things got out. I'd gone and done that. I should've kept my mouth shut. Better yet, I never should've pursued Wes in the first place. I was going to be known for the rest of my life as the boy who slept with his English teacher.

By fifth period, my heart was racing so fast, I thought I was having a cardiac arrest. I asked my philosophy teacher if I could go see Mrs. Callahan, and he sent me off with a pass. I wasn't thinking straight. I was so riddled with guilt and embarrassment, I felt I had to do something to redeem myself. So I wandered down a corridor of the building where Wes usually held class. The halls were empty. I came to a classroom where the door was open, and it was quiet inside. Peeking in, I spotted Wes sitting at the desk grading papers. I perched around to make sure no one else was in that room, and then I stepped inside.

Wes looked up at me, and his face blanched. Then he shuffled over to close the classroom door.

He yanked me by the arm to a spot where we wouldn't be seen through the glass door panel, and he faced me, grim and mean.

"What did you do?"

I couldn't get anything out before he came at me again.

"I spent the morning being interrogated by Dean McGovern and the school lawyer. What did you tell them?"

"I didn't say anything. I told Dean McGovern nothing happened."

"Somebody said something. A somebody who heard it from you. Did you tell your friends?"

I shook my head, but then I broke down, not wanting to lie to anyone no more.

"Just my two closest friends. In a million years, I never thought they'd say anything. And I don't know for a fact they did."

Wes was sweating through his shirt collar and heaving with breaths. "Who? That faggot Dale Knox-Levy?"

I was too stunned to form words.

"You're an idiot. You thought it was a good idea to tell a boy who's the biggest fuck up at this school?"

"Now, hold on there. Neither one of us knows it was Dale."

He launched his open palm, clipping my face so hard, I felt my neck snap and I nearly fell over trying to stay up on two feet.

"You're a piece of shit. Trying to ruin me. After every fucking thing I did for you."

He bullied me farther into the classroom with his face twisted up, looking like the devil himself. A few weeks back, I'd seen he was a finger snap away from letting out the violence inside him, and now it was loose and frightening.

I stumbled away from him, holding my hands in front of my face, still seeing stars from that smack, while he was spitting cruel things at me. When I got some breath into my lungs and felt my strength coming back, I did the only thing I could think to do. I charged at him and shoved him with all my might. Sent him tumbling into a desk chair with a clamor to wake the dead.

It might've toppled two desk chairs, but I didn't stick around to survey the damage. I ran out of that classroom and ducked into a bathroom across the hall before the teachers came out to see what in blazes was going on. I hid myself in a stall, listening to a crowd of teachers and students run out of the classrooms.

WHEN THE COMMOTION died down and sixth period started up, I emerged from the bathroom stall, thinking I might go about my business as usual. Then I caught sight of my face in the mirror above the sinks. My left cheek was puffed up and scarlet. I wadded up some paper towels and doused them with cold water to ease the swelling. Then I skulked over to the dormitory and hid in my room.

I sure felt like a jerk. As mean as Wesley Turner had treated me, things would never had come to this if I had left him alone from the start. I couldn't take it back. I felt trapped and stupid. Everybody was going to hate me now, and I was always going to be responsible for Wes losing his job. I just wished I'd had a chance to come clean before someone reported what was going on.

While I was holed up in my room, I couldn't help noticing a familiar envelope on Jonathan's desk. I took a look, and sure enough it was an acceptance packet from Columbia. I didn't pry into it, but it was the same big envelope I'd received.

I made myself an ice bag from the fridge to hold against my cheek, and around three o'clock, I heard someone rustling at the door with the key. Jonathan stepped in.

He didn't even look at me. He went straight over to his desk, dropped his bookbag, took off his jacket and loosened his tie with his back turned to me.

"You ain't got nothing to say?"

Jonathan sat down at his desk chair sideways, still avoiding my gaze. "Say about what? Did you skip classes again?"

"I skipped a few. But I was talking about that envelope from Columbia. I got one, too."

"Yeah. I got in with a full scholarship for tuition. But I still have to see if my financial aid will cover the dorms and living expenses."

"Congratulations."

"You got in, too?"

"Mm-hmm."

He glanced at me, and his gaze skittered away. "You get into a fight?"

"Could be. Sometime around fifth period. In the humanities building. Supposing you heard something about that?"

He was careful at first. "Some kids said something about Mr. Turner falling down in his classroom. They said it was an accident. He had to be taken to the hospital in Hawthorne."

I set down my ice bag and fixed on him. An intuition was growing inside me.

"You told Dean McGovern I was sleeping with Mr. Turner. Why? That's all I want to know."

"I don't know what you're talking about." He pried off his shoes and went to his closet to pull out a pair of sweatpants.

"Someone told the dean about Wes and me, and I'm thinking it could only be one of two people."

He stopped unbelting his slacks. "Did you tell Dale?"

"I did."

"Then maybe you should be talking to him."

"I could. But I'm talking to you right now."

I watched him step out of his slacks and fumble while pulling on his sweatpants. "Maybe you weren't as discreet as you thought. Another student or a teacher could've seen the two of you together. They'd have an ethical and legal obligation to report it. What the two of you were doing is considered abuse."

"I ain't been abused, Jonathan. I'm seventeen years old. That's one year older than the age of consent."

"It's still illegal. And in the school code of conduct, if you don't report illegal activity, it's grounds for disciplinary action, even expulsion."

I studied him once more. His face had darkened with incrimination. "So, it came from you."

He heaved a breath. "Yes. I reported it. Before someone else did, and I'd get called for questioning by Dean McGovern. It was for your own good, but I guess you hate me now."

"Did the thought ever cross your mind to mention to me you were going to report it? Could've given me a heads up 'fore I was interrogated like a criminal."

"I knew you'd try to talk me out of it."

I shook my head. "Wow. I'm thinking I'm better off being your enemy than your friend. That's the way you treat somebody who brings you home to meet his family for Thanksgiving? Who stood up for you every single time some kid tried to mess with you. I tried, Jonathan, but I never am going to be good enough to be your friend, am I?"

"What was I supposed to do? If it came out I knew what was going on all along, I could get suspended. You remember what Dean McGovern said when we broke curfew last term. I'm sorry, but I'm not going to jeopardize my education and let all the sacrifices my family made go to waste."

I scowled at him. "You really think you could've gotten in trouble? No one asked me once if other students knew about it. If they had, you think I would've told them you knew?"

He pulled up his sweatpants. "I can't afford to take chances. I already have two strikes against me, being Mexican and gay. And I don't have a father like Dale's to bail me out."

I stood up. "You could've told me how you were feeling. That's what friends do. If I knew you felt like you had to make a report, I'd have done it myself. If you bothered to have a conversation with me about it, you would've known Wes and I were through a long time ago. We hadn't slept together since November."

Jonathan shrank away from me. That just got me more riled up.

"I made a mistake, Jonathan. I told you about it all the way back at Thanksgiving. I been trying to work it out, but you didn't give me a chance. You went over my head so I'm always going to look like a dirtbag." I huffed a mirthless laugh. "I'm never gonna understand what I did to make you hurt me that bad. 'Cause if the tables were turned, you know I wouldn't have thought nothing 'bout risking getting in trouble in order to protect you. I thought we were brothers, but I was wrong."

He grabbed his book bag. "You don't know about the choices I have to make every day. I did what I felt I had to do."

"All right. I can accept that. I'll talk to Mr. Ruskin. See if arrangements can be made so we don't have to room together the rest of the term." I looked at him squarely. "I wouldn't want to put you in any more ethical predicaments."

Jonathan glared at me. I walked out of the room to hunt down Mr. Ruskin.

25

I OUGHT'VE BEEN used to disaster cropping up no sooner than I'd gotten ahead. I'd lost my grandparents in a fire just when me and my siblings had found a safe place to live. The first man I ever loved, Nicolas Bondurant, gone and killed himself. I'd been taken in by my real birth daddy, and then came along all the hardships for Dolly and Little Douglas. True to form, life had delivered me admission to the college of my dreams and less than twenty-four hours later, it cut me down to size with the scandal of my relationship with Wesley Turner coming out.

I went back to Dean McGovern and told him the truth. He called in the school counselor and later the school lawyer to talk to me, and everyone acted like I needed to be handled with kid gloves, a victim of molestation. I just felt ashamed of getting myself in the situation in the first place. I didn't feel coerced or victimized.

Everyone said my confidentiality would be protected, but you try being at the center of a sex scandal at a boys' boarding school without word spreading like wildfire. Mr. Turner up and disappeared one day. I don't know the particulars. But the other teachers had to be gossiping about it, and maybe things leaked out to students from there. I got stares around campus, and the dining hall went quiet as soon as I stepped in. Then, one day in my philosophy class, when the teacher was talking about moral relativity, Brad Ellis raised his hand with a big smirk on his face.

"Is that like how in certain parts of the country, like the South, it's okay to marry your cousin?" Brad stared at me smugly. "Or to get boned by one of your teachers during his office hours."

The teacher told Brad to cool it, but not before every single student in the classroom broke out in laughter. I hadn't felt so humble at Middleton since my first day arriving on campus. Then the graffiti started on my door.

Cocksucker

G.A.Y. = Got AIDS Yet?

Inbred faggot

Walking across campus one day, some boy I didn't even know caught up with me and asked: "Did you give Mr. Turner AIDS? Is that why he left?"

I watched him run off to laugh about it with his friends. All the self-confidence and bravery I'd built up at that school had shrank away to nothing. I hung my head and avoided people. It got to the point I stopped going to the dining hall for meals. I didn't have much of an appetite anyway and got by with snacks from the vending machine now and then. In the final weeks of the term, instead of joining all the celebrations for the senior class, I just counted the days until I could get the hell out of there.

They had to tell my daddy what happened, so that weekend he came up to Boston was one long conversation about what we were going to do instead of celebrating my acceptance to Columbia. My daddy said he'd get a team of lawyers to make sure Wes spent the rest of his days in prison. I told him over and over again that's not what I wanted. I did a lot of crying that weekend, asking him to forgive me for bringing shame on him and the Bondurant name.

One thing Gaston Bondurant was real good at was consoling a fellow when he was down. After my tearful apology, he sat close to me on the couch in our hotel suite.

"It's all right son. We all lose our way sometimes." He held my shoulder. "We're going make right what this fellow did to you."

I looked him in the face. "Daddy, he didn't do anything to me I wasn't looking for. I'm seventeen years old. He's the fellow I told you about during Christmas break. Who I was trying to let down easy. The one I was seeking your advice about."

That got him quieting and thinking things over.

"I know it was wrong on both our parts. Believe me, I understand that now. But it don't call for lawsuits. It don't call for bringing any more attention to it than's already been done. That's no good for me, no good for you, and it's no good for the school."

He came around to agree. He told me I'd learned my lesson and didn't have anything to be ashamed about. Daddy even said he'd always be proud of me. That meant a lot. I was looking forward to having a clean slate in college where nobody would know what I'd done.

I did get the school to let me move out of Jonathan's room. The only option was to set up a cot so I could double up with Dale, which was plenty fine with me for the last six weeks of the term. Dale cheered me up by saying stupid things like at least I hadn't caught gonorrhea, and I could parlay the situation into being popular at college for having slept with an older man. I owe a lot to Dale for standing at my side those final weeks at Middleton. He even brought Wally over to hang out with us again a few times so I didn't feel so alone. Dale got into Yale, by the way. We made an oath we'd keep in touch. Yale was just an hour and forty minute trip from New York City on the train. I sure was going to miss Dale.

Then, to put another bee in my bonnet, at the end of the semester, we heard Jonathan and Russell had started seeing each other again.

In May, on the last day of finals, everyone was running amok on campus, screeching and hollering through the halls and joining up with friends in the quad to blast music from boomboxes and throw frisbees and kick around hacky sacks. I snuck up to my bedroom to get a start on packing up my things so I could hightail it out of there right after the graduation ceremony. I heard a knock at the door and went to answer it.

Jonathan stood in the hall looking at me like a lost puppy.

"You got a minute?"

Talking to him wasn't at the top of my list of things to do, but I stepped aside to let him into the room.

He looked at my packed suitcases and boxes. "You must be looking forward to heading home."

I nodded.

"I heard you made magna cum laude. Congratulations."

I nodded again, half-heartedly.

"What do you have planned for the summer?"

"What do you care?"

Jonathan smiled nervously. "Just seemed like a topic of conversation."

"I'm going to Europe for a while."

"I think I heard that. You should have a lot of fun. I'll be back in L.A., working at my uncle's restaurant again."

I went back to setting aside the clothes I'd need for the next few days. "Why'd you come by?"

He didn't answer. I was thinking I shouldn't have bothered letting him in the door. I peeked at him and saw he'd turned pink in the face.

Finally, he said, stiffly, "I wanted to make sure I said goodbye. And that I'm sorry."

I snorted to myself and stacked up a pair of briefs. "Ain't that peculiar. What're you sorry for exactly?"

He swiped his face. "I could've handled things better. Come talk to you before going to Dean McGovern." He met my gaze. "You were right. You've always been a good friend to me. I went through some things this year, and I don't think I was always such a good friend to you."

I looked at him blankly. "How's that?"

Jonathan shifted around. "I don't know what kind of person I'm supposed to be. Feels like I don't belong anywhere sometimes.

Here, I'm too brown to fit in. Back home, I'm too nerdy and shy to be a real Chicano. I get angry. At the world, I guess."

"We got that in common. I thought I'd be leaving school with my head held high. But with what you done, I'm running off like a thief in the night. Just a queer Southern boy with a bad reputation who never belonged here to start."

Jonathan looked down at his shoes. "I didn't know things would get so bad."

"What changed, Jonathan? Me being white and you being Mexican? I can't say I know what it's like to be you, but it used to be we could talk about those things. Used to be we had a friendship where we looked out for each other."

"It's complicated, Arizona." He sniffled. "I'd been trying to tell you all semester how I felt. What it's like being the only brown-skinned kid in our four musketeers. I felt like I was going crazy sometimes. I needed space."

"You got that space all right. Could've gotten it by telling me off instead of letting everyone know the biggest mistake I ever made in my life."

"I only told Dean McGovern it was something he should look into. I didn't think it would turn out this way."

I rolled my eyes.

"I keep going over that day in my head again and again," he went on. "I really thought at the time I was doing the right thing. Not just for me but for you." He hid his gaze again. "But maybe there was part of me that did it out of spite. I could've talked to you about it. I thought I couldn't trust you anymore. Arizona, I was angry at everyone, not just you. You were getting closer to Dale, and I felt like I was being left behind. Then there was that thing with Wally. Everything was mixed up in my head. That's on me, not you. We had our fights about Mr. Turner, but I should've given you the benefit of the doubt."

As much as all that was right honorable for him to admit, it was a day late and dollar short. Over a month late actually.

"Anything else?"

"I don't know. You have anything you want to say to me?"

I almost told him to beat it. But I had been simmering about something I wanted him to hear.

"Y'know Jonathan, I hear it ain't easy being you. And you know more than anyone where I come from, and how people treated me last year. Calling me white trash. Saying I'm an inbred, bayou faggot. I ain't saying what I did was right, but how's the punishment fit the crime? You had to know deep down what would happen when you reported me to Dean McGovern. You know what this school is like."

Jonathan couldn't look at me.

"I can't..." A lump formed in my throat, and I had to swallow it down. "I can't even show myself around school. I get notes under my door, and people calling things out in class, and it's not because I slept with a teacher. It's because I'm gay. That ain't your fault, but where you been, Jonathan? You stop by my room three days before move out day?"

"I stood up for you any time I heard boys talking." He covered his eyes, gasping tears.

I turned my back to him and started packing up some socks. It felt like everything had gone dead in the room.

"I screwed up, Arizona. I can't take it back, but if I could, I would. You think there's anything I could do to repair our friendship?"

I shrugged a shoulder toward the door. "Go on."

"Okay. If that's what you want. But listen, Arizona, you're not bayou trash or any of those things kids are saying. You're a good person. You were my best friend. I fucked it up, and I know it."

I looked over my shoulder before he left the room. Our eyes met. He gazed at me earnestly. He did look real beat up by everything.

"I'll understand if you never want to talk to me again, but I guess you should know, we'll both be at Columbia next year."

I raised my eyebrows.

"I just found out today. They gave me some extra scholarship money, and with a work-study job on campus, it'll cover tuition, books, and the dorms."

I gave him a nod. "Guess we'll be seeing each other."

"Guess so."

He gave me a tiny grin and left the room.

26

I FLEW BACK to Louisiana, and when Buck drove me home, the first thing I did was walk over to the garage and fire up my Corvette. I needed to see somebody real bad, and I was lucky to not get caught in a speed trap on the way. My flight had landed late. I had to lead foot it to make it to Merle's Gas and Go before close at seven thirty.

I made it with a few minutes to spare, and I parked right in front of the shop's glass doors. I waited for Preston to come out and lock up, and when he did, I grinned real hard from the shocked look on his face.

He came over to the driver's side window. "They don't teach common sense at that fancy boarding school? Or did you miss class that day?"

"How you mean?"

"Calling ahead? It's a common courtesy."

I scowled. "How's a person supposed to call ahead when he's forty-two thousand feet in the air? I only landed in New Orleans a little over an hour ago. You got plans?"

"I do now." He came around the passenger's side door and jumped in. I pulled out of the gas station and drove straight over to our spot by the Bayou Teche.

"How was graduation? If you'd called ahead, I could've given you your present."

"You done reminded me." I scrounged out a rabbit's foot keychain from my jacket pocket. It was just a gag gift. I couldn't resist when I saw it on a store display case at the airport. I handed it to Preston. "It'll go nice with the green one I bought you. The summer after tenth grade. You still got it?"

Preston held it up at eye level and spun the rabbit's foot around. "I do. It's on the keys to my pickup. But I dunno. Don't one lucky charm cancel out the other?"

"Then I'll have to buy you a third." I eased back in my seat, feeling happy for the first time in weeks. "It's good to see you, Press. You're looking good."

He lifted his Saints baseball cap to scratch his head. "I still wish you'd let me know. I told you I like taking a shower after working all day."

"Press, I wouldn't care if you just rolled out of the mud." I took his hand and held it against my leg. "I just wanted to spend some time with you. You get my letters this time 'round?"

"I did. Though they trailed off at the beginning of April. Guess you got busy with finals and graduation." He smiled. "You got your high school degree, Arizona Bondurant."

I nodded.

"You don't look too excited 'bout it. Still working off a hangover from the party last night?"

"No. I didn't go to any parties." I shifted my gaze. "Press, there's some things I didn't tell you in those letters."

I gave him the full story about me and Wesley Turner, not sparing him the parts about our sexual relationship, or how he treated me when Dean McGovern found out, and everything I had to put up with when word got out around school.

"I ain't proud of what I done. But it's over now. So how 'bout you take over talking? What's stirring in your head? You think I oughta be back in the loony bin in Baton Rouge?"

"Arizona, I'd be disappointed if you *hadn't* been up to something scandalous and sordid."

I elbowed him in the arm. "Nice of you to be supportive. I nearly lost it up at school. All them prying eyes on me all the time. Like I was a criminal."

"I suppose I shouldn't have joked about it. I guess."

"You know what's still got me hopping mad about the whole thing? I'm seventeen years old, and he was only twenty-four. Don't that kind of thing happen every day? Every hour the day, I'm figuring. What if I'd been a girl?"

Preston chuckled. "If you'd been a girl, your daddy woulda packed up his hunting rifle, drove up to Massachusetts, and used the fellow for target practice."

"Well, what if it'd been a female teacher? I'd have been getting pats on the back."

"Now you might right about that. Though the teacher still woulda gotten into trouble."

I knew he had a point, but I was fed up with the whole thing.

"Are you in love with him?"

"Hell no. I never was." I shrugged. "He was cute. But I never loved him. Take my word. I just had to tell you about it so there's no secrets between us. You sore at me?"

"I ain't happy. But considering where we left off last summer, I suppose I ain't got a right to be sore."

I caught his glance. Then I leaned over to kiss him on the lips. After, he looked out of sorts.

"I missed you, Press. Was that the wrong thing to do?"

He smirked. "Right after you told me about sleeping with your teacher?"

"So, you are sore. Guess I gone and screwed up something else." I sat back in my seat feeling sorry for myself.

"Ain't there some kind of saying about having made your bed and lying in it?

"I've done plenty lying in bed. That's all I've been doing. Tell me you understand, Press. Why, if you slept with other fellas this year, I wouldn't hold it against you."

He scowled. "Who am I gonna sleep with?"

I wriggled my eyebrows. "You might be surprised. You're awfully cute. And you got wheels now. You telling me you never took a drive back to New Orleans to see what was going on at that Café Lafitte in Exile?"

He burned up with a blush. I gaped at him.

"I did fine with the driving. Even stepped out of my car and walked around the corner. But I got cold feet." He shook his head. "That's a real thing, y'know? Thirty yards from that hotel, my feet froze up and wouldn't move. Until I turned around. I got back into my pickup and drove straight home. Wasted a half tank of gas. And I had to park behind the church down the street for one full hour because I told my parents I was going with a friend to the crawfish festival in New Iberia."

"Now that's a tragic story." I gave him a teasing grin. "You went out looking for something to wrap your lips around and come home with your breath still minty fresh, *and* an empty stomach."

"I'm remembering now what a pain in the ass you are."

"Hmm. You got that the other way around. You're the one who's a pain in my ass when I got the gris-gris on my side. What do you say to another kiss?"

Preston placed his hand on my shoulder before I could lean in. "I say, it's not that I wouldn't like that. But I don't know no more."

"Listen, Press. Ever since you came by on New Year's Eve, I been thinking about you a lot. I know we haven't seen each other for a while, but you been thinking about me?"

"I be lying if I told you no. But I don't want to be a fella you just come to see when you feeling lonesome."

"Press, I love you. I always loved you. I'm just always jammed up figuring out how to make things work. I'm going to Columbia next year, but I've got something to ask you." I breathed in some courage. "My daddy bought me a trip to Europe this summer.

London, Paris, Venice, and a half dozen other places. It's a full month, and he said I could take a friend. I was hoping that friend could be you."

Preston looked stunned at first, and then I saw a glimmer of wonder on his face as he imagined it. But my heart sank as that glimmer faded.

"That's a real nice offer, Arizona. But my uncle can't give me a month off from the shop."

"I bet he could give you a week or two."

Preston was silent for a stretch. "Arizona, I don't want you to think I'm ungrateful, but maybe that's not the best idea."

I massaged his hand in mine. "Why? Neither one of us ever been to Europe. We could have a real good time, boy. See Buckingham Palace. The Eiffel Tower. The Sistine Chapel in Vatican City. My daddy booked rooms at some swank hotels. We'd be doing it in style."

He stilled my hand. "That's a real nice trip. But what would it mean for us?"

I maneuvered in my seat a little closer to him. "It'd be like a vacation." I grinned at him. "Some time to get reacquainted. Think about it. *Paris, France.* You could use your French, and I've got three years of classes under my belt. I seen pictures from my Daddy's trips. It's the most beautiful and most romantic city in the world."

"I don't doubt that, and I'm sure we'd have some fun. But I got my heart to think about. We done this before, Arizona. Last summer was one big vacation. And toward the end, reality set in. I can't go through that again."

"You're the only person I want to go with, Press. Neither one of us knows what the future holds. Why, you'd prefer me going on my own, and the two of us not seeing each other until mid-July?"

I watched him shifting around and gathering his thoughts. "You know what I'd prefer, and you know that ain't gonna happen. You can't keep stringing me along."

"What if I told you, I want us to be together. Through thick and thin. You say the word, and I'll wear that engagement ring you bought for my birthday."

He cocked his head. "You really mean that, Arizona?"

I hesitated. I didn't want to. It was just, well, I don't know what it was.

"See there? Now, I can wait on a maybe, but I ain't going with you to Europe on a maybe."

The corners of my eyes burned, and I dropped my head. I felt like I'd ruined everything in my life. Made everyone I cared about turn away from me.

Preston clasped the back of my neck. "Look here, big shot. I ain't never gonna stop loving you. This ain't easy for me to say, but I think you should take that trip on your own. You ain't spent much time as a single man. It was always me, then Nicolas, then me again, and this year that teacher at school."

I swiped my face. "That was a big mistake."

"I ain't arguing about that. But how 'bout slowing things down and sitting with yourself for awhile?"

"Press, I need you. I don't want nobody else."

"Well, I hope you come back from Europe feeling the same way. And if you don't, at least we'll know where we stand."

"I don't know if I can do it. Press, I'm scared. I'm no good by myself."

Preston squeezed my hand. "That's exactly why you should go, knucklehead. To get comfortable on your own. There's a fella inside you I fell in love with. But I don't think you faced him for a while."

It hurt something awful hearing that, though gradually, while we sat in silence, I came around to understanding, even though my heart didn't like what my head was putting together. I was promising him things I hadn't thought through. It wasn't fair to him. If he came with me, soon as we got back home, we'd go back to being two people with different ideas about the future we wanted for ourselves.

"If that's what you want, I'll do it."

He smiled. Then he kissed me.

After, I scowled at him. "How's it okay for you to kiss me, but I can't kiss you?"

"That was just something to say I missed you."

"You could do it again. See where it leads." I wriggled my eyebrows.

He laughed. "You been listening to a damn word I say? We both know where it's gonna lead. How 'bout I fill you in on the latest with my cousin Francine instead?"

That's what we did that night at our spot by the Bayou Teche. Preston got me all caught up on the Montclair family drama. Later, I told him about graduation and my various antics with Dale Knox-Levy. I drove us over to Sonic's for some burgers and fries, and then I drove him back to the shop where he'd left his pickup. I said he better be coming to my graduation party at the house that weekend, and Preston said he would. We kissed goodnight, and I drove back to Darrow.

I WAS DEAD tired by the time I got home. I just stripped off my shirt and slacks and crawled into bed. Though as worn out as I was, I didn't fall asleep exactly. I was in some kind of in-between state, with so much going on in my head. My thoughts just churned and flashes of things passed by my mind's eye while I lay there with my eyelids closed.

I thought about Jonathan and our last conversation, wondering if it was possible we'd go back to being friends at Columbia next year. He'd hurt me real bad, but we'd been through a lot together. That counted for something, and he'd come around to try to make things right.

My mind roved to Wesley Turner, picturing him in bed like me somewhere. He had to be a broken man after his worst fears had come true. I can't say I liked the man he was, but he'd been dealing with the same things as me, being afraid and lonesome in the world. I shouldn't have come on to him so strong. At the least, I could've backed off when I realized we were looking for something in each other that neither of us could give. I'd learned some things about myself I didn't like. I wanted to be an honest and honorable man, and I sure hadn't been in a number of ways. I wondered how a man redeems himself. I'd never been religious and wasn't sure what good prayer would do. But I needed to be washed of my sins, metaphorically speaking.

I got to thinking about Dolly and hoping wherever she was, she was doing all right. Was she still trying to get her baby Dinah? I ought've done more for her. That led me to picture Little Douglas, stuck in bed with his leg braces. I hadn't done a thing to help him, and I was ashamed.

Those moving pictures in my head had me feeling real low, and then I thought about my brother, Duke. Was he happy working as a carny? Or was the living hard and toughening him up to be a man like Gus Fanning with his heart turned cold to the world? I saw Duke's face so clearly, it was like a moment of clairvoyance, though I couldn't read what he was thinking when he was looking back at me. I hadn't told Preston that I felt sometimes like Duke, Dolly, and Little Douglas were ghosts following me around, staring at me like I'd abandoned them and wanting to know the reason why.

Like a dream, those visions spun around, and I saw Dale, hanging out at some crowded bar, scoping things out to see who might take him home. He was another lonesome soul, looking for redemption just like me.

Then, I pictured my daddy in some hotel room, tucked in bed with that mistress of his. I wondered if he was happy, or if keeping that secret only made him feel more lonely the way my affair with Wes had made me feel. He'd been trying to teach me to be a good man, but he could only give me lessons in what he knew, and maybe I needed to look for answers someplace else. Then things drifted in my head to Le Moyne Parish, where I pictured Preston

laying sleeplessly in his room, wondering what kind of person I'd
be when I came back from Europe.

I got to thinking of big things, like all the people who come
into your life, and if there's some rhyme or reason to things
happening in a certain way or if it's all just chance, and what that
means for a person's responsibility. I wanted to be a good brother
to all the gay men I knew, like my hero Harvey Milk. But I didn't
know how to go about it with people like Wes, Duncan Linklater,
and Russell Thorne, who hated themselves for being gay. Meantime, I'd been raised with two brothers and a sister who weren't
related to me, but they thought of me as their brother. Did it
matter in terms of family? I couldn't help feeling like I'd let them
down.

I felt like layers were peeling away from me, leaving just a void.
It was horrible. I wasn't sure who I was anymore. I'd been trying to
be the good son of Gaston Bondurant, but the truth was, the stink
of growing up in poor Acadiana still clung to me, and I didn't
know if I was wrong for wanting to wash that off or wrong for not
being able to shrug it off and fit into my daddy's world. That got
me thinking about conversations with Jonathan again. He was the
only person who understood how hard life's choices could be. He
didn't know where he belonged neither, and somehow, that year,
we'd gone and pushed each other away in spite of having so much
in common. Well, he'd been trying to tell me how it was different
for him because of his culture and his skin color, and I guess I
could've been a better friend and listened to him.

Then somehow, thinking about that, I regained a bit of me. I
remembered how I told Jonathan I wouldn't change who I was for
all the money in the world. I was a poor boy from the bayou and
the privileged son of a wealthy French family that went back generations. I was gay and proud. I was a magna cum laude graduate of
an elite boarding school, and I'd earned admission to Columbia,
and I was going to be a famous writer. That didn't make me a
chimera or a phony or an imposter or a sellout. I just needed to

figure out how to live with all them parts of me and be true to myself.

I came around to thinking Preston was right. I needed to take that trip to Europe by myself. It was going to be lonely, but if I wanted to be the best man I could be, the only way to get there was being on my own for a while. I'd made some big mistakes that year, and I didn't want to be the kind of person who hurt other people. I needed to be comfortable in my own skin and not rely on somebody else to make me feel loved and worthy. I'm not going to lie. I was terrified. But I was also just a little bit excited. I was going to walk the streets of Paris, see the piazzas of Venice, and sit in outdoor cafés in Vienna with strangers who had no idea who I was. That's how I was going to figure out how to be Arizona Bondurant, and I was coming back that summer better than ever.

ABOUT THE AUTHOR

Romeo Preminger has been called the master of the romantic thriller. He's the author of over a dozen books including the Southern Gothic ARIZONA series, the branded romantic thriller series GUILTY PLEASURES EDITIONS, erotic romance stand-alones, and some naughty shorts called STORYBOOK EDITIONS.

Romeo lives on the East Coast with his husband. Beyond writing, some of his favorite jobs on his resume are a brief stint as a zookeeper, an even briefer stint as a hot dog vendor, and a more substantial career as a counselor and advocate for LGBTQ+ youth. For more about Romeo, visit: https://romeopreminger.com or connect with him on Twitter at https://twitter.com/Preminger Romeo.

Sign up for his mailing list and get news on sales and upcoming releases:

https://mailchi.mp/78bc1368af1e/team-romeo

Made in United States
North Haven, CT
05 May 2024

52135951R00141